# RIPPLE
## EFFECT

Published by Swan Lake Press

Printed in the United States of America

ISBN: 978-1-7360908-0-0

Fiction / Literary: FICTION / Historical FICTION / General

1. Young women – New York Fiction 2. Nineteen sixties – Rebellion – Fiction 3. Loss – Family Saga Fiction
4. Regret – Redemption – Fiction 5. Journalists – Fiction

Cover and interior design: Jacqueline Gilman, Gilman Design Larkspur, CA

Photos of author: Stephanie Mohan, Creative Portraiture Fairfax, CA

Front cover art adapted from a photograph by Cathy Rath

# RIPPLE EFFECT

## A NOVEL

# CATHY RATH

*To my exceptional Mom
for her unconditional love
and for believing in me always.*

*In memory of my spiritual guides,
Grammy, Jack & Lauren*

"It's time we stop, children, what's that sound
Everybody look what's going down."

*For What It's Worth*, Stephen Stills, 1967

## Chapter One

# JUNE 1952

# *Walter*

WALTER HAD ANTICIPATED THE tinny wail of his alarm clock seconds before the 5:00 a.m. setting. He hit the button before Bernice could stir. No matter how quietly he shaved, showered and dressed, she'd hear him and want a last word or touch before he left the house. She'd become a light sleeper since the kids were born, but he knew there was a deeper need to be in control, training herself to teeter on the edge of consciousness. He put up with it most days, but today he wanted his weekend to start without her admonitions to drive safe, call her at every rest stop, or pull him in for one last kiss.

He slipped on his khaki pants, guiding his belt through the narrow loops, and put on a short-sleeved shirt, light enough for the summer heat. He clipped his signature pen protector onto his shirt pocket and stuffed his wallet into his back pocket. A last glance at the full-length mirror, Walter followed his hands as they patted down his damp, wavy hair. His eyes shifted to the gold rings on each hand. The chunkier engraved one on his right middle finger had been passed on to him from his own father as a Bar Mitzvah gift, which he rarely took off in fear of losing such an irreplaceable keepsake. The slim wedding band on his left ring finger had a stranger feel, as if he could never quite adjust to its permanency.

To avoid her drama and his inevitable guilt, Walter crept

back to Bernice's side of the bed and leaning down, brushed his lips against her forehead. Her eyes blinked open and before he could straighten up, she reached her arm around his neck and whispered into his face.

"Call—whenever you stop, promise me."

Walter nodded, then rearranged the blanket so it draped over her shoulders. Treading softly into the kids' room, he eased inside and bent over Jeffrey's inert body. Parting the tufts of his curly hair, he planted a kiss on his cheek, inhaling the shampoo residue from last night's bath. Then he turned toward Jeannie, curled in a ball, her tiny frame facing the wall. Crouching down, Walter steered her limp torso toward him. "My angel," he whispered, "you be good." Then he kissed the bridge of her freckled nose and tiptoed out.

Navigating out of Queens was easier than he'd expected. As he merged onto the highway heading south, Walter cranked up the radio. He recognized an Andrews Sisters medley, their harmonious voices bringing him back to the Fort Dix USO mixer where he'd met Bernice. Thin and petite, she had a body built for dancing. When he'd finally gotten the nerve to take her for a swing around the floor, they Lindy-hopped until curfew. The memory summoned an image of two people from another lifetime, when a war brought them together, but didn't prepare him for the struggles that came next.

Streaks of orange light cast a glow across his lap as he crossed the Georgia state line. He'd been driving since dawn and needed a good meal before the last hundred miles to Atlanta, the site of the three-day annual psychiatric convention. After too many internship hours to count, and solid recommendations from supervisors, Walter planned to circulate among the decision makers, apply the charm he'd been blessed with, and set up a bunch of interviews for when he got back home. He felt optimistic, and that alone was enough to justify a rare break from father, son, and husband duties. Other than his stint at Fort Dix six years earlier, Walter couldn't remember the last time he was away from New York and on his own.

Underneath a billboard signaling he'd arrived in Braselton, population 3000, was a neon sign that blinked, "Ray's Tavern, Best Chicken-Fried Steak in Georgia." Walter veered off the highway and followed arrows another half-mile down an unevenly paved road. Encased by tall trees, the flat-roofed building stood alone giving it an eerie, desolate feeling. The spaces close to the entrance were taken, so he parked under a large oak tree at the far end of the lot. The tavern was so dark that Walter experienced a moment of near blindness as he entered. He rubbed his lids hoping it would soothe the strain from his long drive. Before he could head to the bar area, he was greeted by a middle-aged woman with a beehive hairdo.

"Good evening, young man, welcome to Ray's. Bet you got a stomach aching for a chicken-fried steak, that sign don't lie, we make the best in Georgia. Now where can I set you down?" Her faded red lips curved up into a wide grin, while she clutched a menu against her huge chest.

He nodded his head. "Don't need a table tonight, it's just me, thanks." And then pointed to the bar.

He settled on a stool at the farthest end of the counter. He wasn't normally a loner type, but something about being in a new place warned him to keep to himself. There were five men around the L-shaped bar; two seemed to be engaged in conversation, the others hunched over glasses of whiskey. A tall thin-lipped bartender with a bushy mustache sauntered over and laid a coaster in front of him.

"What'll you have?" His southern drawl made him sound more welcoming than he looked.

"Gin and tonic with a twist, thanks. And I'll want to order some dinner, smells really good in here."

The bartender nodded and, in a few moments, both his cocktail and a brown leather menu were placed in front of him.

Sipping his drink, Walter gazed around the tavern's interior. Deep-brown mahogany panels lined the walls from floor to ceiling with glass sconces spaced around the perimeter. One long window framed a view into the parking lot, but beyond the bottles of colorful liquid behind the bartender's runway, the place was like a cave. It felt cocooned, and a little spooky. Now away from his daily routine, where even time with the kids was planned out, he allowed his mind to wander. Something inside of him had been closing down but he couldn't pinpoint the cause. Like the low-lit ambiance he found himself in, it felt as if his inner light had been dimming for months, maybe years.

The front door opened, interrupting his thoughts. A backlit silhouette of a tall man stepped inside. Walter could make out the man's light-colored suit, shirt opened at the collar, and his tie pulled loose. The buxom hostess tottered over to him, touching his arm with what seemed like a familiar gesture. The man looked right at Walter, said something to the woman, then headed over to the bar and sat down next to him. Facing Walter, the stranger put out his hand.

"Well, howdy. Not from round here, I'm guessing."

He nodded at the bartender who placed a drink before him. "Evening, Ray."

He turned toward Walter. "Ol' Gladys figured you must have missed your turn—thought you might like to know where you landed." His mouth curved up in a confident manner. "What's your name?"

Surprised by the forwardness, Walter hesitated. The man

reached out his hand again.

"Walter, Walter Glazer," he mumbled, offering his hand.

Ray the bartender lingered for a moment. The regular tapped twice on the rim of the glass and nodded his approval for what was evidently his usual. "Ready for another, Walter?" he smiled.

"Not just yet but thank you."

Without sharing his own name, the regular slid his hand around the small glass, and downed the shot in one gulp, then turned his head in Walter's direction.

"This is your first time passing through Jackson County, am I right?"

Walter nodded slowly. Though not usually adverse to small talk, he was not keen on engaging with this guy. He didn't want to know any more about the town, not even the man's name.

"On your way to Atlanta, I reckon. Nobody 'cept the locals make it to Ray's unless they're tired of their own home cooking." He turned his head to acknowledge the other patrons.

The man's profile looked as if an artist had drawn a perfect line from his smooth forehead to his strong jaw. Waving at Ray at the end of the bar, the man twirled his index finger in a circular motion, signaling for two more drinks. Walter needed dinner. His stomach had rapidly absorbed the liquor, slowing his brain and tongue. A dark-haired waitress appeared and took his order, and despite the aroma of the tavern's specialty, he went for the char-grilled steak and potatoes. Bartender Ray followed with the drinks and after a few bites, Walter calmed down. With a reason to focus on his meal, he only had to nod appropriately during this guy's monologue. Walter caught fragments through his thick southern drawl, something about real estate business, virtues of the town, being so close to Atlanta. *Gift of gab,* his mother would say, but that never bothered Walter. Listening was his specialty and a reason why he had chosen psychiatry, a six-year investment he hoped would be rewarded with a job offer over the weekend. Like his patients, who meandered through disjointed stories of distant times, he could sense something else brewing beyond his bar mate's amiable, good old boy chatter. Perhaps he was trying to sell him property on a dumpsite in Braselton; the potential pitch enticed Walter to wait it out. But he also began to soften to the man's charm. Cleaning his plate and swallowing the few remaining sips of his second drink, he patted his belly and finally chimed in.

"Now that was just what *this* doctor ordered."

The man turned his body toward him, giving Walter a three-quarter view of his facial features. Even in the bar's muted light, Walter could distinguish the leathery creases around his eyes and mouth. The deep even bronze complexion was interrupted by blotchy veins on the side of his cheeks and nose, the mark of a habitual drinker.

"You're a doctor?" The man leaned in closer.

"Well, yes, but not the fix bones or open you up kind. I'm a psychiatrist."

"A head shrinker? Well, I'll be, yes sir, can't say I've met too many of y'all—don't think we got your types in this whole county." He made a sweeping gesture for emphasis. "But reckon there's plenty of business up north, where you're from, right?"

Walter knew his New York accent, clipped and closed-mouthed, was difficult to hide.

"Well, you haven't said but a few words, but I suppose Jersey or Big A, not too many of y'all come through here. Right after the war though, vets on their way to Atlanta would pull off the highway to find themselves a meal or a new life." The man said, picking up his glass, swirling the liquid around, before finishing it off.

"New York, but did spend some time in Jersey, Fort Dix until D-day. Heading to Atlanta for a convention." Walter waited for his gregarious drinking buddy to come back with a quick reply. Instead, he ordered them another round. After an awkward pause, the man scooted in closer, giving him a sideways glance.

Walter was already over his alcohol limit and recalling that the Thomas Guide put him about 90 minutes outside of the city, a third drink was out of the question. He had to admit though that he enjoyed the company, strange and one-sided as it was, but still reached for his wallet to signal he was done.

"Got kids?" The man jumped in.

Walter paused, thinking about their faces, then opened his wallet and pulled out a photograph. It was from Jeffrey's fourth birthday, the image included his daughter Jeannie, who at two, was nestled under the arm of her brother on their front porch decorated with American flags.

"That's my son, Jeffrey, he'll be 5 next month, and the pip-squeak is Jeannie, just turned 3."

"They're adorable." The man smiled as Ray appeared with full tumblers to replace the empty ones. That's all it took for Walter to open up. As he went on about their playful antics, he somehow veered off to his time at Fort Dix.

"Yeah, 'course I wanted the horrible war to end. And this is going to sound crazy, but what I do miss is the whole army routine, the purpose we had, all the comraderie," Walter said, picking up his drink, "nothing compares to it. Had a few close buddies, there was one guy who wasn't afraid to talk, you know, honestly. After Dix, we kept in touch for a little while, but then with med school demands, a marriage, and kids, well…"

He hadn't talked this much to anyone in years, the liquor loosening up his thoughts and mouth.

"And what about your wife?"

He pulled out another photo of a young woman dressed in a USO uniform. "We were happy then" is how he described Bernice and her toothy grin. He remembered inserting the rectangular image in his wallet six years earlier, before the wedding, but photos of the kids took top billing, so it remained unfaded with sharp borders. Walter didn't want to talk about Bernice; thinking about his married life would deflate the air between him and this charming stranger. He didn't want the detour. The truth, he told the man, was that he loved his kids more than anything, and vowed to never let them down.

"I remember bringing Jeffrey's tiny form right up to my face, kissing his forehead, and falling in love. Yup, and you know, the only other time I got that feeling again was two years later, holding baby Jeannie in my arms." Seeing their happy grins in the photo tightened his chest with longing. His cheeks burned at his sentimental confession. "Hey, didn't mean to go on." Walter met the man's gaze and saw a different person on the next stool, someone who had been listening, something *he* did so well; it was as if he were looking into a mirror. The recognition lingered, and in an attempt to hold back his tears, his right leg began an involuntary tapping that made its way up his torso. The man looked down at Walter's barstool.

"You okay, buddy?" he asked, touching Walter's hand.

"Yeah, yeah, I just miss my children, never been away from them overnight. Geez, getting all worked up, I sound like one of my patients." Walter picked up a cocktail napkin, wiping the beads of perspiration from his forehead.

Ray came over and laid the tab on the bar and mumbled that the place was closing. Walter jerked his head up, looked around and realized that he and this stranger were the only ones left in the dark tavern. He glanced down at his watch, midnight, what was he doing, he had to get back on the road no matter how weary he felt or how slow he'd have to drive.

The man palmed the check.

"I got it, and say, listen you don't look too good to drive. I live just down the road, big place, you can rest your head 'til morning."

"No, no thanks, I'll be okay, some water to drink and splash on my face, that should do it." But as Walter stood, his legs wobbled forcing him to hold onto the bar to secure his footing.

The man slid off the stool, followed him to the restroom but didn't go in. Walter staggered to the urinal, and fumbled to relieve himself, a slight dizziness turned his stomach. How many drinks had he had, 4, 5? But it had been over a four-hour period, so he just needed to wash up, the cold water would help clear his fuzzy vision. The mirror above the sink had one jagged crack in the middle. The image cut his face into two frames, making his eyes twitch with unnerving alarm. Though he felt drunk and sluggish, he also felt an adrenalin surge move down his spine and into his pelvis.

A gentle rapping on the door startled his reflection.

"You okay in there?"

"Yes, yes, be out in a sec."

As soon as he hit the nighttime air, Walter's knees buck-led. The man caught his arm preventing a headfirst fall onto the rocky pavement. Even when pulled upright, he didn't feel strong enough to bear his full weight and so had no choice but to grab the man's torso for balance.

"Whoa, easy, I got ya," The man readjusted Walter's arm

and draped it around his shoulders. "'Fraid Atlanta might have to wait 'til morning."

"No, no, fine, just need to get my sea legs, too much sitting." He shook his head.

"Maybe so, let me help you walk some."

Moving away from the dim light framing the tavern's door, the blackness of the parking lot made Walter's car appear as a faint outline under the towering oak tree. When they reached the car door, Walter began to grope into his side pockets for the keys but could not pry them out. The man reached in and removed the keys. Then, without a word, cupped Walter's groin and pulled him in so their bodies touched.

Walter's attempt to push him away were feeble at best. The man's grip was firm, not forced, guiding him from the car to the wooded clearing just beyond the lot, where he propped him up against the tree. The man buried his head into Walter's neck, raised his chin, planting first his lips, then a gentle hand over Walter's mouth, pleading with him not to protest. The man's mouth then traveled down his body to his waist, hands unbuckling his belt, lowering his pants and taking him in. It was over in minutes, but not for the stranger. He turned Walter around, unzipped himself and leaned into his bare buttocks, his arms encircling him against the tree. The accelerated panting culminated in a moaned release. Before Walter could regain any semblance of thought, he heard the man zip up.

"You okay?" he panted.

Walter felt a wave of nausea, the alcohol and shock mixing together. "NO! I don't know—what was that, I mean, who are you, *what* are you?"

The man shook his head. "What did you think? C'mon, you wouldn't be up against that tree if you didn't know where this was heading. You've done this before, that army friend?"

Walter raised his weary arms and pushed him away. "No, no, *never...*"

"Shit, what, I'm your first?" The man stumbled over his words, and before Walter could respond, they were both startled by a slammed car door, the hue of a red spinning light, followed by a flashlight bouncing in their direction.

A burley figure lumbered towards them; the clanging of police gear was unmistakable. "What in Jesus' name is going on here?"

Walter froze in horror, and before he could let out his next breath, the stranger bolted into the woods and was gone.

# Chapter 2

# AUGUST 1968

# *Jeannie*

"JIM!" She screams over and over, but the throng of bodies sweeps her along.

People are everywhere running, shouting, the piercing sirens drowning out her cries for help. A black van with a twirling red crown screeches to a stop, forcing them to scatter or be hit. A swarm of helmeted men spill out. Jeannie knows she should run but her legs feel paralyzed, her feet stuck in cement. She's never seen so many cops in one place before. Where is Jim? Before any of them could bolt, the pigs bring weighty batons down hard on their heads, shoulders, hips, calves. Jeannie jumps back, missing a cracked skull by inches. Where the hell is Jim?

"Get your asses in there, now!" A beefy cop grabs her arm and drags her to the van. Like an unruly animal, Jeannie is shoved inside, tumbling onto a swell of bodies. The door slams shut cutting off light and air. She is wedged between two girls, one moaning in pain, the other lifting her shirt up to swab her bloody forehead. "Police state, police state" echoes through the small vehicle, fists banging on the sides as it speeds off.

When the van stops and the doors open, they limp out and are told to 'shut your traps, all of you' by a tall, acne-scarred officer who then orders 'just the girls' to follow him. They are led into a holding cell already occupied by six or seven women, all of them in ragged clothes with a stench of stale sweat and fear. When the steel gates clank into place, Jeannie feels like she is going to faint. She wobbles over to an empty space and sinks onto the hard, sticky floor. Leaning her head against the wall, she tries to catch her breath. So hot, so little air, yet her teeth begin to chatter from an inner chill she cannot control.

The girl with the bloody forehead has ripped her t-shirt into pieces and holds it to her wound. No one seems to notice or care that she is now dressed in just a bra. Her face is drained of color except the streaks of blood seeping from her forehead. It is obvious none of the pigs give a shit. A dark-haired girl wearing a cropped "End the War" shirt tries to help, while the others run to the bars screaming at the guards to call an ambulance.

"Back away, and pipe down!"

The acne cop opens the door and inches a few steps into the cell. He points at the injured girl lying on the cement ground. "Let's go, you two, help her to her feet." He juts out his jaw, then yells out for back-up.

"She can't stand up," cropped-t-shirt girl yells back, and then, under her breath, "you prick."

Jeannie catches his beady-eyed scowl. Glaring around the cell, he clutches the club from his belt, pulls it out, then slams it hard against the bars. The sound makes them jerk up. No one, she assumes, plans to charge this armed asshole or attempt a running break into the station lined with more cops. But this officer's disdain for their cause is what Jim and the others had warned her about.

"Where ya from?" The girl with the cropped t-shirt asks in a soft voice. Jeannie is barely able to respond. She can't erase the image of cops with their raised caveman clubs banging heads and then her narrowly dodging the steel fender of a police van.

"New York, Barnard...I'm with, uh, you know, SDS." Jeannie wants to sound proud, or at least virtuous, but her composure has dissolved. Bruised and battered, the tears fall down her cheeks.

"Shit yeah, SDS, man. You guys made every headline. The Chicago cops are nothing like the helmeted fascists out for blood at Columbia." Jeannie watches the girl's head lift, bob, and then, with a smirk, "So, are you with that Rudd guy?" Her eyes widen a bit, seemingly more curious than impressed.

"Yeah, he's the main leader. There's a bunch of others—one's name is Jim, and he's my boyfriend. We've been together since last November," she looks up at the blotchy stains on the ceiling, "but I'm not entirely sure if he sees it the same way." This is the first time she shares her real feelings out loud, and the honesty makes her squirm.

A combination of factors put her in Jim's path along with his radical friends, who could spew locomotive-paced speeches against a corrupt government, inciting crowds into action. Before meeting him, she had been a timid yet eager student, sitting quietly in the first few rows of every class, taking copious notes and letting other girls ask questions. She'd wake up before her alarm, eat breakfast in a half-empty dining common, and rush to be one of the early arrivals.

"We met at a coffee shop on Broadway. The SDS guys, maybe eight of them, all looked the same, the beards, long hair, but Jim had the kindest eyes," she replies with an unsettling feeling in her chest.

It had been too easy to fall for Jim, so much was happening on campus, the charged atmosphere spilling over into her classes. She'd signed up for a political science course and right away, the leftish-bent professor, a bony man with a pointed chin, had shaken her up. He went on about resistance movements, labor strikes, the suffragettes, civil rights with speeches by Dr. King, Malcolm X, and the rise of the Black Panthers. Jeannie's papers were consistently filled with red marks, questions and comments that revealed her naiveté. It was as if she'd been circling the outer edge of a huge pool, not sure if she should take the plunge, and before she had a chance to consider her options, she'd fallen into the deep end with Jim and SDS navigating the way.

Only a small minority of freshman girls engaged with the rebellious campus-wide energy. She didn't get the chance to protest at the Low or Hamilton Hall takeovers or march to Harlem to rip down the gym site fences in the spring. Afflicted with a full-blown cold, she stayed behind watching the jarring chaos unfold from the television screen in the dorm's rec room. Cops assailing students, aggressively pushing, shoving, and battering heads. She'd put her face up to the set, searching for Jim, or anyone she might recognize, but the cameramen stayed at an unfocused distance. The terrifying bust had been happening right outside, less than a mile away, and Jim, she was certain, had been in the thick of it. Jeannie didn't see or hear from him for three days. She'd hounded her dorm buddies for the details, but many had been frightened off by the April riots and stayed away. One of them, a thin Jewish girl from Long Island who spent too much time in front of a bathroom mirror massaging VO5 goop into her kinky hair, had announced that "protesting was a guy thing, and any of you who'd put your faces and bodies at risk of permanent disfigurement needed your heads examined."

"Backs to the walls, ladies," acne-pig commands, as a goofy-looking Abbott and Costello paramedic duo squeeze through the cell door. They didn't bring a stretcher, but from the looks of their fallen charge, they should have. She is clearly unconscious; her slumping body being protected from the cement ground by the laps of two girls. The paramedics kneel down beside them, and the girl wearing the "End the War" t-shirt, spits out, "She'd better not be dead!" The heavier technician feels his patient's neck, turns to his partner, and nods.

"She's okay."

"Hey, wait!" A voice sings out from the back corner of the cell. "When do we get to make our calls, it's been over an hour already, it's our right."

"You should've thought of that when you broke the law. You'll get your calls when we're damn good and ready," acne-cop snarls as he walks off.

For the first time in the last forty-eight hours, Jeannie feels as if she is completely alone, or worse, abandoned. The cell walls begin to close in on her, and the odor of sweat, blood and a dozen unwashed women sharing a cell makes Jeannie pinch her nostrils to prevent a gagging reflex.

She wonders if Jim would even think to come to the precinct if she didn't return to their motel. What if he has been arrested too? Who would she call when she has the chance?

"Hey there, you okay?" Now free from caretaking duties, the cropped-t-shirt girl reengages. They'd probably been locked up for less than an hour, but it seems much longer. Her throat is so dry that she has to force several swallows to respond.

"No, not really. I'm just, well, new to this, all of it." Jeannie shifts her head slowly around the cramped space. "And my name is Jeannie."

"I'm Patty, and you're in luck." She sits down next to her. "I'm a holding tank vet, you might say, been inside a bunch of these over the past six months, but this time, man, the convention protests went way out of control, too many of us in here, could be an overnighter."

Up close, Patty appears more weathered, her brown skin contrasting with her faded denim shorts and exposed belly; her long, dark hair hangs down like slabs. The windowless cell is reaching sauna conditions, and Jeannie keeps tightening her sagging pony to keep her wild, frizzy strands from touching her neck. She is wearing a long-sleeved, muslin top and knee-length Indian-style skirt, her customary summer attire to protect her delicate, paper white skin from turning red and scorched. Three days among thousands in Chicago's heat, with food a luxury, make her clothes even looser.

"Overnight?" says Jeannie, her voice cracking. "What about our calls? Are they just going to forget about us in here? No water, what about using the bathroom?" She goes from a whisper to a shriek. The others turn toward them.

Patty reaches over and puts her hand on Jeannie's leg.

"Hey, hey, you're spinning here. These pigs can be bad asses, but they're not going to torture us or anything. The bathroom tour guide should be here any minute."

Jeannie isn't convinced, and since her bladder is barely holding on, she guesses it is the same for all of them. She stands up determined to make their needs known but is pulled back down by Patty.

"Hold on, they'll be here, you going off and yelling through the bars will just piss 'em off. They'll give us water, crappy vending machine snacks and the phone calls. Trust me." Patty leans back against the wall, closes her eyes, inhales deeply and lets out a deep throated ahhhhhhh. The more alert girls watch her.

"The important thing is not to panic. You see what I'm doing? Keep inhaling, exhaling and you'll get through it. They don't want us here anymore than we do."

Jeannie slumps back down, and again, feels a wave of

gratitude for Patty's calmness and camaraderie. Despite the heat of August, two months living out of her backpack and surrounded by non-stop craziness, the cramped cell is almost a respite from her traveling companions. She did want to talk, to hear her own thoughts about why she jumped into the back of a VW van and headed to Ann Arbor in mid-June.

Jeannie does a few rounds of the breathing thing. "Thank you for, well, it's just…"

Patty cuts her off. "See that girl in the tie-dye? She and I have been through it. I've got one side of the cell; she's working the other. That's what we do for each other, you dig?"

Jeannie is grateful, but also scared. Why hadn't Jim or anyone from her group showed up? She'd spent weeks in and out of smoky meetings in filthy apartments, sitting on laps in death-trap cars, or holed up for what seemed like hours in crummy diners. And still, she didn't understand what all the infighting and grabs for power had been about, or the raucous debates between peaceful resistance tactics and the darker, more violent ones. When the arguments got too heated, she'd be ordered by Jim or one of the guys to either get coffee or make a grocery store run. Looking around the cell filled with battered veterans of the cause, she sees she is in way over her head.

"What about you?" She is interested in Patty's background, but also wants to avoid the sickening feeling that Jim might not show up and get her out.

"I'm with PLP, been with them for a while, maybe a year. I was at Northwestern, and now I'm on the road, you know, 'like a rolling stone'." Her grin lights up her angular face. Jeannie wonders if her relaxed demeanor is real or an act.

"They'll come for me soon enough. Bail money should arrive by morning, I'm not worried." Patty crosses her legs in a Buddha pose, and gives Jeannie a nod.

"PLP, is that Progressive Labor Party? I've heard of you, but I don't know why we're different from each other. Aren't we all about ending the war?" Jeannie's voice goes high.

"We follow Maoist philosophy, and for sure, we want it to end, but the Vietnam war is a distraction. PLP's about over-throwing the capitalist regime, about empowering the working class, the true proletariat, who don't have rights, or any chance to control their destinies. It's about class, race, and the meek taking over someday."

Patty keeps going, "SDS took the anti-war movement in a more militant direction, about the fat cats who control the war machine, and civil rights for all, aligning with the Panthers— very righteous, but like I said, that's not going to get at the core problem."

"So, wait," Jeannie has lost interest in their political differ-ences, "someone from PLP knows you're here?"

"Well, not exactly, but yeah, if I'm not back at the safe house by morning, they'll figure it out. That's the protocol. You don't sound sure your guys will do the same."

"Protocol? No, I don't think so, not that I know of, at least. We were all together outside the convention center, and then suddenly the cops swarmed in, I lost sight of Jim and didn't get away in time."

"Bummer, it's not like that with us. Women aren't just there to carry coffee or spread our legs, we count just as much as the guys. I've met a few people in the SDS chapter out here, and all they talk about is the pecking order, and women?—forget about it."

Patty's glib summary triggers a truthful look at her last nine months. When Jim wanted sex, even if she didn't, they had it, end of story. She and the other two girls on the van journey were not asked, but told, to get coffee, cigarettes, food, do laundry, whatever it took, to keep SDS leaders happy and in charge. It happened just like Patty described; the leaders were all guys, until they reached Ann Arbor, when two women in their mid-20s joined the inner circle. She'd forgotten their names, but it was their explosive debates that made her cower into corners, away from learning about the more serious plans. When the guys would raise their voices proclaiming force and destruction as the only answers, she'd escape by smoking more weed, enough to pass out on Jim's lap or an available couch. The truth was she didn't get involved with SDS; she fell for Jim, and until now, thought it was reciprocal. Maybe Patty was right, that she was just his sex toy and the group's house girl. It kind of seemed like that over the summer, but she blamed it on their hectic schedule, being on the road, in and out of motels, crashing on floors.

No, it can't be what Patty says. Jim truly loves her and wants her by his side. She totally agrees that the U.S. should get out of the war, but it was also more personal; she had too many nightmares of her brother, Jeffrey, in an army uniform, being sent overseas. And obviously, black people were treated like rapid dogs in this country, their leaders obliterated one by one. First, Malcolm X assassinated by one of his own and then King, shot down in cold blood for becoming too bold and powerful. All outrageous and worth the struggle, but to find herself in a jail cell and the possibility that the guy who says he loves her wasn't coming to her rescue is not what she signed up for.

Jeannie jumps to her feet, and navigating around sprawled bodies, puts her head through the bars. "We need a bathroom run! Hello out there, can you hear us?"

Several girls stumble to their feet and begin a spontaneous chant, "We need to pee, we need to pee, come to the bars and bring your keys…" Patty joins the fray, adding, "Water, water, give us bread and water."

Within a few minutes, a middle-aged woman, stuffed into her black uniform like a misshapen sausage, appears and commands them to 'zip it up!' Following her is another cop pushing a rickety cart with a pitcher of water, plastic cups, and airplane-sized packets of pretzels. Jeannie feels almost giddy as these women, like a blurry mirage, approach the cell. An orderly line is imposed with the two matrons working together to hand them water cups and pretzels through the bars. When it is her turn, she drinks too quickly and chokes as the drops rush down her windpipe.

"C'mon ladies, keep the line moving, we ain't room service." The sausage cop's voice is deep and hoarse, her face pinched in a sneer. It makes Jeannie feel like a hardened criminal instead of an innocent college student on a protest tour across the U.S.

After the snack and water service, they are taken in groups of four down a long, dank-smelling corridor to the bathroom. Loud, high-pitched voices bounce off the walls of a cell right next to the bathroom and as they pass, there is no mistaking this group's profession. A tall, black woman with blood-red lipstick and a strapless glittered top that barely holds back her huge breasts is standing up against the bars. She sticks out her arm and catches the gauzy sleeve of Jeannie's blouse.

"You is as white as a ghost, little sista. Ha, did I scare you?" She laughs and slowly lets go. "Looky here, bunch of white girls out for the evening, guess y'all didn't 'spect to spend a summer night with Chicago's finest."

Sausage cop stops and hits the bars with her baton, too close to whacking the black woman's hand. "Shut your trap, Doreen, and back your ass away from the bars. Next time, I won't miss."

Jeannie's temples begin to throb. She feels as if she's on the edge of freaking out. This is too real. If her family had any idea that she is about to pee in a stainless-steel toilet bowl with a guard standing watch next to a cell full of prostitutes, they'd think she had lost her mind.

She tries to keep her head straight ahead when they pass Doreen and her cellmates again. Compared to these ladies, her disheveled, banged-up crew, with dirty mismatched clothes look as if they'd been in a dungeon for years. Jeannie reclaims her spot next to Patty, who is curled up in a fetal position on the floor, and apparently conked out. She spots another red-haired girl across the cramped room, one of the few still awake, and notices a watch on her wrist. Waving to get her attention, Jeannie points to her bare wrist and then in a loud whisper asks the time.

The redhead puts her arm inches in front of her face, and mouths, "it's 11, um, 11 ha, cool, huh?" She shakes her head and grins, but to Jeannie there is nothing funny about being behind bars as midnight approaches.

Rather than staying calm, Jeannie's heart pounds, forming a chilly sweat around her neck. She needs to inhale and exhale slowly, like Patty instructed, but then instead of long, calm breaths, she feels as if she suddenly can't swallow. A ringing in her ears, then a panic surges in her chest; is she hyperventilating? She wants fresh air, and to get the fuck out of this hellhole. Where is Jim? Would they get their phone calls? Calling Uncle Jack is the only option. He'd be upset but would keep his cool until he found someone to get her out.

Heavy footsteps approaching the cell interrupt her anxious thoughts.

"Glazer, J. Step forward." It is an older cop, this time with a full head of whitish-gray hair wearing black square glasses.

He doesn't shout like the others.

Jeannie gets up, almost tripping on her skirt in her rush to the front of the cell. A bunch of the girls rise to their feet, including Patty, who speaks up first. "Well Miss J, guess your man made it. Maybe it's love, after all." The cop fumbles with the keys on his belt, then inserts a larger one into the door panel, opening it just wide enough for Jeannie to slip through.

On the other side of the cell gate, she glances back at the sea of misery. Most of the girls now stand at the bars, hands extended, but it is Patty who grabs her sleeve as the cop twists the key back into the lock.

"Good luck, Jeannie, don't let the guys push you around."

Jeannie is just able to mouth a 'thank you' before being pulled away and escorted through another set of heavy doors that brings her into the brightly lit station. She scans the room hoping to spot Jim right away. But the main processing area is teeming with people, every chair taken, bodies sprawled out on floors, and up against walls. Any of the bearded guys in the crowd could be Jim. She gets on her tip toes, straining for more focus, and in doing so, pulls away from her gray-headed escort. Where is he? She wants it to be like he is picking her up at an airport or train station, peering over the other passengers, searching for his girl in the crowd.

"Hold on there, Glazer." The cop puts his hand on her neck and leads her to the towering desk in the station's center.

The desk sergeant directing the commotion has a block for a head and Italian features, sharp nose, bushy eyebrows, just like the pizza man, Sal, from her Queens neighborhood. Jeannie cowers underneath waiting for him to stop barking orders and notice her from his high perch. Feeling even smaller and more waifish, she swivels her head around the room again, hoping to see her man.

"Sarge," the gray-haired cop calls out, "she's the one." Sergeant Marconi, whose name tag she can now read, holds up one hand to stop a group of approaching officers, and with the other, takes a white business-sized envelope from the desk, and motions for Jeannie to come closer.

"This is for you, Miss Glazer. You can tell your Pop we appreciate the tip. Now get your sorry ass outta here before I change my mind." He shoves the envelope towards her, but it falls to the floor before she can get a grip on it. Crouching down to retrieve it, Jeannie sees her name scribbled in barely legible handwriting. When she stands up, the gray-haired cop is gone, and Sergeant Marconi is back shouting orders.

"My pop?" she hears herself say too loudly. Is this some kind of sick prank? Jeannie brings the envelope close to her chest, then eyes the black-rimmed clock on the wall behind the sergeant's desk; 11:45. The station is hopping, but no sign of Jim. Jeannie feels more frightened in that moment than she had out on the streets or in the claustrophobic cell. She begins to rip open the envelope, but stops mid-way, deciding she needs privacy. She dashes toward the women's room near the station exit and locks herself inside the first stall. Her hands shake as she pulls out a folded piece of lined notebook paper. Inside are four crisp $50 bills and a Trailways bus ticket to New York's Port Authority station. What the hell? She cannot process this; it is as if her brain waves have flat-lined in her head. Someone knew she was there, and it certainly wasn't her father. He'd been dead for over sixteen years. She stuffs the envelope inside her bra and runs out of the station.

# Chapter 3

## JULY 1960

# *Jack*

JACK CROUCHED DOWN TO the bottom drawer of his dresser, his knees letting out a moan like a rusted-out door hinge. Sifting through a pile of old t-shirts and assortment of mismatched socks, he felt around until he found the small velvet box. He stuffed it in his outside coat pocket and stood up slowly. From the surface of his dresser, he slid an envelope with the Yankees logo into his breast pocket. His nephew would appreciate his gift of home plate seats for several games far more than the chunky gold ring inside the box. He'd have felt the same way at 13.

Before leaving the bedroom, Jack glanced at the full-length mirror outside the bathroom door. He had chosen his lightest-weight suit to accommodate the July heat. As a man born with a propensity to perspire, even applying the strongest deodorant on the market, he'd no doubt be drenched by the time he reached the temple. He flattened his shirt over his stomach, adjusted his jacket so the shoulder pads were even, but when he tightened his necktie, it hit the base of his Adam's apple causing an uncomfortable gag reflex. He hated anything around his neck, never wore scarves even if outside temperatures fell below freezing, and didn't own a single turtleneck sweater. Ties were a necessary evil in his line of work, but fortunately, by the time the news day got rolling, he, along with his newspaper staff, would yank down the knot to mid-chest depending on the intensity of the headlines. He jutted his face inches from the mirror and took a deep breath. The tiny gray strands along his temples and darker lines under the hollows of his eyes revealed more than the fatigue of a busy job and two rambunctious toddlers. At 33, the additional burden of caring for his late brother's kids and keeping a devastating secret for too many years, turned his dreams into sweat-filled nightmares.

He checked his watch; time to go. As he emerged from the gold-plated elevator into the pristine lobby, Jack was greeted by Hector, the amiable, middle-aged doorman and fixture at The Hemisphere House for 25 years. No one ever walked past Hector, no matter how hurried or out of sorts, without slowing down to exchange some friendly chitchat.

"Good morning Mr. G. Hot one today. Just saw the missus and the boys, she told me the happy news, congratulations to your family. Will you be needing a cab too?" He nodded his thick neck up and down, pulling open the glass doors.

"Thank you, Hector. No, I'm going to hoof it. Yes, big day and if I don't get a move on, they'll start without me." He lifted the corners of his mouth straining a grin, and then stepped out into the bright morning. It was after 10 a.m.; Jack had cut it way too close. He hadn't planned to make the trip by foot or on his own, but the boys had battled Cindy every step of the way as she attempted to dress them in their miniature suits. He didn't have the usual patience to cajole them into obedience. Instead, he'd hurried them out the door, and despite the heat decided to walk the ten blocks to the temple, delaying entry to a place he never wanted to ever return.

Jack was not surprised to see the streets of his Forest Hills neighborhood already filling up with kids on bikes and a street stickball game in progress. With the steady interruptions by honking motorists, these games could go on for hours. He slowed down to watch a fly ball sail over the outfielder's head, hitting the pavement on a high bounce before rolling under a parked car. "Get it, get it!" his team shouted as the little guy scrambled under the wheels to locate the rubber ball. By the time he threw it back, the hitter had easily run around the chalked-in bases and was getting pats on the back for a run scored. He'd seen this scene dozens of times without pausing for a second glance. But this morning, he saw his 10-year-old self, taunted for his size, staying on the periphery, doing whatever he could to be included with his big brother, Walter and his gang. He could easily rewind the tape of their countless scenes together, recalling almost every frame of their connected lives. Jack had been blessed with loving parents and a sensitive big brother, and while it was sometimes hard to be in his shadow, Walter always took care of him. Even the four years he attended Hunter College as a subway commuter living at home to save money, Walter could be counted on to get Jack through the challenges of high school. Until he had to report for basic training at Fort Dix, Walter had slept in the next room to his every night. Jack had taken that security for granted, believing it would last his whole lifetime.

Alone in the temple's dimly lit foyer, he could make out echoed voices floating down the hallway. The smell of burnt cedar permeated his nostrils and brought back the nauseated memory of crossing the threshold eight years earlier for the funeral. He wasn't that religious and stopped observing any formal rituals after Walter died. With no occasion to force a visit, Jack had not entered the stark building until now. Following the voices, he rebuttoned his suit jacket and caught his breath. The first silhouette in focus was Bernice, and behind her, a collection of relatives and friends engaged in hugs and lively handshaking. She spotted him, and stopping in mid-sentence, hurried to his side.

"Jack, thank God, you're here. I saw Cindy and the boys and got worried." They embraced on cue, Bernice's head turned allowing their cheeks to touch, careful, he knew, not to let her lipstick stain his face.

"Your forehead's all wet. Here," she pulled out a tissue from her pocketbook, "take this and wipe yourself off. Why in heaven's name did you walk in this heat? It's a scorcher."

"Yeah, I know. So where is Jeffrey?" Jack dabbed his face as instructed.

"With the rabbi. We were here at 9:30, but he didn't feel like mingling before the ceremony. Can you blame him? He's got the bar mitzvah butterflies and you know Jeannie; she hasn't helped to settle them. It wasn't a smooth morning at all." She rolled her eyes and tilted her head toward a circle of giggling girls in pastel party dresses. Jeannie was among them, but on the outside looking lost in that separate world of hers, head down, fussing with the hem of her sleeveless dress that revealed her skinny legs.

Bernice turned back toward Jack and gave him a crinkled brow. "How about you, feeling okay?"

"Sure, I guess." He slipped his arms through hers. "Shall we?"

As soon as they reached the others, Jack was sucked into the welcome committee's clutches. Amidst the colorful sea of relatives, he held his breath while they wrapped their fleshy, perfumed arms around his shoulders. He heard his mother's high-pitched voice as she parted the small crowd before seeing her compact figure approach.

"Jackie, honey, why so late?" As she reached up to tighten his tie, her sharp-edged patent-leather handbag, locked in the crook of her arm, nearly whacked him in the jaw.

"Mom, stop, please—I'm fine." He touched her bony hand and she gave his a fragile squeeze.

"Sorry dear, you know, it's a big day. You remember your bar mitzvah?"

Jack nodded barely able to create the saliva needed to swallow. He felt like he was suffocating.

"What a day, so proud of our boy." Uncle Pauley ambled up alongside his mother, leading a cigar-reeking contingent of men, each taking turns gripping Jack's hand.

"Mazel tov, Jack, such a milestone, yes?" A deep voice spoke out from the minion of white-haired men.

Jack began to feel lightheaded. He'd never say it out loud, but he wanted to protest—'he's not my son, I didn't sign up for this job.' He spotted the porcelain fountain to the right of the sanctuary's entrance and politely excused himself. He lowered his lips into the arc of water, then cupped a few drops into his palm and patted the back of his neck. He took in one more gulp to calm the tiny jolts of stomach pain that had already begun their daily assault. Rather than offer to escort his mother or Bernice to their seats, he tried to regain his composure. Since he'd opened his eyes this morning, Jack could not block out flickering scenes of an animated, smiling Walter and then a pale lifeless version of him in a cold hospital morgue. For eight years, he'd put his grief in permanent lockdown, nose to the grindstone, helping to produce a newspaper every single day, but today, his grief felt caught in the back of his throat. Shaking his head to erase both the images and thoughts, Jack hurried through the sanctuary doors.

The cavernous space was nearly full; the sun pouring in through the stained-glass windows spread a rainbow of light on the well-coiffed crowd. Jeffrey's friends filled up the last two rows. Several boys restrained by their suits and ties, stood like statues, while others flailed their arms and twisted their bodies in playful protest. The girls, in contrast, seemed to wear their lacy dresses like a second skin. He noticed Jeannie entering the sanctuary's side doorway and following close behind, was her dark-haired Italian friend, Roz Vincie. He remembered Bernice telling him that she wanted Jeannie to have someone to pal around with so she wouldn't put a sulky damper on the day. He should have stopped to greet his niece with a supportive hug; instead, he took long, focused strides down the regal blue and gold carpeted runway to his own family.

When he reached the second row, he eased into the aisle seat next to Cindy. The kids announced his arrival with a loud 'Papa! Daddy's here', then returned to the prayer books and flyers they had pulled from the shelves in front of their seats, flapping pages in each other's faces.

"Stop it now, you two, you'll rip the book. Settle down… please." Cindy turned toward Jack and gave him a stern, pleading glare.

"You just made it, Jack. Is everything okay?"

"Yeah, you know, I just don't like this place."

"Okay, I understand, but these guys," she tilted her head toward the boys, "have never been inside a temple, and will have to sit still for who knows how long. Can you help me out here?"

Help? What wasn't he doing to help his family out? What about the forty-hour-a-week plus job providing for her and the kids? What about time for any of his needs? He shook his head, giving himself a sliver of self-pity. And yet, he knew too well, nothing in the daily routine would come close to his role as the family's pillar of strength. Jack tried his best to understand the degrees of pain and loss each family member experienced when his brother died. But he'd been the one thrust into the front lines ever since. While one family member after another slipped into despair, Jack had to keep both feet firmly on the ground as they grabbed for him with outstretched arms. Bernice's instant widowhood gave her first dibs and from that minute on, he had been drafted into caring for Jeffrey and Jeannie. Then, his own father, who could have lent a helping hand, got diagnosed with a heart condition and began to shut down, barely speaking, his vacant eyes either tracking words in a book or fixed on whatever program was on TV. Five years later, he died silently of a heart attack in the middle of the night. When his still grieving mother woke up that tragic morning, her precious Bill had been gone for hours, and this time she didn't seem to know how to bounce back.

"Yes, sorry honey; here, give me Maxie." He put his youngest son on his lap. Cindy had every right to feel resentful. He left so much to her and she didn't have a clue why. The only rational thing to do was tell her the truth, the whole truth. Nothing short of the real story of what took place eight years ago would work. He had mustered up the courage during their honeymoon up in the Poconos, but when he couldn't spit out the words, he tried writing out a script on the hotel notepad while she was out shopping one afternoon. Despite his determined resolve, whenever Jack began to relive his journey south on that hideous June day, his mind slammed on the brakes just in time for an emergency detour. After each kid was born, he had tried to convince himself that sharing the tragedy with the mother of his children might finally give his misery the company he longed for, but it could also backfire, and cause more anger that he'd kept her in the dark for too many years. Time marched on, and in the end, he said nothing, and let it gnaw his insides.

The organist to the right of the podium pressed his fingers on the keys, emitting a low, rumbling wail that signaled the start of the service. As the rabbi, cantor, and Jeffrey all emerged from a door next to the ark, the organist began to play a more upbeat sounding tune. He held onto the chords until Jeffrey was seated in the high back chair between the rabbi and cantor, who were now standing at podiums on either side of the small stage.

The Rabbi began. "Good Shabbos, and welcome to the Sabbath service that will be followed by the bar mitzvah of Jeffrey Glazer. Please stand and turn to page 15 in your prayer books."

Jack placed his son on the empty seat next to Cindy and went through the motions, but unlike the rest of the congregation, did not chime in with the Sabbath prayer. Instead, he closed his eyes to conjure up a picture of his 13-year-old self up at that podium, and probably like Jeffrey, praying to get through the haftarah portion without long pauses or flat-out mistakes. Jack, too, had struggled to learn Hebrew, but it had, once again, been Walter who pitched in, dismantling every line and making him practice until he wanted to slug him. On the big day though, he felt Walter's steady gaze on him while he recited every passage all with 'no runs, hits, or errors'…just a new man on the mound.

He raised his eyelids, mumbled through some call-and-response segment, and upon the rabbi's cue, eased back into his seat. The organist started up again and after a few bars, the deep soulful voice of the gray-bearded cantor filled every corner of the temple. Jack leaned forward to check on the boys. Scotty had his hands over his ears and Max was sucking his thumb. He locked eyes with his wife, her hair arranged in a bun showing off her lean neck and high cheek bones. She smiled and squeezed his hand. This was good, he thought, these are the moments to savor.

He inhaled and slowly let out a measured stream of air through his mouth. Shifting his head forward, he casually swayed from right to left and felt his hands clench into fists. His brother should have been here, should have been raising his own children, taking care of his wife and celebrating this milestone like all the rest of them. His own father should be sitting among them, head held high, watching his first grandson up at the bimah with the rabbi. He felt like he could read the minds of the guests. *Poor Bernice, raising those kids by herself.* Then, *poor Helen*, her turmoil the loudest among their silent thoughts, *losing a son, then five years later, her beloved Bill.* His mother was never the same. She stayed busy, she had to, she'd tell him, the more activities in her life, the more distracted she could be from her inconsolable grief. It showed up more and more in her sinking posture, droopy eyelids and deep gray lines barely hidden behind the frames of her large oval glasses.

Bernice was a close second, but he'd seen her abject sorrow turn angry; he did anything he could to avoid being left alone in a room with her those first few weeks after Walter's death. She acted like a junkyard dog, head low, her body in a hunt to survive each day, but also sniffing around for reasons why 'that Georgia sheriff didn't call her first.' Jack had to make up a wild tale about the deputy finding Walter's 'in case of emergency card' in his wallet with Jack's name and number underlined. That didn't satisfy her at all. 'Why you? I am his wife!' She took her hurt out on him for many months and to keep up the façade, he'd let her. Jack had no idea it would end up setting the stage for him to play his brother's keeper right up until this day. A sharp jab of pain in his lower abdomen had him reaching into his pocket for his antacid tablets but he came up empty. In his rush to get out the door this morning, he forgot his most vital accessory. His neck had already accumulated enough beads of sweat to start a drip under his collar, but now he had nothing to relieve his chronic indigestion. He glanced over to the side door and decided he had enough time to make a run for it before Jeffrey's performance.

"Cin—need to get out for a sec." He whispered, then gestured toward the door.

She knew better than to question him, and instinctively put her hand over Scotty's mouth so he wouldn't ask 'where's daddy going?' His mother turned and almost caught his arm as he hurried down the aisle. He didn't look back but could feel their concerned stares.

Out in the silent hallway, he raced over to the bathroom, breathing out a series of airy burps. When he got to the sink, he loosened his tie, and once again, cupped a handful of water and dabbed it on his neck and cheeks. "Pull it together," he commanded himself, and after a quick effort at the urinal, reentered the hallway. As he turned the corner toward the sanctuary, there was his niece gliding on her leather soles over a small expanse of the varnished floor.

"Jeannie, what are you doing?" His voice was quiet, but sharp.

"Uncle Jack, there you are, you didn't say hello to me." She smiled and ran over to him grabbing his hand. "Why'd you leave? Are you sick or something?"

"Oh, I see, you are keeping an eye on me, well that's a nice change. C'mon we're both going to get in trouble if we miss even a second of your brother's show." But when Jack tried to lead her back, she pulled her arm away.

"Do I have to? He'll be fine, he won't even know I'm gone."

"No, Jeannie, he might not, but your mother and grand-mother have got eyes in the back of their heads and they'll be sore at you." Jack's attempt at light humor wasn't hitting the target.

"But *you* won't be mad and that's all that counts." She lifted his arm and tucked her head underneath, trying to entice him into a playful dance.

He stopped her too abruptly and took hold of both of her hands, then crouched down to be at eye level. "This isn't an easy day for you, is it, honey?"

She looked at her shiny shoes and started clicking the heels together.

"Jeffrey's got a big job today; you wouldn't want to trade places with him on that stage, would you?" He reached for her chin, pulled it up, and looked into her eyes.

"He's got the stage all the time. Mommy's always worried about him. What about me?"

"She loves you just the same. Hey, and what about me? I'm here, honey, always have been, and always will be." He pointed to the sanctuary doors. "And if we don't get back inside, even Jeffrey will notice."

"I don't want to go back. I like it better out here, and you're wrong, Jeffrey won't even care, Mommy either."

Her words tightened the muscles around his heart. Jack had such a tender spot for his vulnerable niece. Spirited as a little girl, she seemed to have entered some new phase, more quiet, somber, less social, and according to Bernice, preferring to read a book alone in her room than engage with the outside world. If she only knew how much Walter loved her, how he'd fallen hard for his red-haired curly top beauty. Watching Jeannie care for her dolls, his brother shared his dreams of her following him into the health field, as a nurse, or even, he'd touch his own chest, a doctor. Jack tried to make her feel special by being there as often as he could, but he knew he could never replace his brother. With his own family to love and care for, not to mention taking over a daily newspaper where the pace never let up, he just didn't have enough reserves for her and Jeffrey.

He stood up and gently took hold of her arm.

"I'm wrong about a lot of things, but honey, not about this, trust me."

He pulled her in for a tight hug and kissed the top of her head. "You know I love you like a daddy."

She didn't look up and held him a little longer than usual. Then, unraveling from his embrace, she smiled, turned and skated across the floor. Before going back inside, she waved and lifted the sides of her dress in a silly curtsy.

Jack waved back but didn't move. His legs felt heavy as if a layer of cement had been wedged inside his shoes. Since that fatal day, he'd had no time to grasp the full weight of his family responsibilities. It was go, go, go, take care of it, fall in love fast, have babies, be the devoted son, and without objection, assume on-call brother-in-law duties. It was painfully unfair; Jeffrey and Jeannie, Scotty and Max, his mother and Uncle Pauley, Cindy and her two sisters, all alive and well. But he had been cheated and robbed in the most tragic of circumstances. Siblings are supposed to live through the loss of parents and elderly relatives together and travel the rest of the way side-by-side until their own aging bodies gave out. Jack had been far too young for a solo journey.

He pulled the velvet box from his pocket. Rolling his thumb over the top, he watched his hands shake as he opened it for the last time. Wedged in the white satin fold was the chunky gold ring that had been in the envelope at the Georgia morgue. It was a bar mitzvah gift from his grandfather who passed it on to his father Bill, and then on to Walter when he was 13. Jack took it out, rubbed his fingers along the raised inscription and slipped it slowly onto his right ring finger. He'd found an old jeweler on the Lower East Side who took a week to decipher the words. It had come from the 121st Psalm, all about trusting the Creator for protection; the translation said God would guard 'our' going and coming both now and forever.

"It says all that?" Jack had asked the old, hunched man with the magnified glasses.

"More or less." He shrugged back.

Jack extended his right arm, spread his fingers wide and stared at the ring, just as he imagined Walter had done on the day he received it and the hundreds of days after that, until God's protection had expired. He headed to the sanctuary door, weary and upset with himself for falling into a maudlin well of despair. Before reentering, Jack pulled off the ring, placed it back into the box and put it in his pocket. It would be Jeffrey's legacy now, and if Jack could help it, would protect his nephew from knowing the truth about how his father's ring had actually been found.

He took one last breath and crept back inside.

## Chapter 4

## JUNE 1968

# Grammy Helen

THE 6:00 CBS EVENING NEWS with Walter Cronkite was blaring throughout the small living room. While Helen had difficulty hearing specific details, she could always follow the lilt of his staccato voice and derive some solace watching his unwavering expression of calm as he cycled through one catastrophe, it seemed, after another. Helen likened him to a brave fireman hosing down flames, then sticking around to sort through the smoke and rubble.

She made sure dinnertime began somewhere between 5:00 and 5:30 p.m. so that she had the time to wash up, put the dishes away and join her older brother, Pauley, who'd be nestled into the leather recliner once occupied by her late husband, Bill. Helen would pitch forward from her spot on the couch, straining to absorb the nightly reports that sadly, over the past year, left both of them shaking their heads in audible sighs of disbelief. The clips of Vietnam were the worse, all the disturbing battle scenes ending with the body counts made Helen anxious and afraid for Jeffrey. As a junior in a college Upstate, her grandson was temporarily safe from the draft. But sometimes when she'd watched too much news, her mind would drift to images of Jeffrey in an army uniform, a gun on his shoulder, boarding an aircraft, and landing in that murderous jungle. It would make her stomach leap, her throat to close up, and at times, force her to bolt from her chair to

RIPPLE EFFECT                    39

pace, clean, or if all else failed, call Jack at the newspaper.

A couple of months earlier, on April 4th, toward the end of the news hour, Walter Cronkite announced to the world that Martin Luther King, Jr. had been shot and killed on a balcony in Memphis.

"Oh my god! How could this have happened?" Helen moaned to Pauley, shocked, heartsick for his family, and frightened for what would come next.

The next 24 hours, they didn't take their eyes off the set, staring at black and white faces twisted in pain and tears, heads in hands or raised in agony, and then, disturbing scenes of riots erupting in nearly every Negro community in the country. Helen thought about Harlem, within walking distance from Barnard College where Jeannie, her 18-year-old granddaughter, was attending school.

Pauley blurted out, "It was just a matter of time, I'm sorry to say that, but there's too much hate for the coloreds, especially down south. I think it's going to get a lot worse."

Three weeks later, it came closer to home, when the somber Cronkite, surrounded by photographs and chaotic film coverage on the screen behind him, reported that antiwar protesters had taken over the Columbia campus next to Barnard. Helen watched choppy images of students scattering, waving fists and signs, arms linked together barricading doorways chased by swarms of police grabbing, hitting and shoving them in vans. Could Jeannie be in those crowds? Helen rolled herself off the couch and peered into the screen. Would her granddaughter get involved with this sort of craziness?

Both she and her daughter-in-law, Bernice, who talked every day, repeatedly dialed Jeannie's dormitory to reach her, but no one ever picked up. Pauley kept telling her that if Jeannie were in trouble, they'd know, and anyway it was guys on the front lines, not girls like Jeannie. "She's smart enough to keep her distance."

After watching days of alarming footage of hundreds of police with clubs pounding kids' bodies, she was not convinced and reached out to her son.

He picked up his private line after a dozen rings.

"Jack Glazer."

Helen didn't like that he never greeted callers with a simple pleasantry.

"Hello dear, can you spare a minute?"

"No, Mom, I've got every reporter on both shifts, it's mayhem. We need to keep all the phone lines open. We do know that anyone out there not in a black police uniform is likely getting arrested or being sent to the nearest hospital, including reporters."

"Okay, okay, just another minute, what about Jeannie? Do you think she's okay? Why hasn't she called us?" Helen felt her voice rising. Her hearing seemed to drop off more in the evenings, and phone conversations with noisy backgrounds were very frustrating.

"It's just been a few days, I'm sure she's okay. Look, we're in unprecedented waters; these kids seem to have some kind of plan and are standing firm."

Helen not only kept the television on throughout the day but read *The Globe* without fail. Between the pictures of striking students and then more mobs of young people marching together down the streets of Harlem, she didn't know if it was about protesting the war or more outrage at Reverend King's assassination. Helen kept her son on the phone a little longer and asked him why the students were so upset.

Jack exhaled into the receiver. "It's about Columbia's contracts with the Pentagon; the students say the school is contributing to the war effort. On top of that, yes, it's also about race. The university wants to expand their gymnasium into Morningside Heights, and both the black and white student groups agree it would prevent the Harlem community's access to the school's gym."

Helen adjusted the phone right up against her ear. "So, these young people believe that violating property and worse, getting beaten and arrested, is going to stop the gym from being built, *and* the Pentagon contracts from being carried out?"

Now she was shouting, but her anger came from being worried sick. "Oh, I don't care about all that. Where is Jeannie? Find her, *please*."

• • •

THE CALL SHE'D BEEN praying for came four days later.

"Hello Grammy? It's Jeannie."

Helen wanted to shout with joy; instead she twisted the phone cord around her fingers and took a deep breath.

"Darling, are you okay? We've all been beside ourselves with worry. Why didn't you call sooner, you know we've been watching the news and..."

Jeannie cut her off. "I've been sick with a horrible cold—it turned into some kind of chest thing. I couldn't get out to the protests even if I wanted to."

While concerned about her cold, Helen wasn't sure what she meant. Would she have joined the protests if she had been well? A strange feeling gripped her stomach. No, she'd never take those dangerous risks, that wasn't how she was raised.

Three more weeks passed before the police, including a special patrol force, ended the school standoff, though not before hundreds of arrests and dozens of beatings. The only relief she felt was knowing that Jeannie had not been among them.

Newscasters reported that in retaliation for the police brutality, the protesting students had gathered enough followers to block access to buildings for as long as it took to shut down the Columbia campus. Several days later, the administration gave up and announced that classes would be canceled for the rest of the semester. Helen monitored it all, turning up the volume so as not to miss a single new development.

"Helen, it's too loud, please!" Pauley rarely raised his voice; she knew he'd had enough.

Her progressive hearing loss was probably the only point of contention between them. Since her widowed brother moved in a few years back, he badgered her on a daily basis to see a doctor for hearing aids, but she wasn't ready for those contraptions. Mostly she fought with her own vanity, and how she would be forced to restyle her heavily lacquered bob-cut to hide her condition. Helen, more than her brother, had been blessed with genes from the healthier side of their family. She'd always been steady on her feet; her compact five foot one-inch frame kept its resiliency despite reaching her sixth decade. She had inherited her boxy shape from her own mother. And after two children, and then four precious grandchildren to cook for and spoil, she put on a solid 20 pounds that settled around her midriff, though her narrow hips and birdlike legs stayed taut and lean. With just a hint of make-up, Helen still received compliments about her soft, peachy skin and high cheekbones, and looked at least a decade younger than the ladies in her canasta club. Her hearing though, was getting worse, but it only made her dig in with more stubbornness every time Pauley gave her the business.

Bernice called with the best news she'd heard in over a month.

"Hello Mom, I wanted to let you know, Jeannie's back and in one piece, but thin as a rail and tired." Bernice's voice was high and much louder than Helen needed it to be. "So to celebrate, Friday night dinner is on. You and Uncle Pauley can come any time after five."

Helen lit up inside. "Oh, so happy, dear. Please tell her I'll make her favorite dish."

• • •

FRIDAY NIGHT DINNER WAS the last semi-religious tradition that survived both Walter's and then Bill's passing. It began when Walter and Bernice moved into their neighborhood after the war. What the kids didn't know was that she and Bill had been on a real estate hunt as soon as Walter announced his marriage plans. After months of calling agents and visiting open houses, they found an affordable two-story home between Kew Gardens and Forest Hills, only ten minutes away from their son and daughter-in-law. Helen would never forget walking up the short path, seeing the SOLD sign on the miniature front lawn, and stepping inside to see Walter and six-months pregnant Bernice, twirling around the empty three-bedroom detached home. Tears spread down her cheeks as her daughter-in-law rushed over to give her a hug, and then linked arms to show her around. "So perfect," Bernice pointed at the white fence in the backyard, touching her extended belly, "for kids."

Years later, she and Bill got their second wish when Jack and Cindy were married and moved into Jack's one-bedroom apartment in Rego Park, also close by. Then, after ascending to *The Globe's* editor-in-chief job, Jack found a spacious place in a high rise in Forest Hills. It was an older building with a marbled lobby and a doorman. Best of all, the property bordered a tree-lined neighborhood close to the temple and the sprawling grounds of the Forest Hills tennis courts, a safe community to raise her two rambunctious grandsons.

Friday could not have come fast enough. Pauley decided to spend the day visiting his old buddies in Brooklyn and asked if she'd like to come along; he told her it might do her some good to get out of the house, but she waved him off.

"I've got too much to do today. I'm making my scalloped potatoes for dinner tonight. Jeannie's favorite," she added as she followed him to the front door. "Now go, but don't be late coming back. I want to get to B's early."

Helen watched him get into the taxi double-parked on their street. She had convinced the old coot to forgo the subway and treat himself to an air-conditioned ride to Flatbush. She closed the door quickly to keep the cool air inside, and rather than return to her spot on the couch, she settled into the cozy recliner.

She had drifted off into one of those fuzzy catnaps where the ringing phone was a fire alarm in her dream. A scene of strong men, one-by-one, sliding down poles and then, racing to their trucks, gave her a sense that help, or some kind of rescue was on its way. After what must have been several moments of ringing, she opened her eyes, and popped off the chair.

"Hello?" Her voice came out thick and groggy.

"Mom, it's B, are you okay?" Bernice spoke faster than usual.

"Yes, yes, dear, I guess I'd fallen asleep. What time is it?"

"Well, that's not like you. It's almost three. I was just calling to check on when to expect you. Like I said, any time after five is good for me."

"Oh no, oh my goodness, I haven't even started my dish.

I have to go. At this rate, we won't be there until 5:30, and that's if I can make water boil faster!"

"Wait, Mom, don't go crazy. I was also calling to say only Jack is coming, and he'll be late. Scotty is sick with some stomach thing, so Cindy is staying home with the boys. Come when you're ready. I know you and Uncle Pauley would prefer eating earlier, but I'm thinking 6:30 is more realistic, that okay?"

"Wonderful, we'll be there before 6." Helen hung up and dashed into the kitchen.

"For goodness sake," she said out loud, realizing she'd slept for two whole hours. Bernice was right; it was unusual now for her to nap during the day. After Walter and then Bill died, she'd often dream about them, with vibrant images, sometimes younger, sometimes older, but always alive and well. Then, she'd open her eyes, suddenly conscious of the empty space beside her, and the reality of a son no longer a 10-minute drive away. By mid-afternoon after those restless nights, she'd doze, often finding herself waking up on the sofa or even in her bed, disoriented enough that she'd have to turn on the television or pick up a newspaper to know what day it was.

Moving as quickly as her body's creaking joints would allow, she filled her biggest pot with water and placed it on a burner. Then she began the tedious job of peeling and slicing the spuds into neat slivers. Just as she was dropping the potatoes into the water, she heard her brother calling from the front door. Pauley did that now so she wouldn't be startled if she didn't hear him come in.

"Hi Helen, I'm not too late, am I? Just need to change my clothes and..."

She stopped him. "You could probably take a short nap if you wanted to, the potatoes won't be ready for another hour. I dozed off on the recliner, and if Bernice hadn't called, well I don't know what. She said dinner is at 6:30, but I still want to leave as soon as the dish is done." She turned on the oven and dug into the Frigidaire for butter, milk and cheese. The recipe was from her Betty Crocker Cookbook. Not being the most creative of cooks, she followed the directions to the letter; the dish was a consistent crowd-pleaser.

"Well, I suppose you needed the shut-eye." Pauley turned back toward the hallway.

"Wait Pauley, tell me about your visit, how's the old gang?" She wanted his company.

"Let me go change and I'll tell you all about it." He paused a moment, then shuffled over to her side and planted a gentle kiss on her cheek. It was just what she needed from her big brother.

Since the dinner was getting off to a later start, they decided to take a cab to Bernice's place. Helen didn't like to drive in the dark, and besides, Jack took his car on Fridays when there was a dinner gathering so they could count on him to give them a ride home. She and Pauley had barely settled into their seats when the cab driver screeched away from the curb. The short distance wouldn't give him much of a fare and no doubt he wanted to drop them off even faster.

Bernice was already at the front door and scooting down the steps to greet them as they arrived. Helen leaned in for the customary cheek kiss, then handed over the casserole dish while Pauley gave her shoulder a quick squeeze and led the way.

"Is Jeannie here?" Helen asked as the three of them reached the porch landing.

"She'll be back soon. She said she had some errands to run." Bernice had a buoyancy in her step, and a glow on her face. Helen saw she'd put in some extra effort with her hair, and even a hint of red stain on her lips. She still had that skinny frame, although a bit of a paunch had thickened her midriff.

Inhaling the aroma of Bernice's roasting chicken, Helen let out a long sigh.

"How are we going to make it another hour, B? I guess I should have eaten a bigger lunch."

"Not to worry. I figured you'd have too long to wait, so I made hors d'oeuvres to tide us over." Bernice told them to settle into their spots in the living room.

It was after six when Jack let himself in through Bernice's screen door. Helen pushed herself up off the couch and was the first to greet him in the entryway. With outstretched arms, she gave him a chesty hug and then looked up into his eyes. His pasty face showed deep divots between his brows and around his mouth. She felt her face responding to his pain.

"You look exhausted, son, been such an awful few weeks." She reached up and touched his cheek.

"I'm that and then some, but mostly starving. Jeannie here?" He turned his gaze toward the kitchen. "It smells like a four-star restaurant. You made the potato supreme dish, I hope?"

His grin put a smile on her face, and she nodded, then looping her arm through his, led them both into the small dining room.

"No, Jeannie's not here, she'll be back any minute." Bernice came through the swinging kitchen door, her arms holding the challah tray draped with an embroidered silk coverlet. She placed it in the center of the dining room table, and then untied her apron before leaning up to give Jack a kiss on his cheek.

"Well, aren't we being fancy tonight?" Jack picked up a chunky crystal wine glass from one of the place settings. "Looks like you broke out the china, almost too elegant to mess up with food. Where's Uncle Pauley?"

"He's here, in the bathroom. We've had a bit of a head start on the crackers and dip. You know it's late for us to be eating dinner." Helen spread the candle holders further apart to allow more space for the challah tray.

"What's wrong with Scotty? Nothing serious, I hope." Helen felt a twinge of concern but also relief Cindy and the boys wouldn't be joining them tonight. Jeannie needed to be center stage and she believed all four of them wanted it that way.

"Nah, he just ate something that didn't agree with him; Cindy says he'll be fine by morning." Jack was about to sit down when the front doorbell buzzed in short rhythmic beats loud enough for Helen to hear. It was Jeannie's signal that she had arrived. They were all familiar with her entrance ritual, something she started when she was still in grade school.

Helen scurried down the hallway, Jack on her heels.

"Sweetie!" She wrapped her granddaughter in her fleshy arms.

"Hi Grammy." She was carrying a long, ratty canvas bag slung across her body. "Please loosen up the grip. You're choking me."

"Okay, okay, let me look at you." Helen released Jeannie and looked her up and down.

"You are all skin and bones, and pale. Oh my, that cold must have been something. You need to eat and get some rest, honey, you're home now."

"Okay, okay, please stop being so dramatic; it's not like I've been away for so long."

"Well, yes you have my darling girl, for us you have." As she took hold of her arm, Helen's eyes began to water. She had a special relationship with her only granddaughter. Maybe that was how it was between grandmothers and granddaughters, who knew, but for her, having two sons and three grandsons, Helen was eternally grateful that Walter and Bernice had a little girl. Jeannie had melted her heart from the first moment she held her fragile body. Living close by was also a godsend; not only could she watch all of her grandkids blossom, but in Bernice's single parent household, Helen had been allowed to remain in the thick of their day-to-day lives. She could even discipline them when needed, but that never happened. Her role was to spoil and arrange fun outings to zoos, museums, movies, shows and all kinds of restaurants where the kids were free to order anything they wanted. She never ordered anything except a cup of coffee, and then waited patiently for them to eat like birds before swooping in to make sure nothing went to waste.

Helen grew more concerned about Jeannie's weight loss as Bernice reached up to her daughter's face, pulling back her curly auburn locks elongating her hollowed cheeks. Jeannie's shmata of a dress hung on her too loosely. It was one of those hippie outfits with swirling circles of color, a canvas belt with beads knotted at the ends cinched her waist.

Jack entered the foyer, followed by Pauley. Moving out of the way to let the men join the welcome party, Helen sensed their collective joy. After a tumultuous few months, they all wanted the chance to squeeze her bony frame and exhale.

"C'mon now, let's eat, the food has been ready for an hour." Bernice led everyone into the dining room.

"Gosh, Mom, what's the occasion?" Jeannie asked as she sat down in her usual place. Helen could detect a nuance of appreciation from her granddaughter.

"You are home for one, and we're almost all together. I wish that brother of yours would consider a visit, even a short one; you know he hasn't been back home since Thanksgiving,"

Bernice replied while placing the roast chicken, already cut in pieces, next to Helen's scalloped potatoes, along with a string bean platter and a green salad.

Jack opened the red wine and filled everyone's glass, except Helen's. He knew she didn't like to drink wine or any kind of alcohol anymore; it produced a dull ache at her temples even if she only indulged in a small glass. Bernice lit the candles and led the prayer over the wine, then quickly took the coverlet off the challah. Pauley, per their tradition, recited the blessing, and then the temporary decorum was replaced by a flurry of arms passing around platters and piling food on plates. This always made Helen relax; delicious food and wine brought both contentment and conversation, reminding her that despite all the tragedy in their lives, they were still a unit, a family.

"Fill us in Jeannie, we're anxious to find out where you've been during all the protesting." Helen couldn't wait any longer to blurt out the first round of inquiry.

Jeannie finished swallowing, drank from her water glass, and squinted across at her. "Sick, in bed sick, I told you all." Her tone took a hostile twist.

"Hold on there, honey, why are you talking like that to your grandmother?" Bernice put down her fork, stared at her daughter, and then shook her head.

Jack jumped in. "And was that such a bad thing? We haven't heard from you in a month. You could have been seriously hurt in those protests. Your grandmother, like the rest of us, was just hoping for an inside scoop. My reporters had a helluva time avoiding blows to the head. One of them wasn't so lucky and got whacked in his back and can't work for another week." Helen noticed that Jack had poured himself another full glass of wine.

"Seriously?" Jeannie turned her face toward him. "Sorry,

Uncle Jack, about your reporters, but you know, I had friends
with stitched-up head wounds too, and a whole other bunch
sent to jail or the courthouse just for asserting their rights to
free speech. And who knows how many ended up in hospital
beds. I should've been there too, should've been marching with
Jim, Ted, Mark, all of them!"

Helen shifted her head around too quickly giving her one
of those painful cricks in her neck. Jeannie's forceful voice
seemed to suddenly go limp, as if after spilling her guts, she
didn't trust her audience to provide the empathy she was
seeking.

Helen's generation never would have questioned the government's decision to go to war but over the past year with
what seemed like millions of people, not just young kids, out
in the streets, would she be unpatriotic to believe President
Johnson and the Congress were wrong? And then there was
Jeffrey, maybe just one year away from being drafted. Back
in their day, boys like her Walter knew that when it was time
to serve their country, they reported for duty, no questions
asked. That didn't mean she wasn't worried sick about him
and would pray every moment for a posting far away from the
front lines. Walter finished college in May of '44 and a week
after his induction, the Normandy invasion meant no more
troops would be sent to Europe. Adding to their good fortune,
Walter's flat feet inherited from Bill's side of the family kept
him safely on U.S. soil until victory was declared the following
year. It had been a worldwide battle to stop and destroy an evil,
fascist dictator who'd already annihilated millions of innocent
people. Everyone served in any way they could. Sending troops
to Vietnam was not like WWII, she wasn't that naïve, but until
all the dangerous protests against this war, she still had faith
in her government to make the right decisions. But just like

every other frightened parent or grandparent with boys, she wanted the Vietnam war to end.

"Okay, I'm sorry, I wasn't thinking," Jack lowered his voice. "The protests certainly have some merit, but like you said, things got out of hand and dangerous, wouldn't you agree?" Jack pushed his chair back and crossed his legs. "I mean your friends knew that eventually the cops would be summoned. It's been like that all over the country. A losing street battle has been the outcome every time."

Jeannie slammed down her fork, "But we didn't lose at all! Our demands were legitimate, and they knew it. If it wasn't for all of us out there shutting down the school, that racist gym project would be in full swing right now, no one would have made a stink about Columbia's Pentagon contracts that keep this fucked up war going."

"You calm down this minute, young lady, and watch your language!" Bernice stood up and glared at Jeannie, whose flashing eyes and hand waving made Helen fear she might flick a forkful of potatoes at either Jack or Bernice.

"Are you kidding, Mom? My language is what you want me to watch? You're all just spectators *watching* it happen on TV. Were you even able to see that students and the Harlem community are joining together to promote racial equality? This is historic. And yes, we're not going to stop, because every day this government is sending boys like Jeffrey into a jungle we have no reason to be in. There's no war to win, and in fact, you all have to know by now, we're actually losing it. But all everyone sees are privileged white kids, bored with school, nothing better to do than incite riots so they can justify missing classes. Call in the cops, restore order, and if anyone gets hurt, well, then they asked for it…" Jeannie pursed her mouth into a sneer as she ranted, then stood up as her eyes shifted around the table at all of them.

"Alright, enough! Please sit down. You've been sick and in the middle of this craziness for months now. Can you give the soapbox speech a rest?" Bernice's sharp words silenced the room.

Jeannie didn't look up as she pushed food around on her plate. Dinnertime was clearly over.

To ease the tension, Helen spoke up and asked about her plans for the summer.

"I have a boyfriend, I told you about him, right? We're thinking of going on a road trip sometime this summer." Helen could detect a tentative defiance in her voice.

"What? A road trip, to where?" Bernice leaned forward in her chair.

"We don't know yet," said Jeannie. "Jim, that's his name, has some work leads for me too. I'll be fine."

Helen rotated her gaze around the table, saving Jeannie's face for last. When their eyes met, she felt herself flinch, that soft innocent look was gone. Helen stared harder, momentarily unable to recognize the young woman sitting across from her, the sweet pea she'd help raise, thinking: Who had put these thoughts in her head? Jeannie looked away, then picked up her plate and carried it into the kitchen. Helen rose too and glanced at her son. He gave her the nod of approval, and so she followed her granddaughter.

Jeannie stood by the sink with her arms folded across her chest, staring into the big picture window overlooking the backyard. The sun had just set and a faded orange hue filled the small kitchen. Helen stepped toward her, and out of habit, gently turned her shoulders allowing their faces to meet.

"Sweetie, what is wrong, *please*, you can tell me."

She could see her granddaughter's jaw twitch, and after too

long of a pause, she responded, "Nothing is wrong with me, or the others. It's been a tough time. I'll be fine. I just need a break."

Helen had watched Jeannie's lips extra carefully so she wouldn't miss a word.

"Is this about that boyfriend of yours? Maybe we could meet him—"

Jeannie shook her head. "No. Not now, and I don't know when. Please just trust me, okay?"

Helen had more questions about this new person in Jeannie's life; who was he and why couldn't they meet him? But she knew she'd get no more information tonight. It was now up to Jack to set things right, a role he'd taken on since Jeannie was three years old.

• • •

"PAULEY, OH NO, NO!" Helen shouted through the front door screen from the porch landing. She always woke earlier than her older brother to use the bathroom and get the coffee percolator going. While the machine hummed into action, she'd make her way to the porch and retrieve the morning paper.

"What's going on, where's the fire?" Pauley shouted but Helen couldn't answer, her brain struggled to absorb the paper's screaming headline: RFK SHOT! Underneath was a grainy photo of Bobby Kennedy's body, his head encircled in a halo of blood.

*Not again!?!* She skimmed the first paragraph and placed her hand over her mouth when she read that moments before he was gunned down, Bobby had been declared the winner of the Democratic presidential primary in California. She began shaking her head back and forth, like one of her grandson's bobblehead figurines.

"Helen dear, what's the matter?" Pauley opened the screen, coaxing her back in.

"He was shot last night! Good heavens, Bobby Kennedy was shot right after he won the primary; who could have done this? Why? I don't believe it. *I can't believe it!*"

"Come in now, Helen, try to calm yourself. I'll turn on the set, and you get us some coffee." He held out his hand and helped her across the threshold, and then veered off into the living room.

Helen kept her head down, scanning the paper's details on her way to the kitchen, then stopped in her tracks when she read that "*RFK was still in critical condition...*" So wait, maybe, God willing, he'd pull through. *Please don't die*, the words coming out in rapid succession as she poured their coffees. A saucer in each hand, Helen carefully made her way down the hallway.

"What are they saying, Pauley? Is he still alive? The paper said he's in critical condition, so...

Pauley cut her off. "Yes, yes, dear, he's still in surgery, but they don't give it much hope. It was several bullets to his head. They got the guy though, some Palestinian. I don't understand either." Pauley's last words were indecipherable to Helen.

Had only two months passed since Dr. King was gunned down? Blinking back tears, Helen felt as if the world had gone mad, that this deliberate act of murder was the last straw. Her mind reeled at yet another young promising leader, another Kennedy too, killed in the prime of his life. Reports of his failing condition dominated television and newspaper coverage for 24 hours, until Helen and Pauley woke up Friday morning to learn that *Robert Kennedy was pronounced dead at 1:44 a.m. PDT.*

Their quiet living room was still dark; neither she nor

Pauley had taken the next steps in the daily routine to draw back the drapes. She lifted herself off the couch, shuffled over to the curved bay window and tugged at the curtain cord. It was just past 7:00; she gazed out at the familiar cars parked along her street, the early morning sun reflecting off windshields wet with dew. Opening the window, she glanced up to see a few birds land on the magnolia tree across the street. She leaned her ear against the screen to better hear their high-pitched tweets. Everything looked so serene and peaceful like a landscape painting. Turning back toward the neatly arranged room, she scanned the sea of framed photographs lined up in waves on the antique cherry cabinet. Helen picked up her favorite image, pushed her oval glasses to the top of her head, and studied the faded sepia-toned figures of her young family. The boys in their swim trunks, she behind Walter, resting an arm on his scrawny shoulder; and Bill, his hand atop Jack's head, smiles of pride and joy on both of their faces. She traced the heavy gold-leafed frame and noticed how wrinkled her veined hands had become.

Placing the picture back among the others, Helen did not have the courage to visit any more eras filled with grinning children, grandchildren, or Bill. Beyond sharing her day-to-day existence with him for 40 years, he had been her last link in body and soul to Walter. After they lost Walter, Bill did whatever he could to care for her crushed spirit; he'd been the rock for all of them, setting aside his own grief. Or so she had believed.

A breeze from the open window carried the scent of cut grass. It took enormous willpower to distance herself from Walter's accident and the agonizing weeks and months that followed. Her sunny disposition had evaporated, replaced with a cloud of despair that could become so disturbingly dark, she'd find herself weeping at any hour of the day. And nothing, not a look of sympathy, or even Bill's touch could erase the harrowing image of her son's lifeless body crushed behind a steering wheel.

While she struggled through every day for months on end, it was her stoic Bill, never much of a talker, who had become even quieter, she having constantly to ask him to speak up, and this was long before her hearing problems began. He'd answer her questions with only a few syllables and put up the best front he could with the rest of the family. She woke up before dawn one morning, Bill wasn't in bed, and the bathroom light was off. "Bill?" she called out. She found him in Walter's old room, sitting on his narrow bed, with one hand on his heart and the other holding his forehead, restrained sobs coming from his chest. Hurrying to his side, she sat beside him and they held each other until he caught his breath. "You're not sleeping, dear," she whispered into his ear, "let's go see the doctor, maybe he can give you something to help." Bill reluctantly agreed, and a few weeks later began to take medication that did bring him the oblivion he needed to get through the sleepless nights. After a month or more of swallowing a tiny white pill before bed, Bill had leaned over and asked her if he was becoming an addict. Would he ever be able to fall asleep on his own again? His eyes pleaded with hers for hope. Staring into his chronically sad face, she reached up and caressed his cheek, uttering the phrase that would become her lifelong motto, "This, too, shall pass, my dear. But in the meantime," she had tried to reassure him, "you are entitled to grieve in any way you need for as long as you want." Bill's sorrow, she knew, had included his regret that he didn't accompany Jack to Georgia to settle up the affairs and retrieve Walter's body. But Jack had insisted that he go alone, and raged like a wild man, commanding Bill to stay 'with Mom' and that he didn't need any help.

Jack had left early the next morning, but not without his marching orders to call them collect every time he stopped for gas or food. She and Bill spent those long, heartbreaking days adrift in shock, and comforting poor Bernice and the kids. While Jack stayed true to his word, phoning in at regular intervals, their relief was quickly eclipsed by the brutal reality that only one son would be returning home alive.

She was in no mood for breakfast but thought Pauley might need something to off-set the coffee on an empty stomach. Stepping outside, she saw her brother sitting on a padded patio chair, hunched over, his head dropped into his chest. A sliver of sunlight peeked through the trees and spread out onto the porch. The glow landed on a row of colorful pots arranged around the porch's perimeter. Every spring, she'd make the trip to the gardening center and select the most vibrant and resilient annuals, the ones that wouldn't turn brown or wither if she lost track of watering days. By June, the reds, oranges, and purples stood tall in their leafy pots; their time to thrive, she'd marvel. Helen never had much of a green thumb, but took up the garden project the first spring after they moved in. Walter had just turned six and Jack was a one-year-old toddler. For Helen, this stretch of years before the Depression were filled with idyllic memories where she believed she was the luckiest girl in town.

"Ready to eat, Pauley?"

"No, but it'll do for distraction."

She nodded and as she helped him out of the chair, they heard the phone ringing.

Helen scurried to answer it.

"Mom, it's Bernice."

"You saw the news, yes? It's beyond tragic, the poor Kennedys." Helen pulled a tissue from her sleeve and wiped her nose.

"I know, unbelievable, I've been in tears...but Mom, listen, I'm calling about Jeannie."

"What's the matter?" She flattened the receiver to her ear.

"She packed up a suitcase and snuck out this morning."

"Oh no! Where to? Did she leave a note?"

"No, just an unmade bed."

"This isn't like her, not at all." Helen's heart pumped with a beat of fear.

Bernice let out an audible sigh. "I left Jack a message; he'll know what to do."

# Chapter 5

## AUGUST 1968

# *Hank*

T HE NIGHTMARE WOULD VARY, but it always ended the same. He'd be running hard and fast, faceless men in suits bearing down in black cars, the deafening sound of sirens. They'd get close enough for a man to thrust an arm out of an open window, repeatedly firing a long pistol at his head, the piercing explosions ringing in his ears. Waking with a jolt, Hank swerved onto his side, crashing his arm on the marble coffee table and knocked over a tumbler of melted ice onto the shag carpet. He didn't jump up in reaction; passing out on his narrow couch and the disorientation it produced had become routine. He gently lifted himself into a half-sitting position and massaged his temples in an attempt to stop the awful buzz. He opened his eyes to a dark house, the only light coming in from the patio doors, the moon painting white lines into the spacious living room. It took another few seconds for him to realize that it was the phone ringing from inside his bedroom. "Jesus!" Easing off the sofa, he followed the beams to his nightstand and grabbed the receiver.

"It's Tony, sorry to wake ya."

"What's up?"

"They got her at the main precinct. She's banged up, but alive and kicking." Tony Dallopena didn't mince words, he was a savvy professional who delivered, and his efforts didn't come cheap.

"Good, get going then. I want her out as fast as possible." Hank felt a rush of adrenalin spread through his bloodstream.

"Yeah, but there's a problem with the amount. These guys have been through 48 hours of hell. Desk sarge has about the greasiest palm I've ever squeezed. The city wants their streets back, a real war zone here. It's three Gs or she's staying with the rest of the scum—his words, not mine." Tony's snappy tone gave away his New York roots.

"Fine, fine, just do it—did you get the ticket?" Hank sunk down onto his bed, relief easing down his shoulder blades.

"Yup, but like I told ya, long shot she'll use it."

Tony thought the bus ticket to New York was a waste of money, and a bad idea. "Getting bailed out without knowing who put up the dough is confusing enough," he said. "The free ride home will drive her nuts." Hank didn't care, he was going to see it all the way through, no matter what.

"Follow her until she gets on board." Hank now felt in charge, the liquor clearing from his brain.

"Okay, I'll ring ya from the station." Tony hung up before Hank could respond. That was typical of their relationship. Hank was the boss, but somehow Tony called the shots.

He stood up and groped his way back into the living room. The air conditioning hummed through the vast room, but the place still felt muggy. Summers in the south defied modern technology. Although he had discarded all but his boxer shorts, now bunched up into the crack of his backside, he was hot, sticky and starving. It was after 2:00 a.m. and he couldn't remember the last decent meal he'd eaten. He walked into his stark kitchen, flipped on the light and let his gaze rest on the take-out food remnants stuck to cardboard boxes on the Formica counter. Dirty dishes filled the stainless-steel sink, and the stale fried-chicken stench should have turned his stomach, but instead, he pawed the boxes for a stray drumstick. He opened the refrigerator and got even more depressed; bottles of beer, coke, and tonic water dominated the shelves. He grabbed a Schlitz and headed out to the patio, picking up his Camels on the way.

As his slovenly household behavior intensified, Hank spent more time in the backyard. A sanctuary of sorts, it was dominated by a large, rectangular pool and a stylish cabana with a built-in mini-fridge and bar. Weeks after he moved in, he added a few chaise lounges, a white, round wooden table, and an umbrella stand with wheels that he could easily move around to shield direct sun. The space had a simple quality to it and that was just fine with him. After 11 years in a smaller home with a family that filled every cranny with stuff, Hank veered more toward a "minimalist aesthetic." As a real estate agent who'd entered hundreds of homes to evaluate their market value, Hank always felt like a cop arriving at a crime scene. He had witnessed plenty of attics crammed with boxes of junk and been assaulted by rancid odors from neglected basements. Hank had come through his sales stint with a serious aversion to clutter and filth. He vowed to clean up the kitchen when he heard back from Tony, and then try harder to maintain a modicum of order, starting with a little less booze.

After he bought the new place, it took Hank several years to hire an interior decorator. He naturally had a lot to choose from and picked a woman known for her sleek and sparse designs. He had fallen in love with the property's backyard and the spectacular view that stretched far into the surrounding neighborhoods of manicured lawns, more pools and tennis courts. It was an ideal set up for entertaining, but in the five years he'd taken ownership, no one outside of his parents, the kids and, on very rare occasions, a random overnight guest, had crossed the threshold.

Settling into one of the lounges, Hank put the bottle between his sweaty thighs and lit a cigarette. Smoke billowed out of his mouth and into the cloudless black sky. He took a long swig of the icy beer, the fluid flowing down his throat and into his empty stomach. The combination of beer and cigarettes would ease the hunger pangs until morning, he hoped.

As he lay back adjusting the chaise to a reclined position, he stared up at the nearly full moon. The sound of chirping crickets and tree dwellers interrupted the silence around his concrete and grass trimmed patio. Neighbors' voices rarely drifted up to his enclave, and for that he was grateful. He had engineered the solitude for his protection but hadn't thought ahead to his lonely march through time. When his father retired, he handed Hank the reins to Carlton Realty, but that turned his more casual work life into a true full-time job. To boost the business, Hank decided to become involved in a variety of charitable causes with his nights spent hobnobbing at fancy fundraisers. It kept him out and about, with a payoff of temporary company, more listings, and his agency achieving a top rating in the state. When the lull between events grew longer, Hank spent his nights with a bottle of liquor and too many cigarettes. The alcohol helped blur the flashbacks and ease a guilty mind racked with regrets.

He finished the bottle and raised it to the nearly full moon. Tonight though was cause for celebration, and so he toasted his victory. Jeannie was free and, on her way back to the family. He had gotten her out of a serious jam, and perhaps, back on the right track.

It had been a tiring and stressful summer. Her hectic pace cost him a lot more cash than he had anticipated. Hank imagined Tony relaxing on the plane back to New York, sipping a scotch and adding up all the money he'd made off his secretive employer, not only during the past two months, but for the last five years snooping for him. Hank didn't care anymore. To even find a guy like Tony, a diamond in the rough, took several trips to New York and three scurrilous wannabes before he landed the real deal. With his olive complexion, wiry body and tough-as-nails demeanor, the guy was a natural sleuth. After retiring early from the NYPD, Tony earned his stripes as the most reliable and well-paid private eye in the business. He stuck to the job and never asked questions. This was critical for Hank as he never felt confident about his cover story. "Promised an Army buddy killed in a car accident after the war that if anything ever happened to him, I'd check on his family from time to time." Tony knew to keep his mouth shut. Would he continue to keep an eye out for her? Hank hadn't really thought about his benevolence in those terms. The scholarships he arranged as a blind trust for both Jeannie and Jeffrey were a drop in the bucket; academia couldn't have cared less who shelled out the fees, but this last intervention was far more dangerous. He had gotten her out of jail, and on a bus back to New York. Though nothing would ever make up for Walter, Hank felt that at least a small piece of his debt had been paid.

## Chapter 6

# AUGUST 1968 – JUNE 1969

# *Jeannie*

JEANNIE MADE LONG STRIDES away from the Chicago precinct, scanning the streets in a succession of nervous tics to see if she was being followed. A few stray souls like her scooted around plastic bottles, coke cans, food wrappers, discarded bandannas and t-shirts scattered on the city streets. She clutched her macramé bag in front of her chest and quickened her pace. Was she even going in the direction of the motel? She looked up at the concrete skyline of office buildings, surprised to see a checkerboard pattern of lights still on past midnight. Wouldn't everyone be home or somewhere safe by now? Jeannie remembered that the shabby two-story stucco motel had only been about a ten-minute walk to Grant Park, where they all gathered for the protest, but now disoriented, she had no idea how far the police station was from the convention center, and what direction to take to the motel. Nothing felt familiar. She'd have to find someone to ask and hoped it would be a Chicago local. In New York she could have stopped anyone walking by and nine times out of ten, would get accurate directions and an amusing anecdote to go with them. Out-of-towners assumed New Yorkers were pushy and uncaring, but that had never been her experience. By the third block she hadn't seen any men in uniform, no police or armor-suited National Guard troops, and told herself she'd find the motel and Jim. She felt anxious carrying $200 in cash and willed herself to get back safe.

Jeannie's whole body ached, especially her feet. She looked down at her sandals, and even in the darkness, could see the grime between her toes. Certain the back of her skirt was streaked with jail soot; she ventured a sniff under one of her armpits and had to jolt her head up to breathe in fresher air. Could her SDS crew have been arrested too? If that was the case, she certainly would have to forgive Jim for not showing up at the station, but then how would she get into the room? She didn't have the key; would the motel office be open? And if no one was there, would she actually resort to using the bus ticket and return to New York? She thought again of Patty and the PLP's arrest and release protocol, where she'd be walking out of the station in the morning on the arm of a fellow comrade. She, on the other hand, was on her own.

*But wait, was she really?*

When she'd snuck out of her home two months earlier, Jeannie delayed calling her mother for nearly a week until they reached Ann Arbor to let her know she'd gone out west with Jim and the others. She had just enough coins for a three-minute call, revealing their final stop was the Chicago convention in August. Her mother 'didn't like it one bit' and before she could beg her to return to New York, the operator cut them off. No doubt the whole family had watched and witnessed all the hysteria on the news. She knew it was wrong not to keep them better informed, especially during her extended stay in Ann Arbor, but Jim kept telling her that she needed to be free. "You're not a baby anymore, Red."

She picked up her pace. Could Uncle Jack have been keeping an eye on her? Yes, that's it...the only explanation. One of his reporters covering the convention, of course. She tapped the heel of her hand on her forehead to jolt her common sense back into place. *"If she gets arrested, Mac, get this envelope to the station, pay the bail…"* She could just hear the tenor of her uncle's calm, yet unmistakable command.

"Damn!" She spit the word out, then said it again and again. She reached for her chest and patted the envelope. It had her mother's fingerprints all over it too, and likely Grammy's. "Jackie dear, do whatever you can to find her."

After wandering the streets for half an hour, she recognized the flashing "No Vacancy" sign of their motel. She should have felt relieved to have made it back in one piece after such a crazy day; instead, she felt like a fake, a little girl who needed to be rescued by her family and then comforted by her boy-friend. She walked up the stairs to the second floor and crept up to the door. Turning the knob, thankful it wasn't locked, Jeannie opened the door and edged inside the dark room. One of the double beds held two passed-out bodies, and on the other lay Jim, snoring in measured rhythm. No one stirred when she closed the door and headed for the bathroom. Dying of thirst, she grabbed the plastic cup resting on the sink and filled it to the top with water. She gulped almost all of it, then looked at her reflection in the mirror. Even with her hair tied up in a loose ponytail, the frizzy tendrils had created a red afro. Her face and neck were smudged with dirt; the dark crescents underneath her eyes were almost as thick as the ones baseball players draw in to shade the sun. She was only 19 years old but looked a little too much like her mother. She bent down and began a furious soapy wash, and then snatched a towel from the floor to dry off. How could Jim have fallen asleep when she had not returned? If not so freaked out, she would have started shouting at all three of them, making them bolt up and take notice. "Hey remember me. I got lost and arrested! Did anyone give a shit or think to look for me?"

But where would that get her? She sat down on the toilet seat and rubbed the back of her neck. She pulled the envelope from her bra and hid it inside the zipped pocket of her bag. With just enough energy to brush her teeth, take off her clothes and put on the oversized T-shirt she'd left hanging on the bathroom hook, she hobbled over to the bed. The mattress creaked loud enough for Jim to stir. He turned his naked body toward her, he smelled soapy. "Oh, Red baby, where've you been? Searching, everywhere, we all did, up, down streets, calling you, so worried..." He groggily kissed her mouth, spreading her lips with his tongue, pulling her body into his, and reached between her legs, speeding up their sexual rhythm and giving her the reassurance she needed so badly. He did care, it was love, he had been looking for her after all. But then why not at the police station? Patty said her PLP group would assume if she didn't get back to their digs, then she was likely locked up. There would be no way she could come clean and tell Jim, or any of them, about being arrested and released with an envelope of cash and a bus ticket back to New York. At security trainings in Ann Arbor about FBI informants, they were warned to watch their backs if things didn't 'add up', that a slip-up could get them all busted. It wasn't even safe to share her speculation that her uncle might have arranged her bail, because if he hadn't, then someone else had pulled the strings. So, the next morning, she told them all a story of getting lost in the crowds, hanging out with girls from other groups and then somehow, finding her way back to the motel.

On the long van trip home to New York, she joined in with the others inhaling leafy joints and kept quiet. She half-listened to their animated discussion about the convention, arrested leaders, how LBJ sold them out, Humphrey being a joke, and

Tricky Dick, if elected, sending more troops to Southeast Asia. It was time to tighten up the reins, they all agreed, and that meant a serious pledge to the cause. High enough to lessen her guilt, she whispered to Jim she was 'all in,' having no idea what that required, or the dangerous risks it would involve.

School started a few weeks later. Jeannie told Jim she had to return to her dorm and register for classes, but that she'd meet him at the apartment over the weekend. His face went slack and then dark.

"Oh yeah? Was this just a summer vacation for you, Red? You know there's so much to be done, not a part-time thing, and for you too baby. I need you."

She looked up into his riveting blue eyes. "Me too, I know, but Jim, please understand, I also need to stay in school. That's the only way I'll get my scholarship money. I can do both. Trust me."

Jim wasn't the only one who pressured her to drop out. The others, especially Sally, the only other female in the group, who was shacking up with Kurt, the main leader, had adopted the party line and was in 'a hundred percent.' Kurt was not someone to trifle with either. A stern organizer with beady eyes and a mouth that changed position only to speak, he wore a black faded baseball cap with the words *No BS* above the lid, which he never took off. Sally had gone to Hunter College and should have been starting her junior year, but after Chicago, she decided it was pointless to read textbooks and take inane tests. Kurt and the cause, she confided to Jeannie one morning in the apartment bathroom, were the "only realities she could live in."

But Jeannie wasn't going to give up her scholarship and, unlike the others, didn't have the courage to disappoint her three parental figures. Returning to her empty dorm room, she found a flurry of phone messages on her bed and desk. All had the same theme scribbled in in capital letters. "CALL YOUR MOTHER" or "Your UNCLE called again" and one that read "Christ, ARE YOU DEAD?!"

She would call them, but only after she was officially registered for the fall semester. This would be the peace offering for her inexcusable negligence in being out of commission all summer. They'd all be furious; even Uncle Pauley, who typically remained neutral, would convey a chilly reproach for her poor decisions. She needed a good night's sleep to clear her head; then, she would see them. Her mother and grandmother would be more forgiving, but only after cranking up the guilt quotient. It was Uncle Jack she feared. When she had been crushed against the window seat during the journey back from Chicago, she obsessed about their confrontation. Being high for most of the trip home sent her into a paranoid place and she began to have doubts that it was her uncle's reporters who tracked her whereabouts. It was still possible, of course, checking the police stations was an obvious move, but the probability of finding her? This was a leap even she couldn't buy. If she confronted Uncle Jack about his hand in her jail release, and he admitted it, then she'd feel a sense of relief. And though it brought a tight spasm to her stomach to think no one trusted her, that she needed to be watched like a little child, it did mean she wasn't being followed by an FBI informant and could continue to keep her secret from Jim and the others. But it was still a gamble. She'd have to look hard into her uncle's eyes; there had never been any deception between them. He could be exceedingly abrupt at times, but he'd never lie to her. Though, if he hadn't masterminded it all, then who had? Would she then have to come clean with everyone? Was she putting the group in danger?

It was too much to absorb. She wondered how much of it was Jim and his seductive power that turned her from a part-time anti-war protester into an evolving militant. She could picture her family's troubled expressions, concerned that she was running amok with a bunch of lunatics. Did she want to stop the war by any means necessary? Before the arrest, it had been an exhilarating adventure in Ann Arbor; she had been in the thick of an established organization of brilliant orators, everything they spoke about made sense, they gave passionate speeches and eye-opening classes. She felt import-ant, like she belonged to something so much bigger. Jim was so affectionate too, an arm always around her, stroking her curls, nibbling at her neck, and pulling her into hallway cor-ners for soulful kisses. Once, in the women's bathroom at the community center where they had most of their meetings, he straddled her over the toilet, pulling up her blouse, his tongue making its way down her body where before she could moan with pleasure, he'd reached up and cupped his hand over her mouth. Nothing, she had thought, could top this experience, and even if she had understood his intoxicating spell at the time, it would not have mattered. He was older, wiser, and her first, so as if on a titillating roller coaster ride, Jeannie was going to hold on tight for as long as possible.

After tossing her phone messages into the trash, she lay down on the thin mattress. It wasn't a comfortable bed, but it was hers. She had to think back to early June to recall the last time she'd slept a night alone. It felt like she'd gone a lot farther than Chicago and that reentry would take some effort.

Jeannie turned her body toward the window, a faint scent of her herbal shampoo lingered on her pillow. She had spent a tedious morning in long lines signing up for courses. She had space for a few electives and chose an introductory course in journalism. This would make her uncle proud that she might be following in his footsteps one day. She'd tell him when she saw him, maybe it would diffuse the confrontation. They'd all be anxious to see her, but she'd decline their Friday night dinner deal. She'd gone through the ganging-up crap in June and would not subject herself to the four against one scenario again. She drifted off trying not to let the images of their disappointed faces invade her dreams.

Several days later, Jeannie arranged to meet her mother at Sal's hoping the boisterous crowd and aroma of pizza ovens at full tilt would melt away some of the anger she'd no doubt built up all summer. Once settled in a corner booth, her mother's fury unleashed for 15 minutes, "How could you think we wouldn't be worried sick knowing you were in Chicago? Cops all over, kids getting beaten up, the National Guard, where were you, we cried. It was like Columbia all over again, for god's sake! It was your Uncle Pauley who calmed us down and told us that if you were in any danger, we'd get a call."

Jeannie knew not to interrupt. With eyes lowered, she took in the reprimand; she even let her mother's hand remain on top of hers when she switched into, "At least you got back safely, but never again, young lady, never again will you not stop at a phone booth and call me collect!" More of the same ensued at her grandmother's house. It ended with Jeannie, at her Grammy's command, raising her right hand, index and middle finger entwined in her signature Jewish honor gesture, promising that she'd never again leave them in the dark like that. "It was not how you were raised," her grandmother pronounced.

The following week, she met with her uncle. This didn't go as she had hoped.

Arriving early, Jeannie waited in the hallway outside the

elevators. At precisely noon, she stepped into the newspaper's inner pandemonium. The 'pit' was a vast exposed square of hectic men, and a few women, all banging on typewriters, yelling into phones, and rushing into offices. Jeannie's earliest memory of visiting her uncle at his office was when she was six or seven, holding onto her mother's hand as they walked around the perimeter of the noisy place. She vividly recalled the smell of tobacco and ink, the plumes of smoke from dangling cigarettes, and the vibration from loud drums of black liquid pumping out papers beneath the floorboards. She became obsessed with those drums and begged her uncle to take her inside the bowels of the press room. Shy with just about any grown-up outside of her immediate family, Jeannie somehow found her voice when she crossed into that portal, and asked one question after another, her curiosity insatiable. She was mesmerized by the men nudging the metal letters of copy into the typesetter. "How does this work? Where does the ink go? How does the machine know where to find the words and cut the paper just right?" That one-hour tour was the most fascinating process she'd ever seen, and right there and then, she decided she was going to do what those guys did for a living. Naturally, they all laughed her off; the idea of women running a press machine obviously absurd. Not in a million years, they told her. "But upstairs, they could use your help keeping the reporters and your uncle happy." As if that was the honor only a few "pretty ladies" like her were offered.

Jeannie approached Barbara, her uncle's secretary, whose swivel chair was turned in a right angle as her delicate fingers clicked rapidly over the keys of a large, black Smith-Corona.

"Hey Barbara, how are you?"

Barbara's small head turned up at the greeting. She wore

her hair in a neat bun with bobby pins hidden, never a strand out of place.

"Well, well, *Miss Glazer*, you're back! Good to see you, truly." Her petite frame twirled around the rectangular desk, skinny arms reaching out for a hug.

"Chief's expecting you. But he can't leave the office today, too many fingers in the dam since the Chicago tidal wave. I'm going to order lunch from the deli. What would you like?" She looked up at her with a wide smile.

Jeannie didn't have the appetite for a mound of spicy pastrami, her nerves were too knotted up, so she politely ordered a Dr. Brown's and a knish. Watching Barbara deftly dialing the phone, Jeannie wondered if Uncle Jack had enlisted her in his covert spying operation. She had direct access into her uncle's life and no doubt knew about 'the rebellious niece' who had traipsed to the convention with her band of bearded activists. She was loyal to the chief and the paper; it wasn't something she'd ever question. The ends justify the means: if that's what Uncle Jack ordered, Barbara would comply to the letter and in the spirit of the command.

"Okay, lunch will be here in 15 minutes. Go on in."

Jeannie thanked her, turned and walked through the half-opened door. Uncle Jack was on the phone, facing his window. A streak of sweat darkened the back of his white, rumpled shirt. Jeannie could see his animated reflection and then caught a glimpse of her own worried face as she got closer to his desk.

"Okay, run with it, but be careful, no mistakes and I mean it." He hung up and swung his chair toward her, popped up and met her in front of his enormous desk.

"Jeannie, sweetheart, you're home!" He wrapped his big arms around her and held her longer than usual. She inhaled and took in the familiar smell of her uncle's Old Spice aftershave. It did feel good to be back, but she wasn't going to share that out loud.

He didn't go right at her about not calling all summer. She guessed her mother and grandmother had already chewed each one of his ears off with recaps of their rebukes. He chided her, but gently, eyebrows slightly raised in concern, or more likely, some displeasure with her choices. Then he switched to small talk about her upcoming classes, and how her two cousins, Scotty and Max had enjoyed their summer at a sleepaway camp up in the Catskills so much, they were not at all ready to return to the high school grind.

Lunch arrived and they made themselves comfortable at the small round table in a corner of his cluttered office.

"So, Uncle Jack, I need to ask you something about Chicago; you had reporters there, right?"

He stopped in mid-bite and tilted his head to one side.

"Of course, sweetheart; I guess you haven't read the papers since you've been back. We got some excellent coverage, and the usual backlash too. Two of my men got caught in some tussles, but luckily they'll be okay." He waved his hand toward the piles on his desk. "I've been putting out fires ever since."

He put down his sandwich. "Why do you ask?"

Jeannie looked down at her hands and inhaled.

"Was wondering, uh, were you watching out for me, you know, keeping tabs, making sure I wasn't in trouble?" Her head moved up slowly from her chest, until she met her uncle's eyes.

"What are you talking about?" He stared back.

"C'mon Uncle J, you know what I mean."

"No, actually I don't. What happened? Is there something I should know?" Her uncle leaned forward, his eyelids wide and when she squinted at him, all she could detect was an earnest and bewildered expression.

"Okay, nothing, really nothing, I just, well, I just thought I'd seen someone from *The Globe*, that's all. I know that's crazy, right? Just forget it."

He reached over and took her hand. "Are you sure there isn't anything else you'd like to tell me?"

It was just like him to hit the ball back with a targeted stroke and watch it gently sail into her side of the court. Making a concerted effort at a cheerful poker face, she assured him that she was still processing the whole trip and needed to sleep for a week straight to regain her wits. This time though, she could see he wasn't buying it. Their honor code had been broken. The rest of their exchange didn't register at all. She now had a far more serious dilemma; if it wasn't him, then who had arranged her jail release and why?

From that moment on, Jeannie felt as if her 20-20 vision had blurred. First it was her classes at school; words, meanings, concepts began to merge together. Pages of text, no matter how compelling, had to be read and re-read before she could make sense of them. She blamed the shuttling back and forth between her dorm and the SDS apartment, as the steady fatigue, too much weed, and nightly sex with Jim turned her brain into a mushy mess. She'd return to her dorm room each morning and spend 20 minutes preparing a list of every assignment for every class, with estimated time blocks for each item. But she failed to include time spent falling asleep on library desks, or spacing out in classes, where she'd get lost in a cascade of problems generated from that damn envelope of cash and its mysterious source. It was all so disturbing, from the guilt of lying to Jim and the rest of the SDS guys, possibly putting them all in danger, to an imposed isolation from her family who would have seen right away that something was gnawing at her insides, to more seriously, a plummeting GPA.

She often found herself feeling as if someone was follow-ing her, then furtively glance over her shoulder, and regain composure only when she was inside her dorm room or the apartment. And then there was Jim, who wanted her "body and soul," relentlessly pressuring her to drop out of school. At his urging, she sat through all the late-night political diatribes, inner circle meetings, and strategy rants like a good soldier, believing their mission was just and inevitable. No middle ground, they asserted over and over again.

The fall semester ended on a frigid day in mid-December. By then, Jeannie had been spending five out of seven nights in the lower Manhattan SDS apartment, stealing precious moments to study for tests or complete assignments amidst a chaotic communal living space with no privacy. As one of the girls, she was automatically assigned cooking and cleaning duties, and sex with Jim was not negotiable. Her diminishing study time was wholly inadequate for any student attending Barnard, so Jeannie was not shocked to find inside the envelope with her shameful 2.5 GPA report, a letter from the dean indicating she was not only on academic probation, but her remaining $6,000 scholarship fund was in jeopardy. A copy also was sent to her mother, which sparked another furious pile of phone messages on her neatly made dorm room bed to get in touch immediately, and to *please* return home for the holidays.

She didn't have the strength to spend the holidays with them and instead called her mother to assure her she was just overwhelmed with a heavy course load and she'd take care of it all. She lied and said she and Jim were going to Florida for the break, his treat. Her mother threatened to come and get her for one lousy day, "I'll get your cousins to kidnap you if I have to, now be reasonable!" Luckily, no one knew the apartment address, so she felt confident that she could stay under the radar. The deeper truth was, she'd lost her bearings. Of course, staying in school was the only way to land a career, especially an exciting one like Uncle Jack's. That was all she ever wanted, and no matter how challenging the work was—from digesting endless pages of fine print to grasping fundamental concepts—she always managed to get excellent grades and get ahead. Failure was not an option. Until now.

By mid-January when school resumed, she felt that the SDS apartment was no longer her temporary crash pad, but rather a secure safe house they all inhabited to protect against outside intruders. She also realized she no longer had a choice to leave the group. Made to feel accountable for her comings and goings by Jim and the others, Jeannie had been pulled in and then trapped into maintaining inside loyalty, at all costs.

Right after mid-terms in April when she received D's or flat-out Fs on her exams and papers, another warning letter arrived from the Dean. By then, she had moved into the SDS apartment full-time, but only granted trips to campus to get her scholarship money, handing over most of it to the group's household kitty. Wanting her financial contribution, the SDS leaders knew they had to approve some quiet time to study. To minimize campus inquiries about her involvement with Jim, who had been a recognizable leader in SDS at Columbia, Jeannie was warned not to return to her dorm or go to the library and risk bumping into anyone she knew. She needed to find another place to work and chose the Chock Full O' Nuts coffee shop near campus where she had first met them all. She even sat at the same corner booth. The bottomless cups of coffee, hot food, surrounding noise, and the odd sense of loyalty to the cause allowed her to concentrate enough to bring up her grades.

One late morning in early May, she arrived to find her booth occupied by a dark-haired guy wearing an army fatigue jacket; a cup of coffee and a half-eaten donut on a small dish rested at the table's edge. It would have been rude to ask him to move, but she had become attached to the booth, and needed its cocooned ambiance to prepare for final exams.

As she stepped in closer, she noticed a nick on his neck, a spot of blood from the morning shave. He looked at her right in the eyes and smiled as if he'd met her before.

"Can I help you?"

"Maybe. This is going to sound weird, but this is kind of my spot where I do my schoolwork like almost every morning." She clutched her big canvas bag in front of her body, and continued, "Are you almost done?"

He extended his arm. "Name's Phil. Join me for a minute, tell me why this is *your* spot, and if it's a good reason, then I'll give it up."

His warm, inviting smile and uncanny sense of familiarity drew her in. She didn't crack open one book that day. Eventually leaving the coffee shop, they walked all the way to the river along the West Side Highway. He did most of the talking, and when she learned he'd just returned from Vietnam, she probed for more stories, drawn in by the deep lyrical tones of his voice. He answered her in broad terms, no details. She'd never met or had any interaction with a real soldier, and believed boys were drafted against their will, but not Phil, he had actually enlisted. Everything that day seemed so out of context, as if she'd been granted a free pass and should embrace every moment of this random respite. She asked if he had a job. He told her he worked several nights a week as a bartender at Frankie's on 75th and Broadway while trying to figure out what he wanted to do with the rest of his life. He wasn't in a hurry, he said, "I'm just glad to still be alive, with both arms and legs still attached."

"So, what brought you to a coffee shop twenty blocks uptown?" Jeannie had been asking most of the questions. She'd been careful to respond to his occasional inquiries only with bland anecdotes about her upbringing in Kew Gardens and the grueling load at school. Nothing about her politics, and certainly not a hint about her current living arrangement.

"No particular destination, just a day off to wander and see where I'd end up." They were sitting on a bench overlooking the water; the easy conversation, spring-scented air and setting sun, had generated a calm she hadn't felt in over a year. A perfect high without a toke of weed.

A pause descended between them.

"Unless you want me to show up unannounced at your reserved booth tomorrow morning, how about giving me your phone number?" He smiled at her and then suddenly as if a flashbulb had popped in her face at close range, the spell was broken. She jumped up. "Oh my god, what time is it? I gotta go!" She turned and began to jog toward the avenues.

"Hold on there, Cinderella, let me help, you need a cab?" He stuck by her side.

"No, please, I, I, have to get back. Good to meet you, Phil, really." Before she switched into a run, she touched his arm and smiled.

He slowed up and didn't pursue her. She was relieved, but also disappointed.

Barreling through the tunnels back to 14th Street, she held onto the subway strap, so deep in thought she didn't mind being pushed and squeezed by the other riders. Arriving more than an hour late would send up flares at the safe house. Everyone had taken on an edgier demeanor over the past six months. Jim came down the hardest, routinely drilling her about where she'd been and who she'd ran into—more for the group's safety than her own. There was a regular schedule of meetings, planning sessions and dinner prep, and missing any of it had repercussions, he warned her. His tone was meant to scare her, and it worked. Naturally, she couldn't give Phil the apartment's phone number. Totally out of the question. It wasn't until she got off the train and hit the button in the apartment elevator that she envisioned another night of fist-pumping rhetoric, and the usual demand for total solidarity. Another trip was being planned to Chicago for the national SDS conference in June, and from the sound of it, some blow-up was anticipated. She was the only one of the six apartment dwellers who rarely spoke up, and thankfully no one cared, including Jim. Her neck sunk into her shoulders as she inserted the key into the lock. She pushed open the heavy metal door and there he was, looming like a giant bear ready to pounce.

"Where have you been, Red? It's late, too late." Jim's voice was deep and harsh.

"I, was, studying, then the train, well, I missed it, and I'm sorry…"

He cut her off. "Go help Sally in the kitchen now, we can't start until everyone's here. No more of this, you understand me?"

She didn't respond and instead hurried into the kitchen where Sally was cursing a pan of hot lasagna that she had evidently burned her hand on taking it out of the old oven. She turned her head, and in a shrill tone, one Jeannie had never heard from Sally, commanded her help. "*Not* cool at all, I'm not down for your job too."

It was Kurt, not Jim, who pulled her into the bathroom

after the long night had ended, and got right in her face, his breath a mixture of tobacco and garlic. "You're on watch duty for the rest of the week, and no more fuck-ups, you hear me?"

Jeannie nodded, but kept her head down. He walked out and closed the door behind him. She turned toward the tiny window that overlooked the metal fire escape railing. From her angle, the railing looked like prison bars.

# Chapter 7

## JUNE – DECEMBER 1969

# *Jeannie*

OVER THE NEXT THREE weeks, Jeannie's mood shifted with the prospect of Phil waiting at the booth for her to arrive. He didn't disappoint either. Anxiety about finals and constant scheming to avoid the June trip to Chicago temporarily receded to the edges of her mind, like a low tide that ignored lunar forces.

Phil guessed she was living with another guy. "Can't give me your number, right?" She nodded her head, and then told him it was complicated. It didn't seem to matter to him though, he wanted to get to know her, he was okay with letting things take their course. She wanted that too, but knew after finals were over, there would be no legitimate reason to leave the safe house. Before she met Jim, during the summer of '67, there had been another guy who shared a room with Kurt at the apartment. Then right after the May campus strike, the guy just "upped and split" and according to Jim, "no one has seen or heard from him since. We found out later that the guy's father was a cop, and either he'd been sloppy or leaked something. Can't have that, not from our own people."

Security got tighter when a bunch of East Coast SDS chapters experienced a huge clamp-down after the April protests at Harvard and over 200 members either had been hurt or arrested. Kurt, with full agreement from the other leaders, decided to extend street surveillance to a 24-hour watch schedule where one of them would be perched at the window, recording observations at 30-minute intervals. A weekly calendar with their time slots was pinned on the bulletin board next to the cluttered array of newspaper clippings and a daily synopsis of actions from other SDS chapters.

Jeannie managed to pass all her classes and was rewarded with her last scholarship installment for the semester. Winding through the crush of bodies at the subway campus stop, she hurried over to the administration building, retrieved her check, cashed it, and then met Phil at the coffee shop. She only had a two-hour window and if she wasn't back at the appointed hour, she'd be reprimanded and given the dreaded graveyard shift of watch duty. Wanting to enjoy the fresh spring air, she and Phil returned to their bench by the riverfront, where she let her head rest on his shoulder. A few moments passed before she lifted her face to look in his eyes; he returned her gaze, then leaned down and kissed her lips. It sent a charge through her body and with unusual boldness, she wrapped her arms around his neck and let him explore her mouth and stroke her hair. They kept it up, until an inner timer went off. She pulled away, knowing she'd be in deep shit if she didn't return to the apartment as required. He walked her to the subway, but then handed her a business card from the bar where he worked; on the back he'd written his address and phone number. "Please call me, anytime. I mean it." From that moment on, she became obsessed with finding ways to hear his voice again.

That wouldn't happen until the end of June, and on the rare occasion that she could get away, she'd call from a phone booth. They spoke only three times; the first two conversations were brief exchanges. His soothing tone evoked hazy rescue scenes conjured up from novels she used to read, all about the handsome hero arriving at the scene just in time to whisk the innocent damsel from imminent danger. The second time they talked, she was on the way back to New York from the June trip to Chicago. There had been so much chaos and hostility at the conference, causing SDS to splinter into another faction, the Weatherman, with a manifesto written by new leaders. Jim assured her that they were finally getting somewhere, but she avoided the heated debates, slipping out into bathrooms or hallways. She had no idea how serious this had become.

On the way back to New York, she felt confused and frightened. She woke much earlier than the others at a Cleveland motel where they had stopped overnight, crept out to a phone booth near the manager's office and called Phil collect. Her knees wobbled when she heard his tired voice accept the call.

"Where are you, are you okay, what's wrong? It's been so long..."

She couldn't hide it any longer, and told him she needed help, she'd been out of town, and missed him very much. He begged her to meet him when she got back, but she said she couldn't commit. She listened as Phil kept up his protests, until she saw Jim running toward the booth and gasped. Before she could hang up the receiver, Jim burst into the booth and yanked it from her hand.

Slamming it into the cradle, he hissed, "What the fuck are you doing? Who were you talking to?" He grabbed her neck with too much force and pulled her out of the booth. She stumbled and fell to the ground, hitting her face on the pavement.

A stinging heat on her forehead spread to her hands and knees. Slowly raising herself to a standing position, she examined the streaks of blood on her palms. Jim took a menacing step toward her.

"Who was that?"

"My *mother*, if you must know," her brain silently fired all the curse words she knew.

Jim's eyelids squeezed into slits; his bearded face remained stern. She'd been with him long enough to interpret that sneer of skepticism.

"Bullshit, Red."

A surge of gutsy adrenalin dispelled her fear. "I'll give you her number, go ahead and call collect, and please tell her I wasn't the one who hung up on her."

She touched her forehead, a tender lump was forming, it pounded as fast as her heart. She needed an ice pack and a couple of aspirin.

"I promised to let her know I was okay, that's all. You were out of line."

They stared at one another, neither of them backing off, then he reached out and put his arm around her. She recoiled, but he pulled her tighter to his chest.

"Baby, listen, I'm sorry." He released her and gently put his hand on her face. It made her wince in pain. "But you know the rules. We just went through god damn hell; we're in over-drive, you heard it for yourself. Jesus, half the people at the conference were probably informants taking notes and names. No phone calls, not now, not until we get our shit together. Okay?" Then he softly kissed her bruised forehead.

*Informants?* The statement rocked her; did they actually suspect she might be one? Did Jim believe she could have been recruited? Did this justify his sudden outburst? As if reading her mind, Jim showed his apology by keeping his arm around her for the rest of the ride back to New York, and leaning down, kissing her in that deep soulful way he did when they first met. It never failed to ignite the vibration between her legs. She liked that feeling, but their intimacy had shifted. She knew it, and so perhaps did he.

. . .

ON A SWELTERING SUNDAY in late August, Jeannie was left
alone for the first time in the rundown Lower East Side flat.
Everyone had important jobs to do that day; her orders were
to stay on watch. Relieved not to be engaged in plotting some
dangerous activities that lately involved destroying property,
and with a fan cooling her off, she enjoyed the rare silence.
The street below had been emptying for hours; people were
either ducking into air-conditioned bars or restaurants, or
off splashing in beach waves or swimming pools outside of
the city.

Why was she still there? Too weak-minded to consider the
larger getaway, Jeannie realized she did have a slice of freedom
she couldn't pass up. If they came back early, she'd tell them
she had gone to the store to get a cold drink. She had proved
her loyalty by staying alert at meetings, even inserting an occasional comment to let them know she was actively listening.
She didn't complain to Sally about the housework chores, and
purposely signed up for more watch shifts. All done to allay
their suspicions, the perfect 'cadre' and loyal girlfriend. What
she didn't anticipate is how long it would take to earn their
trust, and she didn't feel sure enough of herself, or what they
might do to her if she just left. Her racing thoughts frightened
her; she'd been so cut off from everyone else in her life except
for Phil, a guy she barely knew, that she had lost perspective
and didn't trust her own judgment.

There was a phone booth half a block away. She locked up,
ran down the stairs and hit the pavement running. It would
take ten minutes at most. She reached the phone booth damp
with perspiration. She had memorized his phone number, the

name of the bar and even his address. She called his home first, collect and after eight rings he picked up.

"Jeannie! Where are you? I haven't heard from you in two months. Are you alright?"

"Yes, and no, I only have a few minutes, but listen, I know this sounds weird, but just promise me something, will you?"

"Of course, but please let me come and get you, is your guy or anyone hurting you?" Phil's voice went into a high pitch.

"No, I'm okay, truly, but even if it takes a little longer, please be there when I knock on your door soon, I hope very soon." Her throat got thick with the emotion of her own words.

"Yes, Jeannie, I am here, but you sound scared. Just tell me where you live and I'll keep an eye out, I promise I won't..."

She cut him off. "I have to go, thank you for, well, just thank you." After she hung up, she ran back to the apartment, her tears mixing with sweat. Hearing Phil's voice had given her a lift, she clung on to every word. But could she really count on him? She made it inside, resumed her post at the window and spent the rest of her watch shift deciding that she could—she had to—and plotted a way out.

. . .

IT WAS EASY ENOUGH to slip away from Jim's embrace. Most nights after sex, he'd roll to one side and in seconds she'd hear his uneven breathing turn into a deep snore. Still, she waited another ten minutes before sliding off the mattress onto the floor. Crawling over to the closet, she pulled out a small backpack of clothes she'd hidden earlier that evening. Then she tiptoed to the bathroom and crept inside. Even on this chilly winter night, the one tiny window was propped open in a futile attempt to oust the lingering odor of sweat, shit and mildew. Jeannie quickly got dressed, then snuck through the small living room space. At the front door were piles of cast-off shoes; she bent over and picked up her clunky boots but decided not to risk putting them on until she was safely out in the hallway. The two other bedroom doors were closed; thankfully no one had passed out on the saggy couch the night before. In slow motion, she unlatched the chain and turned the knob. Crossing the threshold, she guided the heavy metal door until it clicked gently back into place. At the elevator, she put on her boots, pressed the button and waited. She should have taken the stairs down from the fourth-floor apartment but the stairwell was not safe. Beyond the used condoms, broken needles and syringes littering the floors, she often heard vicious arguments, and once saw a guy slapping a girl across the face on the second-floor landing. She held her breath until the noisy contraption arrived, and then rushed inside, hitting the lobby button too many times.

As soon as the rickety doors reopened, Jeannie darted out of the building and rushed down the deserted street. Grunting like a hunted animal, she forced her body through the biting wind that penetrated the layers of her clothes. The avenue was empty, but that didn't stop her from imagining Jim's feet on the pavement racing up to catch her. She didn't look back. Two more turns and one last block to the 14th Street subway station and then she'd be free. The few people she passed, wrapped in scarves with woolen caps tugged low, kept their heads down and hands hidden in deep pockets. A gusty tail wind caused her to stumble over a curb slick with black slush from last week's storm. The night was so bitter, even the neighborhood bums and their shopping carts had fled. Hooded doorways lay vacant littered with blown trash. Jeannie pulled the straps of her backpack tighter, then shoved her gloved hands back into her pockets and scooped the penny-sized tokens she stole from the apartment kitty.

She slowed her gait down the pockmarked cement steps into the station's underground tunnels. The journey so ingrained, Jeannie confidently navigated the winding route to the turnstile, dropped the y-shaped coin into the slot, and descended another flight to the uptown tracks. A tall black man in a puffy coat with a matted fur hood covering his head stood mid-platform. The three wooden benches between the uptown and downtown trains were occupied by sleeping bodies, all curled up like babies; two men had crumpled newspapers over their faces. A semi-warm refuge for the lucky few. Where did the others go? Were there even shelters in her neighborhood? Who took in these men and women? Why didn't she know, or until now, care to know? She had routinely handed spare change into their outstretched palms, and almost never turned away from the women, some with desperately thin dogs, or worse, babies and small children. It would break her heart, and she'd give whatever she had in her pocket, then get out her wallet for a dollar. How could this tiny drop of kindness or pity ever matter? She hated when so-called friends or random strangers told her "not to give those drunks liquor money," as if every ragged street person drank themselves into poverty. She edged closer to the passed-out middle-aged man without the newspaper over his face. Every inch of him, from his tangled, stringy hair and bearded face to the small open rips in his pants and worn-out laceless boots, cried out: *Help me, help me, please help me.*

Jeannie jumped back as the crescendo of the approaching train made the old guy shift his position. She turned toward the tracks, crisscrossing her arms to shield her body from the blast of cold air charging down the tunnel. As the train screeched to a halt, Jeannie did not have to shift an inch to walk straight into the open doors, the mark of a habitual rider. Her uptown express passed through midtown along the West Side up to the 116th Street station, to a convenient perimeter stop at the university. She had been making this long ride twice a day, five days a week until the semester had ended in May. Tonight, she hoped, would be the last time she'd make the trip from the 14th Street station.

Inside the heated car, there were several riders, isolated spirits like her, camped out in distant corners. As a rule, there wasn't much chit chat in the subway cars even during the day, and at 2:30 in the morning, not a chance. No one was looking down at newspapers or books either. All men, and this should have made her squirm, but once the doors closed and the train took off, she felt for the first time all day, and probably all year, relief that it was really over, all of it, because this time she trusted the man waiting for her at the end of the ride.

The train squealed to its next stop. The doors opened, and she watched an emaciated man with a ratty beard wrapped in a filthy blanket shuffle on board.

He turned toward her, staring right into her eyes, and then held out his hand, "S'cuse me Miss, spare a dolla?"

She dug her hands back into her pockets and pulled out the rest of her coins.

"Here you go." She said, looking away from his face.

He took the change. "You got a dolla in there too?"

An older guy, wearing a woolen cap, the only man left in the car, stood up and zig-zagged toward them.

"Hey buddy, you go on and take a seat."

The homeless man's face went even more slack; his drooping mouth and curved posture set off a pounding sadness in Jeannie's chest. He turned his head and held out his hand again.

"You got a dolla, mister?"

The older guy reached into his pocket and pulled out a money clip. He unclasped it and peeled off a $10 bill.

"Get yourself some food and a place to sleep tonight, you go on now."

The blanketed beggar took the bill and stuffed it in his front pocket.

"Thank you, Jesus, thank you." He repeated in a scratchy voice, his head nodding out the words like the beat to a song.

At the next stop, Jeannie swiveled her neck to track the homeless man's exit from the train. The woolen cap guy followed him onto the platform. As the doors closed, she and the beggar locked eyes. Suddenly, she began to cry.

Now she was completely alone in the car with six more stops to go. Staring out the black window beyond her own reflection, Jeannie saw flashing images of hollowed-eye homeless guys interspersed with frames of young, bearded men huddled over diagrams, arguing about targets and fuses. Had she consented to any of it? Had it been her own free will? Those ragged vagabonds used to live somewhere, used to make decisions that didn't only involve asking for money from strangers. But now, for these sad souls, it was all about survival. Jim and the other Weather guys used to be smart, eager, ethical students. The war changed all that and turned them into fierce rebels whose purpose had become surviving their own violent tactics. Where did they, or she, go so seriously off-track?

She wiped her nose on her sleeve, took a few deep breaths and hugged her arms across her chest wanting so badly to believe she'd be okay. At the 72nd Street station, Jeannie stepped onto a nearly empty platform, a few folks wrapped in heavy coats dashed up the stairwell ahead of her. She wanted to hail a cab to Phil's, but she was down to her last five-dollar bill. Pulling the scarf tighter around her neck, the backpack straps secured on her shoulders, she broke into a slow jog. Panting in front of his building, she buzzed the apartment number to get through the foyer entrance. She could have taken the elevator to his floor but was too charged up and instead climbed the three flights. A door at the end of the hallway had been opened. And there, with outstretched arms, stood a sleepy man named Phil.

# Chapter 8

# MARCH 1970

# *Hank*

THE CALL FROM TONY D came in just after he'd returned from lunch. It had been a slow Friday, and with no more appointments on the calendar, Hank looked forward to a quiet afternoon to catch up on paperwork.

"Mr. C, ya sittin' down?" Tony's Brooklyn accent brought Hank's shoulders to attention.

"Yeah, what's wrong?"

"Huge bomb just exploded on 11th Street. It's the Wilkerson place."

"Hold on, hold on." Hank slid open the middle desk drawer, fished out the miniature key, inserted it into the bottom right hand file cabinet, then thumbed through the manila folders until he located the "SDS/Weatherman" tab, and pulled it out.

"Okay, just a minute." Hank rifled through the file until he found the page and stopped. "Her name is Cathy, Cathy Wilkerson, right? Must be her family home. Jesus Christ, who's dead? *Jim?*"

Hank pushed back from his desk, pulling the phone cord along with him, as he stretched to turn on the transistor radio on the side credenza

"Yeah, she's with the Weather group, but no news yet on who was inside. My guys on the force say two women got out, one might be the Wilkerson girl, both naked as jaybirds. I'm sticking around. Will call ya back when I know more." Tony didn't wait for a response. Hank endured a few moments of the grating dial tone before hanging up.

He rotated the tuning knob of his red and white toaster-sized radio, adjusting the antennae to lock in a station. Even in the sprawling city of Atlanta, Hank still had to navigate around the dials to find a station that carried national news. Bombs had been exploding all over the country for the past 18 months, but this one apparently demolished a four-story brownstone in an upscale Manhattan neighborhood. The reporter on the scene had choppy reception and could barely be heard over the sirens wailing in the background. Hank learned that at first, police believed it might have been a gas-related accident, but they quickly switched to speculation of another random act of violence in protest of, as Hank had begun to say, 'fill in the blank'.

He turned it off. He'd get a lot more of the facts from Tony. Shaken up to hear another senseless act in a youth movement turned deadly, Hank knew if it hadn't been for Jeannie, he'd have been just another distant and disdainful southerner.

His heart still racing, he paced around the spacious office.

Was Jim one of the victims? Hank needed to know; it would make a difference for his next move. Tony would have to get in touch with Phil right away to make sure Jeannie didn't do anything rash or take it upon herself to find out.

Pivoting toward the glass window, Hank watched his head shift from side-to-side in the reflection, then adjusted his focus to the picturesque view of trees, sleek office buildings and oblivious workers going about their day.

"Damn," he said out loud.

If he hadn't arranged the Phil connection, she might still be with those losers, and in that townhouse blown to bits. He sat back in his black leather chair and let out a long exhale.

Hank owed this close call to Tony. Sure, he still pulled the strings, but it was Tony who found Phil, the son of an old police buddy. The three of them, he, Tony and Phil helped Jeannie escape that agitator Jim and his delusional revolutionaries. It had been an onslaught, the past few years of assassinations, protests, and unbridled aggression in the country, but never could he have imagined himself, a Georgia-born real estate broker in his fifties, becoming so involved.

He stood up and returned to the window. Pressing his face so it grazed the glass, he could see waves of heat rising from the pavement. The air-conditioning had switched into a high frigid mode, and while an unseasonably warm day for early March, the coolness generated a chill along his neck and spine. He needed to get out of the office. He wanted to be home in his own backyard pool, submerged in water, the soothing diversion he did almost daily. But today it would feel different. The bombing news had made him antsy, unnerved by just how narrowly Jeannie escaped from this deadly event or whatever next disaster these commie kids would cause. He picked up his keys from the desk, walked out of his office and glided into the sterile hallway. Tammy, his loyal secretary, stopped typing and looked up at him. Her black butterfly glasses gave her face a buggy look rather than the enchanting winged creature she might have desired.

"Need something, Mr. Carlton?"

Hank had to suppress the urge to take her by the shoulders and reveal his bold news.

"No, but go on and finish up what you're doing, then close up." He gave her a reassuring smile and added, "Have yourself a good weekend," then he headed for the stairwell.

It wasn't hard to find his royal blue Mustang convertible among the sea of cars in the crowded underground lot. The two-year old vehicle still gleamed, as if it had just been driven off the showroom floor. It was his baby, he told friends, and any day with a modicum of sun, he'd flip up both visors, lifting the metal handles underneath to unlatch the roof, and press the button on the dashboard. Like a schoolboy, he never grew tired of watching the top slowly fold itself into the waiting hull.

As he emerged into the blue skies, Hank breathed in the fresh air and knew he made the right decision to leave work early. He wanted to feel the sunshine and wind on his face for as long as possible, so decided to take the long way home. After a brief stint on the highway, he veered off the exit and onto the winding back roads, where, with no one around to slow him down, especially on an early Friday afternoon, pushed the speedometer up to a steady 55 miles per hour. The constant breeze provided a sensual feeling through his whole body. It loosened strands of hair that he instinctively styled back into place. Checking the driver's side mirror, he was pleased to see the rest of his graying scalp had hardly moved thanks to the daily Brylcreem regimen he'd kept up for decades. Hank had taken excellent care of his hair, starting when he was a scrawny teenager with family, friends, lovers complimenting his thick, wavy locks, a feature that kept him feeling attractive even now, in his early fifties. He believed applying the daily goop had been responsible for delaying the eventual cue-ball genes that loomed ahead.

He didn't turn on the car radio, preferring the sound of rushing wind to music or news, and allowing his mind to wander. It had been during his nightly benders, before passing out on the couch, when he'd flip on the television, mostly for the company, and stumbled onto a program called *The Mod Squad*. It was a crime drama about three young people; a hip black guy, a pretty blond girl, of course, and a handsome rich kid, all with troubled pasts and criminal records, who become undercover cops to work off their sentences. If it wasn't for the booze, he'd have dragged himself off the couch and immediately changed the channel. But something about those compelling young faces, the realistic plot lines, and the whole detective theme got Hank hooked. He made sure to be home to catch the weekly episodes, and that's when he came up with the idea of getting a third person into the mix with Jeannie and Jim, someone to lure her away from her dangerous boyfriend enough to get her out. It was a long shot, but he wasn't about to give up on Jeannie. For weeks, Tony had sent him prospective candidates, and they spent hours narrowing down the criteria. Mid-twenties, out of draft range, eager for under-the-table cash, and some attractive appeal. Tony eventually found Phil and did the screening to reassure Hank that his former police buddy's son was a 'good egg' with no troubles or stories that stood out. Hank needed a photograph to make sure, and while Phil's picture gave no particular sense of security, Hank thought he had a nice smile. He recalled having to bring the photo close to his face to see the black letters spelling out "Reeder" on the left front pocket of his army jacket. Tony told him "Phil don't much like those anti-war cowards." That was just fine with Hank. It would make it easier to convince Phil that Jeannie had been brainwashed, or worse imprisoned by Jim, and that his mission was to get her out of Jim's clutches before it was too late. With no other options and the clock ticking, he gave Tony the okay. Phil took on the cause without hesitation, and while the money seemed to be the initial impetus, Tony wasn't surprised to learn that he hadn't cashed any of his checks. "Phil's like his dad, two tough guys when their jobs call for it, but holding on to their softer sides no matter how beat down they get."

Turning up the long hill to his home, Hank pressed down hard on the pedal. Not in his wildest dreams could he have predicted this project would extend beyond setting up the Glazer kids' scholarship fund and turn into his own *Mod Squad* detective story, complete with stakeouts and nefarious characters.

He slowed up as he entered his quiet cul-de-sac. Steering into the driveway, he reached into his glove compartment and pressed the garage door opener, then gently rolled into the clutter-free space. He had sold his ten-year-old mint condition Le Mans a few years back and had considered replacing it with a snazzy sports car, but after seeing the Mustang convertible in a downtown showroom, it was love at first sight. The garage was detached from the house, and that had been the only drawback when he decided to buy the property. He would have liked the discretion of an inner door directly into the kitchen, particularly at night in case someone was watching. Luckily, he had learned a long time ago to be stealthy; from nosey clients to scary encounters with shady strangers, the passing years had made him a pro.

Hank strode up the limestone path to his front door. Two years prior, he would have celebrated this occasion with a strong scotch and soda, a self-congratulatory salute to his intuition in keeping Tony on the payroll from Columbia to Ann Arbor to Cook County Precinct, and finally back to the boroughs of New York. His involvement might have ended if Jeannie had hopped on that Trailways bus back to Manhattan, but Tony was right; all that bus ticket did was make her even more confused, it backfired, costing him a lot of dough, time and worry. Since then, Hank had learned so much from Tony about SDS and what they were up to that he became obsessed with figuring out their game plan.

But today's insanity was the last straw.

It was in the early mornings, when on the cusp of awakening that his thoughts would stray to 'if only' scenarios. If only he had insisted that Jeannie's father, Walter, too drunk to drive, come back to his home that night to sleep it off. He'd have gone on the next morning to Atlanta, returned home and lived to see his kids grow up. Eighteen years later, he was still making up for it.

After inserting the key into the front door, Hank took his customary deep breath before heading inside. He could feel his shoulders release as he crossed the pristine threshold. The ritual was always the same; he'd place his briefcase on the stand by the door next to a vase of fresh lilacs, and then take a moment to inhale the sweet scent that infused the small circular foyer. Gliding down the few wide steps into the sunken living room, Hank loosened his tie and peeled off his jacket.

From left to right, the renovated room's open expanse covered roughly 900 square feet. Adorned with new beige leather couches, two recliner chairs, and pillows in a variety of burnt orange, gold, and jade colors, the design had been mostly his, along with some finishing touches from the last interior decorator. No matter how dark the clouds became, the airy space enjoyed plenty of light through the sliding glass door off the patio. He carried his jacket on his arm as he unlatched the door and stepped outside into his backyard Shangri-La. The rectangular pool, heated when needed and cool when the humidity became intolerable, was long enough for Hank to get in some decent laps. New deck chaises, the repainted picnic table shaded with a white umbrella, and an embankment of magnolia, fig and lemon trees enclosed the setting to preserve his privacy. His favorite feature was the west-facing panorama that in the autumn months displayed stained glass sunsets.

Anxious to start his weekend, Hank went back inside and headed for the bedroom. He'd also done a complete remodel of the master suite, as he liked to call it, when he'd gotten sober. After browsing through dozens of *Architectural Digests*, he spared no expense on the king-sized bed, matching headboard and night tables, modern light fixtures, and best of all, a 200-square-foot walk-in closet that required pushing out a wall to construct. It was his reward for emptying his liquor cabinet for good. He carefully hung up his jacket, put the tie into the rack, and took off the rest of his clothes, piece by piece, placing each item in its proper drawer or in the hamper. Naked, he padded out to the spotless kitchen, opened up the fridge and poured himself a glass of iced tea, then strolled out to the pool.

He moved one of the cushioned chaises into the sunlight next to the Weber barbeque, a sobriety gift from his father. Not one for beating around bushes, his daddy's gesture was a hint that his son begin dating and entertaining again, even consider remarrying the 'right woman' this time around. Hank didn't invite anyone into his private world, and if he did on rare occasions, they were carefully vetted. This was his sanctuary, the only place he truly felt safe. It was why it had been only his parents and his two teenage girls who enjoyed his perfectly charred burgers and grilled hot dogs in his backyard; otherwise, the barbeque was covered over to protect against rain and neglect. But glancing at the Weber now, he decided to fire up the coals later, and cook up a thick steak he had in the freezer.

Hank got up from the chaise and now warmed by the afternoon sun, strode to the pool's edge and dove in. The water sent a chill through his body, but after a few laps, he had adjusted to the temperature and the sensual gliding it generated between his legs. He hadn't been in the pool in a month, too busy or lazy, and very rarely did he make the plunge if the Atlanta winter required him to turn on the heat inside. Today, however, was warm, cloudless, just right for a swim. He leaned his wet hair back into the water and then lifted himself out. Wrapping a towel around his torso, Hank stepped carefully to the cabana bar, reached under and retrieved his secret pack of cigarettes, along with a silver lighter and ashtray. Settled back in the chaise with iced tea and smoking paraphernalia in place, Hank allowed himself the guilty pleasure of a celebratory cigarette.

The smoking habit stopped after the booze ended, but over the past two years, particularly when days, sometimes weeks would pass without hearing from Tony, or when he'd allow his long list of regrets too much room to wander, he'd sneak through the sliding glass door, sit at the bar and puff on one, or maybe two, out of the pack. It was the only time he had the chance for a slightly altered state; the dizziness was just ephemeral enough to put his anxiety and loneliness on hold.

As he lay on the chaise, sunglasses blocking the strong rays, Hank stretched his arms to rest on the chair handles, spreading his legs wide to give the sun full rein. He closed his eyes and exhaled with a groan of pleasure. The gentle heat on his cool skin made him hard and as he took hold of himself, he tried to be patient, prolonging the erotic sensation for as long as he could. Afterwards, a wave of peacefulness descended slowly from head to toe. He sat up a little straighter to sip his tea and enjoy a smoke, but only got in two drags before he heard the phone ringing inside, the sound instantly dissolving the calm that had just settled over his body.

Hank got up too fast, and woozy from the nicotine and his one-handed joy ride, had to grab hold of the chaise to steady himself. He reached for the towel covering the lounge and rewrapped it around his waist as he raced to answer the phone.

"Hello?" He sounded out of breath.

"Got more dirt." Tony wasn't alone. Hank could hear voices in the background. He had no idea where or in what circumstances Tony did his digging, and in their unspoken arrangement, Hank knew not to inquire.

"It's hard to believe, really, boss. Emergency crews, smoke, fire, a war zone. So, a neighbor, older woman, sees these two girls staggering down the street, and offers her help, lets them into her home, gives them clothes, and then the girls asked for some dough for food, so the lady pulls out a twenty and boom, they split without so much as a thank you. Seeing what's left of this townhouse, it's a miracle these gals survived."

"Hold on a sec." Hank put down the receiver, walked quickly to his TV set at the far end of the living room and turned it on. He didn't have to spin the knob to find the news, something this big would be on all three networks. Smoke billowing from a burning building, jumpy scenes, the cameras panning to show what was left of the bombed-out home. He returned to the kitchen and got back on the phone.

"I see it, looks really bad. So, wait, are you saying these kids were the bomb-makers? That they accidentally blew themselves up?"

"Yup, well, that's what I'm hearing. My guys guesstimate at least two or up to five more inside, but they didn't make it out. It's nothing like I've ever seen."

"Okay, you know the drill. Get in touch with Phil, we need to know if Jim was one of them."

Hank hung up, went back to the television, and watched for a few minutes more, then punched off the power. He wasn't interested in any of the details about the bomb's real target. That would come later. For now, he wanted the names of the

Weather folks inside. He had to make sure Jeannie didn't have any romantic notion of helping out her surviving comrades, or more specifically, Jim.

His stomach, for the first time since his light lunch, had started to rumble. He made quick strides back to his bedroom, and instead of showering off, donned his terry cloth robe and returned to the kitchen. Opening the freezer, he pulled out and unwrapped the porterhouse steak, filled the sink with water and dropped it in. Back out on the patio, Hank uncovered the barbecue, filled the base with coals and after a thorough dousing of lighter fluid, threw in a match. The flames shot up with a vengeance. Barbecues were usually social events and for a brief moment Hank pictured Tony and Phil standing there with him, drinks in hand waiting for their steaks to grill to the peak of perfection. The improbable scene reminded him of that classic joke introduction, 'okay, so a swarthy private eye, a bearded Vietnam vet and a southern, middle-aged ex-alcoholic walk into a bar...' The punchline would not elicit laughs though, just some sad irony. Hank never would utter the real story to anyone, even to those guys, who knew only his tale of benevolence. He paid his handlers generously to keep their mouths shut, and while Hank did not worry about Tony following orders, he wasn't so sure about Phil. For the past three months, Phil and Jeannie had been living together, and Hank fretted that in a moment of intimacy, Phil might spill the beans.

One late night in February, after receiving Tony's snapshots of Jeannie and Phil at Rockefeller Center, bundled up and holding hands, Hank made an impulsive call to Tony. He wanted to know if it was at all possible Phil would tell Jeannie that their meeting was never a coincidence.

"No way, boss." Tony mumbled back into the receiver.

"Why are you so sure?"

"Because without a doubt, soldiers don't snitch, and I'm guessing he's fallen hard too, he wouldn't mess it up if he didn't have to."

Tony's logic had calmed him down a little, but Hank had nothing solid to measure love by. His own marriage had been shaky from the start, mostly built on betrayal and lies, eroding any sense of loyalty. He had no insight into how his parents managed to stay together for 55 years, nor in what universe his surly sister and her shell of a husband could conceivably be months away from celebrating their 20th anniversary. Too late for him to find that kind of soul mate.

It all meant he'd have to trust Tony that Phil would stick to the plan, and maybe Jim had not been among those obliterated in the townhouse explosion. He and Tony would sort through it all, get a hold of Phil, and together, they'd figure out what to do next. Then it would be over. For his own sanity and from a nagging fear that it had gone on long enough, he'd end the Glazer project once and for all. While he'd never be totally exonerated for his own complicity on that tragic night in 1952, Hank had served his sentence.

Back in the kitchen, he lifted the thawed steak from the sink, plunked it onto a large platter, then sprinkled it with generous amounts of salt and pepper. He slipped back outside and stared down into the beckoning white squares of heat. He placed the steel grate into place and lowered the meat to the hot center. Within a few minutes, the savory aroma filled the patio. He was ready for the next chapter of his life to begin.

## Chapter 9

# APRIL – OCTOBER 1973

# *Jeannie*

NOTHING HAD BEEN QUITE like the coverage of the Watergate hearings, and Uncle Jack and his right hand man, Ernie, felt it was even too much for the Globe's seasoned reporters to handle without full staff participation. Just before 5:00 p.m. on a hectic Friday, Ernie announced a mandatory all staff meeting for 10:00 a.m. the next morning; something about new assignments, extra ones, who knew, but no one, at least in her pod of reporters, was happy about giving up a coveted weekend morning. Jeannie had met Phil at his bar per their usual Friday night routine, and by the time they'd gotten home, she was too drunk and forgot to set the alarm. Luckily, Phil had plans to take the train to Jersey for a family breakfast and set the buzzer for an 8:30.

In her drunken slumber, she didn't hear the annoying tone the next morning. Phil leaned over, kissed her and then nudged her body a few times until her eyelids lifted. He jumped in the shower while she slowly made her way off the bed and into the kitchen to start the coffee. She shuffled back to their bedroom to find something more presentable to wear than her boring skirt and blouse set. She went with the new dress she'd bought a few weeks back, and rather than bite off the tags with her teeth, went into their spare room, the size of a walk-in closet, to find a pair of scissors in Phil's desk. She began rummaging around, not feeling quite right doing so. For one thing, it was a mess, but more so because she respected his privacy. It was still his apartment, his possessions, and even if she'd lived there for nearly three years, there were certain lines she didn't cross. Some of the reason was that Jeannie hadn't been entirely straightforward with Phil, just parceling out bits about her time with SDS, and that the extra hours of research at the paper had been to find out what happened to Jim and the others. In a moment of vulnerability, she told him about being arrested in Chicago and getting mysteriously bailed out but didn't tell him that she had been pursuing the source of that money ever since. All those notes with lists of phone numbers, call logs, and dubious speculations were nestled in her tightly guarded bag, and if anyone, including Phil, had been caught looking through her yellow pads, it would be an intrusion she would not forgive.

She flattened her hand and felt the scissors in the back of the drawer. As she pulled them out, an envelope slid along with them. Phil's name and address were typed on the front, the return address a bank in Atlanta. Jeannie tiptoed to the door, stuck her head out in the hallway and crept across to the bedroom. She could hear the loud rush of water cranking through the bathroom pipes; Phil was still enjoying his shower. Hurrying back into the room, she took the scissors from the drawer, cut the dress tags, then gently lifted the envelope out. Her morning grogginess quickly disappeared as she could feel her senses on full alert. It was bulky, the slit open across the top, and as she parted the sides, she felt like a sneaky hypocrite. Inside were neatly arranged papers, all the same, maybe a dozen or so. She pulled out one; it was a bank issued check, multi-colored with lots of official print and in the amount of $500. She fanned through the rest, maybe 10 or more just like it, and gasped. Over $5,000 in uncashed checks!

"What the hell?" Her voice came out charged, angry.

When she heard the bathroom door opening, she shoved the envelope back in the drawer and pushed it shut. Confronting him now was out of the question. She slipped out of the room and headed into the kitchen, poured herself a cup of coffee, and drank it black. She took a big sip of the hot, strong liquid and looked up at the wall clock; if she took a quick shower, and could dress without any mishaps, she might still be able to catch the subway in time for the meeting. But later on, would she come right out with it? "Hey Phil, I found an envelope addressed to you in your drawer, looked in it and found $5,000 in uncashed checks…" Of course, she had to know the source, and the part of her brain, the one without the guilty conscience for snooping through his mail, would demand answers. Was he working for someone else in Atlanta? And why hadn't he cashed those checks? She needed to look at them again, to all the dates they were issued. For a moment, she felt badly for not trusting him, but then her reporter instincts kicked in; follow all the leads first, then strike.

"Hey J, shower's free, hurry up or you're going to be late."

She took another sip from her coffee; it tasted so bitter without her usual two scoops of sugar and heavy pour of cream.

When she came back into the bedroom, he was all dressed and ready to go, and gave her a quick kiss goodbye. She sent regards to his parents, and then slipped inside the bathroom.

*The Globe* was a madhouse for two straight weeks, with a satisfying ending on April 30th when Nixon's two lieutenants, Haldeman and Ehrlichman, resigned from their White House posts. It had been coming for sure, but still sent shock waves throughout the country. Nixon was on borrowed time, and while his loyal supporters could try and point the finger at his backstabbing staff, the walls around the President were crumbling, and *The Globe* reported on every falling brick. Jeannie had been in the fact-checking pool which gave her legitimate excuses for coming home late and not having the energy for the talk with Phil. She did, however, begin a list of possible sources for the mysterious stack of checks. Was he involved in some shady deal? What connections did he have down south? She knew the last three generations of his family were born, raised and still lived in and around the Tri-state area. Drugs? That crossed her mind, but only for an instant. The other, and more alarming explanation that she didn't want to consider, was that Phil had been the one who'd been paid off, the FBI informant who arranged her bail, and stuffed that envelope with $200 in cash along with the Trailways bus ticket. It was crazy, yes, but plausible, she wasn't idiotic to think it, the only sticking point was the quip made by the Cook County desk sergeant about thanking her 'pop' after handing her the envelope. But Phil could have been working with an older veteran FBI agent. It was this scenario that kept her spinning for two suspicious weeks.

She had also avoided his intimate advances in bed. The first week she told him she had her period, and the last, feigned a work fatigue that left her without a shred of energy. It all blew up after they'd gone out to see a movie and then went for drinks afterwards, mostly for her benefit. Phil had been a borderline teetotaler since returning from Vietnam, one beer was his limit. He wouldn't say much about it, only that he'd seen too many people lose their minds to alcohol and all variety of drugs overseas.

As soon as they stepped into the apartment, Phil closed the door and reached out for her arm, then tucked her into his chest. Lifting her face, he went in for the kiss. She let him explore her mouth, stroke her back until his hands rested on her bottom. With the two weeks of abstinence, and a good buzz from two hefty glasses of wine, she let him go. Their mouths stayed glued as they hobbled together into the bedroom, their clothes creating a twisted trail behind them.

When it was over, he held her under his chin where she could feel his heart, still beating at an accelerated pace.

"That was so nice. I missed you. You've been pretty distant." He whispered into the top of her head.

She wiggled slowly out of his embrace, "I'm going to get some water, want a glass?"

"Sure, but hurry back." He patted her vacated space.

She hadn't meant to spoil the night, but there was a calm between them now, and maybe that would help her get through the talk. She handed him a glass, put on her robe and sat at the edge of the bed. "Phil, I do need to talk to you about something I found in your desk."

He sat up straight and turned on his nightstand lamp. "What?"

She needed to get it all out, that was her style; she started by apologizing for going into his drawer, but then asked about the envelope of checks.

From the moment he opened his mouth, Phil didn't sound like himself, something was off, the story too cliché. A rehearsed tale about an army buddy, someone he'd gotten close with, who before he was killed by a landmine in Laos, asked Phil to get in touch with his parents if he didn't make it; they'd hear the tragic news from some military goon, but as an only child, he wanted a friend to soften the blow for his mom and dad.

"When I returned from 'Nam, I kept the promise, but instead of calling them, I flew down and met them in their home just outside Atlanta. I had his last letter and wanted to give it to them in person. They were so grateful, they offered to reimburse my plane ticket and expenses. Of course, I refused." He got out of bed, reached down for his boxers, put them on, and went into the bathroom. Jeannie heard him use the toilet and when he came back, he sat down next to her.

"A month later, I got the first envelope; there's no note inside, just a cashier's check for $500. I saw the Atlanta bank address and immediately got in touch with my buddy's parents. It was from them, and they wouldn't take it back, told me to use it to go back to school or pursue whatever career I wanted, that's what they were saving it for when they thought their boy was coming home. Ten checks in total arrived over the year, and as you saw, I didn't cash them. It stopped at $5,000, and that was about two years ago."

"Why didn't you tell me? We've been together for three years, Phil; that's not a little thing, not at all! What was his name?" Jeannie stood and moved away from the bed.

"I can't tell you that, and don't get mad, please, these folks insisted on their anonymity, and I agreed. When I left their home that day, I thought I'd never hear from them again, and then the checks started to arrive like I said. I can't explain it either."

She stared at him, shaking her head. "I believe you had army buddies and that some of them died on the battlefield, but the rest of your story sounds like bullshit."

He got up and walked toward her. "Why would I lie to you?"

"How come you haven't cashed them yet? It's been years...!"

Phil shrugged, "I don't know, but if it makes you happy, I'll go to my bank tomorrow."

"No, it won't because you're not telling me the whole truth, are you? A bartender by night, but you've got a day job, don't you?" She couldn't stop herself.

"Oh, really? And what's that?"

Jeannie inhaled and then, at last, let it out. "We met at the coffee shop, my coffee shop, the one I went to almost every day, and while I didn't share many details back then, you knew, didn't you, that I was in SDS because you showed up just when things had heated up for me, when the group had turned into the Weather Underground, and then hung in there despite how little I told or could promise you. It was enough though, enough to get me away from them. But then I did tell you, remember? About the Chicago arrest and the whole bailout thing, and that there could be an informant, someone who had been watching me. But I'm guessing you already knew that."

Phil looked at her as if she were truly out of her mind. His eyes squinting, brows in a deep furrow, his mouth puckered. "What are you accusing me of?"

"Being an FBI informant."

His shoulders relaxed, and he began to smile, then broke into a breathy laugh, "Oh man, you've really gone off the deep end. It's the paper, right? Nixon, the tapes, the break-ins, all of it. It's you who needs a break, Jeannie, maybe you should take a weekend away, and calm the heck down."

"You're right, I do need a break—from you!" She shouted at him.

Then it was like a scene from a cheesy B-rated movie; she running around, grabbing her suitcase, opening drawers and stuffing in random clothes, and Phil, trying to stop her, the yelling and protests, racing out the door, down the stairwell, and out onto the street, waving her hand wildly to hail a cab. Without thinking, she gave the driver her grandmother's address. Grammy would pry and plead for answers, and understandably be alarmed by her actions, but unlike her mother, would give her space and the time to sort it out.

. . .

SIX MONTHS LATER, JEANNIE remained as obstinate as ever, and no matter how many scenarios she considered, it always ended with not believing Phil's story. He was lying about something or else he'd have coughed up the name of his deceased army buddy. If he had nothing to hide, why wouldn't he just tell her, and then, case closed. Her grandmother and Uncle Pauley said she could stay for as long as she needed, and like the rest of the family, they eventually stopped bugging her about the abrupt break-up with Phil. She'd gone back to the apartment on 72nd street when she knew he was at work to collect the rest of her stuff, and then shoved her key under the front door. She even snooped around the apartment one last time, but found nothing incriminating, and naturally, the checks were no longer in the drawer. He called her at paper, but when she had consistently screened his calls, he stopped. He could have gotten in touch with her brother Jeffrey, or even her mother, but he knew better than to involve any of them. He had a secret and she needed to find out what it was, but the gut-wrenching part was she still loved him, very much. Her heart wanted to believe him, but those anonymous checks collecting dust instead of interest at a bank convinced her that he wasn't able or willing to tell her the truth. She woke up on that dark, cloudy October morning before Jeffrey and Roz's Sunday brunch in a foul mood, dreading the commute to Brooklyn.

Huddled against the glass doors, Jeannie pressed Jeffrey's apartment buzzer. The awning was flapping so wildly that she barely heard the signal to let her in. As she climbed to the second floor, a mingle of voices could be heard drifting down the stairwell.

She wore a beige slicker that touched the tops of her brown leather boots. She didn't bother to compress the frizzy tendrils around her head, knowing the humidity and rain would render that task useless. Smudging her lids with bright colors or waving a sticky wand of mascara over her lashes was only performed for weddings or super special occasions; this brunch clearly didn't meet that criteria. She rarely left her apartment though without tinting her pale lips, yet even that habit had been dropped from the morning routine. She was a half-hour late, so wasn't surprised to see her mother's outstretched arms ready to greet her on the landing. When Jeannie didn't return her embrace and couldn't muster the effort to change her stony expression, she knew she'd sent up a red flare.

"What's the matter, honey?" asked her mother with a concerned frown. "We've been waiting for you. You look, well, I don't know, tired, mad?"

"I'm fine." She followed her inside, and saw Roz and Grace Vincie fussing over the table, like two giggling schoolgirls. Roz glided over to Jeannie.

"Great to see you, Jeannie Beanie." She gave her a peck on the cheek. "Here, let me have your coat."

Jeffrey came out of the kitchen holding a platter of bagels. "Hey sis, nice of you to show up." He gave her a thin smile, and then set the plate in the center of the table.

Jeannie didn't need his sarcasm this morning. It was still hard to believe that he and Roz had managed to reunite so many years after their junior high sex scandal, when the two of them were caught in their underwear rolling around the shag carpet of the Vincies' basement. Roz and Jeannie had been best friends since first grade, but after the basement incident, the Vincies banished both her and Jeffrey from their home and lives. Outside of the school hallways, there was no social contact until Jeffrey went away to college, and then the Vincies lifted the ban, but it was never the same between her and Roz. With her own life in shambles, she hadn't kept in close touch with her brother, so it came as a shock when he announced that not only had he reconnected with Roz, but that it was serious. "Meant to be" he was fond of reminding all of them, as if his and Roz's destinies had been justifiably sealed in that drafty basement ten years earlier.

Jeannie noticed the champagne flutes and was glad to see that alcohol had been added to the brunch menu. She managed a civil greeting for the Vincies, not able to fully let go of the faded grudge between them.

"C'mon everyone, I'm sure you're starved. Find a seat. Let's eat while the bagels are still warm." Roz seemed to float through the room like a cloud-skipping cherub. Jeffrey was right there with her, pulling chairs out from the table to seat his guests, a grin locked into place.

He did the honors of popping the champagne and filling everyone's flute halfway as Roz followed behind with a pitcher of orange juice, carefully topping off glasses. Conversation began to buzz around the table, all about the lovely spread and the imminent storm. Dominic Vincie's loud, deep baritone contrasted with the high tones of the chattering women. Jeannie didn't pipe in, keeping her head either tipped down to her plate, or turned toward the window. The sky had become a dark gray canvas. Jeffrey picked up his knife and tapped the side of his glass.

"Okay, so this may look like a typical brunch, but the Vincies are here for the first time, and besides the good food and drink, there is something else to celebrate." Jeffrey pulled Roz close to him.

Her mother's mood could not have been more buoyant, she seemed so happy that everything was going as planned. Jeannie was relieved that her mother hadn't brought her boyfriend, Marty, to the brunch. She did like him and enjoyed his sense of humor, but ever since they had become a couple a few years back, her mother had turned into a silly teenager whenever they were together. It irked her more than she wanted to admit.

Still standing, Jeffrey nodded toward Roz, a signal for her to raise her left hand and dangle her fingers up by her chin. She must have slipped on the small square diamond ring in the kitchen, and while no one was really surprised, the congratulations were boisterous. Mr. Vincie's smile was so wide that perhaps for the first time, Jeannie saw his teeth. She waited until everyone made their fuss, and then got up and gave her brother and Roz each a kiss on their cheek.

While they all ate, Jeannie continued to fill her flute with champagne so by the time dessert and coffee were served, she had gone from tipsy to semi-drunk. She had been too anxious to engage in any table chit-chat. Besides, it was nearly impossible to get a word in edgewise with her mother and Mrs. Vincie talking over one other. They both at least agreed on a June wedding.

Roz, clearly noticing her silence, jumped in and asked Jeannie what she'd been working on at the newspaper.

She straightened up for the first time all morning. "Watergate, of course, the White House tapes, something is about to blow with that, but now it's also about Agnew's resignation. One crook gone, another to go. There's a feeding frenzy with all the reporters falling over Mr. Editor-in-Chief to be picked for the trips down to D.C. I mean, who wouldn't die to be in the room when impeachable intelligence is revealed?"

She suddenly felt revved up by the champagne. "Obviously every correspondent from here to Timbuktu will be there, so the seasoned guys made their pitches; they know it could boost their careers. Hell would have to freeze over before a 'cub' like me gets on that bus. Besides, all the veteran guys have their favorite gophers, and turns out, I wasn't on anyone's list."

"Well, it's really just beginning, isn't it, dear?" Her mother's voice came out too shrill. "I mean, with the way Washington works, there will be plenty of stories to write about, especially with the war finally over and done with."

Jeannie countered more sharply. "Things aren't done at all; according to our sources, the Paris talks are a joke."

"Alright, enough politics. We're supposed to be celebrating our engagement." Jeffrey swung an arm around Roz's shoulder, and then picked up her left hand again, waving it over the table. He, too, seemed to be more than a little tipsy.

"Yes, and a toast to Jeffrey never having to step foot in that jungle, being right here, alive and safe." Her mother's voice had that shaky, pre-tears quality to it. Turning to the Vincies', her mother went on, "You know, Grace, Dom, it was a miracle, truly."

Oh no, Jeannie silently groaned, knowing what was coming next. The infamous story. This was clearly for the Vincies' benefit. She looked over at Jeffrey, who normally would have given her a shared eye roll, but instead, kept his focus on their mother.

"There I was at work flipping through a stack of magazines getting them ready for shelving, when I saw that handsome George Hamilton's photo in a small inset on a *Newsweek* cover. Anyway, the story wasn't about his dating Lynda Byrd, no, it was about how he'd gotten out of the draft on account of him being the only surviving male in his family. I stopped dead in my tracks. This was it, a way out, I thought, and we still had a little more than 90 days to make it stick." Her mother was talking at a fast clip, having told and retold the details of her ingenuity and perseverance with all the paperwork, and Marty, a lawyer with all his legal help, blah blah blah, it seemed to glide off her tongue. She didn't add that Jeffrey had buried his fear of the draft by smoking marijuana most of his senior year at college and had been no help at all.

"Mom, they've heard it, they know, we all know the story!" Jeannie's voice boomed over the heavy rain now pelting the bay windows. She stood up, stormed into the kitchen and headed to the back door leading out to the fire escape. The rain was hitting the metal frame so loudly, she didn't hear her mother come up from behind.

Bernice's hand rested on Jeannie's back, "What's really going on, honey? It's not the paper, or my tiresome story. It's about Phil, isn't it?"

"You wouldn't understand, *no one does*, and I can't talk about him either, please just leave it alone. I just need everyone to leave me *alone.*"

Jeannie turned away from her mother and walked slowly out of the kitchen. She went straight for the front door, put on her raincoat, then turned and announced, "Sorry. I've got a deadline. Gotta run." She didn't wait for any words of protest before scurrying out of the apartment.

*Damn!* She shouldn't have said anything to her mother about Phil. A good reporter doesn't get that emotional about or even reveal that there is a story until most of the facts are in. Even if she could make any connections between Phil and whoever set him up, here or in Atlanta, no one would believe her. Everyone loved Phil. He'd given her the courage to leave Jim and the group, and they had truly fallen in love. She could never share her speculations with any family member; they'd look at her sideways, shake their heads, and in typical reaction, blame the SDS 'cult' for her persistent suspicion about everything.

The rain was coming down in solid sheets, but it didn't matter, she couldn't get away from Jeffrey and Roz's apartment fast enough. She felt suffocated by the mismatched furniture, all the framed photographs of cheerful faces, along with tiny statues of the Virgin Mary and angels crammed into bookshelves or on windowsills. Their engagement had been no surprise at all, and while Jeannie was genuinely happy for them, it had been over a month since she'd gotten an invitation from either of them to hang out. Her hurt turned to envy. Then her mother had to control the conversation, redirecting topics to impress the Vincies and eventually contriving a chance to retell her heroic mother story. Over the years, Jeannie had come up with a bunch of headlines, *"Clever Librarian Saves Son from Combat"* or, *"No Father, No Draft for Only Son,"* and the least catchy, *"Draft Evaded: Kew Gardens Graduate Joins Hollywood Hamilton in 2A Decision."* Not that she wasn't totally relieved and grateful for her mother's intervention, it was just that Jeffrey's plight had everyone's unconditional support. Not so with her. Since she'd been out of the group, no one except Phil knew the details of her experiences with SDS and the Weather faction they became, about her daily palpitations when she'd listen to their illicit plans; and how they or rather, Jim, essentially held her captive.

It took a long time for her to trust Phil enough to share her stories, especially the terrifying ones about building explosives, and all the recurring nightmares of nearly being blown to bits inside the 11th Street townhouse. It had been a huge weight off her chest. In the darkness, Phil had stroked her head and said he understood. By cutting that lifeline, Jeannie had returned to her dark cave of isolation, forcing her to rely on her wits to find a way out.

Cranky and unsettled, she trudged back to her grandmother's house. The windy downpour blew her umbrella inside out two blocks before reaching the subway. In the near empty train car, soaked and shivering, she vowed, at whatever cost, to prove her theory. Phil, if that was his real name, had become another tentacle of her research, and even if her speculation that he was linked to some FBI informant network was wildly off-course, she needed to be certain. After her humiliating scene at her brother's apartment, she'd have to work even faster.

# Chapter 10

## NOVEMBER – DECEMBER 1973

# *Jeannie*

J EANNIE RIPPED THE SHEET of paper out of the typewriter with such force that it almost tore her final draft in two. She wasn't on a strict deadline, but all the reporters were on edge. Fortunately, the guys in her pod were either off the clock or, as they crudely liked to share, taking a whiz. The small bank of windows at the pit's ceiling height let in little light, making it difficult to determine the time of day, but the clock read 5:00 p.m. The darkness was settling against the fluorescent lights. The winter sky had turned the day too quickly into night.

Being the editor's niece played a huge part in Jeannie securing a cub reporter spot at *The New York Globe*. That only made her work harder to dispel any hints of nepotism. She always came in earlier than the others and would rarely leave the building before 6:00 p.m. Press deadlines often forced reporters to work through lunch, where half-eaten sandwiches and crumpled wrappers were lost among piles of papers, turning the pit into messy chaos. She, however, managed to keep her desk neat, complete her work efficiently, and stay as unobtrusive as she could, pleasant, helpful, anything to discourage co-worker curiosity where they might lean in or ask personal questions. A pattern was established; she'd linger past the 5:00 p.m. staff exodus, shuffling piles of paper or fumbling with her purse. Then, when everyone had cleared out, she'd sit back down. Phil had always been understanding of her crazy hours, and because of his accepting attitude, Jeannie would try and wrap things up as fast as she could to get home before 7:00 p.m. But now that he was gone from her life, she arrived early and stayed late, *The Globe* becoming her primary hang-out.

Without the swell of other bodies, and their billows of cigarette smoke, noisy patter and banging typewriters, Jeannie could relax and truly concentrate. She put her coat over her shoulders and settled in. She had become an after-hours fixture to the janitorial staff and appreciated how they'd clean the whole floor before coming back around by her desk. She unlocked the file drawer to retrieve her canvas bag, pulling out the most recent yellow pad. Flipping through the pages of fragmented notes, arrowed diagrams, names with bubbles around them, and long lists of phone numbers, she looked around once more before starting her nightly calls. She had been careful to keep her bag out of sight. Even when she went to the bathroom, she would tug at her desk drawer to make sure it was locked.

Like a smoker to nicotine, Jeannie had become addicted to her privacy. She began sneaking into empty offices to make phone calls. At her desk, she whispered into her phone even if it was a legitimate work-related call. Often, she used her lunch hour to slip into a phone booth a block away from the building with a handful of coins. Most of her attempts were wrong numbers, or lines that had been disconnected, but then she'd get a live one, a friend of a woman who dated Jim's brother, and it would be enough to keep up the search for him or any of her former comrades who clearly, as she was learning, didn't want to be found. It helped to have access to phone books from most of the bigger U.S. cities at her disposal. The paper taught her to be patient, persistent and unyielding; if not for the two investigative reporters at *The Washington Post*, her uncle repeatedly admonished staff, Watergate would have just been another office complex in D.C.

Jeannie absorbed it all, not only in preparing her fluffy articles, but from late April on, the Watergate scandal that had grabbed universal readership. Any other news stories just took up space. Intent on being seen as a team player, she offered her research skills to seasoned staff, and in her own work double-checked everything to make sure her stories were flawless. Her efforts paid off with a bunch of consecutive pieces appearing in the paper, but they didn't bump her up in the pecking order for the D.C. beat and despite how hard she worked, her uncle would not override the seniority system.

Her social circle had narrowed to Jeffrey and Roz after the break-up with Phil. Single again, she had at first been satisfied with their invitations to go out to bars, dinner or an occasional movie. But just as it was in junior high with those two, she often felt like a third wheel squeezed into their plans. She spent whatever free time she had tiptoeing around her Grammy's home, and if not for her grandmother and Uncle Pauley's compulsion with watching the Watergate hearings, her stealthy comings and goings would have been more scrutinized. Fortunately, she had become adept at distracting them, often leaking tidbits of *Globe* reporters' breaking news that hadn't yet gone to press. When she finally went to bed, her body sunk into the mattress, though her mind kept buzzing. No matter how much she dwelled on the torrent of unanswered questions about her lost comrades, or more urgently, Phil's so-called army buddy from Atlanta, eventually she'd conjure up his handsome face, and for the first few months at her grandmother's, she had cried herself to sleep.

At work she became more furtive, trying to sort out possible leads from dead ends, and would have jumped at the chance to share her half-baked theories with her Uncle Jack. He was now the one person in her life who listened, and even when she wasn't making much sense, she never felt judged by him. At the paper though, he was her boss, and at family gatherings, she rarely had a chance to get him alone. Dozens of times since she'd left SDS, and especially after the bombing, she had wanted to tell her uncle what really happened in Chicago, to talk openly about Jim and the others, what they said and did. Like a good reporter, she would have loved to show him her yellow pads with all of her notes on tracking down who paid her bail, gave her the money and bus ticket, and eventually her speculation about being followed by an FBI informant. She truly believed he'd have given her the benefit of the doubt. But when she broke it off with Phil and started down a slippery investigative slope, she backed away from confiding in him. She needed more courage and proof, and that would take effort; until she had a more grounded case for his help that didn't sound so absurd, she would have to wait.

The holidays had arrived on a grim note. Even with decorative wreaths, flashing lights strung around massive cookie-cutter evergreen trees, and poinsettia pots placed in every visible setting, to Jeannie it all seemed like a façade. The endless Christmas tunes enticing shoppers to gleefully spend hard-earned cash on overpriced gifts had the opposite effect on her. She'd hear "Rudolph" or "Winter Wonderland" and bolt for the exit doors. She'd then return to the office where no pretense about the holiday spirit existed as reporters continued to act like competitive bulldogs. After Nixon's famous "I'm not a crook" speech, in which he continued to deny his role in the Watergate break-in, a troubling shift descended in the newsroom. Instead of the usual pitching in to meet deadline press runs, all the guys jumped on their own horses and raced to the finish line. More bylines on front section column space meant more name recognition, and the reward of a week's assignment in D.C. Jockeying for the lead had never been the way things worked at *The Globe*, but as seasoned reporter Howie told her one afternoon, "There's never been a story as big as Watergate on our watch."

Still, there was plenty of news to cover on the local scene. After Nixon's loyal secretary, Rosemary Woods, "inadvertently" erased an 18½-minute recording of an incriminating oval office conversation, impeachment demands dominated most news cycles, while random protests began erupting in all five N.Y.C. boroughs. For Jeannie, the tumultuous events canceled out all the Christmas cheer; and while *Globe* readers could choose to toss the distressing news in the trash, or fireplaces, she and the other reporters on the front lines didn't have that luxury. Spending several years now in her uncle's world made her appreciate his personal sacrifices to keep the public informed.

But tonight, she couldn't stay late at work; it was Uncle Jack and Aunt Cindy's yearly Hanukkah party, and no excuses were accepted. It was her first holiday season in three years without Phil. She had always looked forward to the gathering, but without him by her side, she'd be alone and even more untethered. When she had finished putting on a tight-fitting navy blue silk dress for the party, she lingered in her room until Grammy and Uncle Pauley called upstairs, saying they were ready to go. She was quiet in the taxi over to Forest Hills. A doorman was waiting as they pulled up. Leaning down, he opened the rear door.

"Ready, darling?" Her grandmother patted her knee.

No, not at all, she thought. To be upbeat and chatty with

her family was like walking into a final exam unprepared; she had no choice but to guess or make up answers. She let her grandmother and Uncle Pauley lead the way, staying silent in the elevator and down the hall to her aunt and uncle's apartment. The front door was partially open and there, hovering in the foyer, were her mother and Marty hanging up their coats.

"Hello sweetheart, Happy Hanukkah. Here give me your coat, I'll put it in next to ours." Marty leaned over and gave her a kiss on her forehead. "You look lovely, such a pretty dress."

Her mother went in for a quick hug, "Yes, honey, it's a wonderful fit." She then squeezed in between Grammy and Uncle Pauley interlacing her arms through theirs.

The living room couches were moved around to accommodate rental chairs and small tables where guests could sit comfortably. Aunt Cindy did it up every year with delicious platters of latkes, cold salmon, raw and cooked vegetables, salads, fruit bowls and dessert trays of rugelach, cookies, and chocolate-dipped macaroons. Jeannie headed straight for the bar area, where her Uncle Jack was pouring red wine for a couple she recognized from the building.

"Oh well, now we can start the festivities, my beautiful niece has arrived." He leaned down to give her a kiss and then handed her a glass of wine.

She raised her glass in a toast, then pointing to the buffet, smiled and scooted away. For the rest of the party, she kept her distance hoping not to be pulled into pockets of conversation. She paused only to refill her wine glass. Roz and Jeffrey were not coming; the Vincies apparently had dibs on the same night for a family event that could not be missed. Nevertheless, she picked up fragments of Roz and Jeffrey's June wedding plans with Grammy's voice in the lead. Marty had staked a spot in the center of the room, delivering his usual stand-up comedy routine, joking about work, life, whatever. It never failed to evoke fits of cackling laughter from her overzealous mother, making Jeannie cringe. She spent a few minutes catching up with her cousin Scotty, who was in good spirits, a cute new college girlfriend by his side, nicely dressed, a freckly redhead like her. She chatted a bit with her younger cousin Max, still in high school, who she saw sneaking liquor from the living room bar, so he was either more outgoing than usual, or nearly drunk. She, in contrast, was like an unmoored schooner, adrift with no Phil, no anchor. She'd almost rather be at work. After the candle lighting and gift exchange, she escaped into the den until Grammy came in and announced that she and Uncle Pauley were ready to leave.

Silent on the ride home, Jeannie said goodnight to Grammy and Uncle Pauley, then scooted up the stairs to her room. She shimmied out of her tight dress, slipped on a flannel night-gown and plunked down on the bed, inhaling the familiar soapy scents of her grandmother's home. As a young girl, she'd always loved this time of the year. There seemed to be lots of parties, culminating with the New Year's Eve overnight at her grandparents' house with Jeffrey. Grammy would make her delicious roast chicken with scalloped potatoes, allow them to drink unlimited 7-Ups with cherries, and finally, treat them to dishes of ice cream and cookies. Her grandmother delayed dinnertime as they tried to stay up past midnight, but after a night of watching TV snuggled in the crook of Grammy's arm with a full belly, she never made it, at least not until she turned 11 or 12 years old. Jeffrey would always boast the next morning how he had stayed up 'til midnight, although according to Grammy, he'd be fast asleep by 12:01.

Now, a decade later, she would be spending it again with Grammy, and Uncle Pauley, but this year she planned on being too drunk to stay up past 10. Jeffrey and Roz had come through with a last-minute invitation to their friends' party, but she had declined, deciding that nothing was more depressing than being single at a New Year's Eve party surrounded by happy couples giving each other big sloppy kisses at midnight.

This December was such a stark contrast from the year before when she and Phil had spent the holidays in festivity-hopping mode. Phil's bar started the ball rolling with a big private party, followed by *The Globe's* annual cocktail dance at the Hilton, then it was Christmas Eve at Phil's parents, back to Queens the next day for the Vincie's Christmas Day extravaganza, ending finally, at a New Year's Eve party in Jersey with Phil's old high school buddies. It had been the best holiday season ever; she was in love and felt loved back.

Jeannie had a standing invitation to the Vincies' on Christmas day, and despite her foul mood, RSVP'd that she'd be there. It was nearly impossible to feel lonely or glum when dining at the most pleasurable Italian eating fest in Queens. Until the Jeffrey and Roz basement incident when the families had parted ways, Jeannie had been a frequent guest at their Sunday dinners. Pizza man Uncle Sal, along with relatives on both sides would arrive with their own specialty platters which would then be arranged on the enormous dining room table. Veal parmigiana oozing with cheese, savory meatballs and perfectly cooked spaghetti, saucy dishes she could never remember the names of, plenty of crusty, warm Italian bread, and then, those powdered sugar cookies and custardy profiteroles. Mrs. Vincie always told Jeannie to bring her mother and Jeffrey along, but the last thing Jeannie wanted was her mother's reserved expressions or Jeffrey's judging eye squints to dampen the fun. No, this was Jeannie's time to be on her own, where no one cared if she ate too much, got goofy with Roz, or laughed too loudly listening to the animated stories and jokes from Roz's hilarious family members.

• • •

THE MORNING AFTER THE Hanukkah party, Jeannie slipped out of the house before Grammy or Uncle Pauley had stirred and walked two blocks to the corner diner. It was her new weekend hiding spot. After a glass of orange juice, a pot of coffee, and a toasted bagel had been delivered to her table, she reached into her canvas bag, pulled out her calendar, and penciled in the Vincies' party. She guessed Phil would be with his family, or maybe his bartender friends, or worse, with a new girlfriend. In the three years they'd been together, Jeannie had only been to his parents' house for the Christmas Eve dinner. She had met his co-workers who, in addition to the holiday event, would occasionally all get together at another bar; but the banter was all about their gang of regular alkies, sports, and who was shacking up with whom. Never in their company had she heard a peep about politics or current events. They rarely asked her questions either.

Naturally, she'd asked Phil plenty of questions about his life before Vietnam, but he either gave vague answers or just shrugged, letting her inquiries die a quick death. His life was 'apple pie' boring, he told her. "Nothing to write home about." She had met his father during their first months together, when he'd come in from Jersey for a retirement dinner, and the three of them went for cocktails before his event. Alfred Reeder had risen to Detective Sergeant in the NYPD and after 30 years on the force, was able to call it quits "with 90% of his salary," he said with a huge grin. Phil's mother, Betty, was a housewife and apparently enjoyed the routine of their quiet suburban neighborhood. "She'd had enough of the crowded, crime-ridden streets of New York for two lifetimes," Alfred told her. Jeannie liked Phil's dad immediately, the soft way he spoke, his directness, honesty, and easy conversational style. He didn't ask her many questions, and for that, she was grateful. Phil also had an older sister who was married and living in Vermont with a lumberjack husband. There were no secrets or family drama, according to Phil, at least not until the two years he spent in the jungles of Vietnam. It seemed like no matter how gently she'd bring it up, she couldn't get him to share any of his army experiences. Instead, he'd shake his head, turn away from her, and stare into some void for a few moments before turning back and changing the subject. She got the message; besides, she was always the narrator in their social life, the inquisitor, and the lively storyteller. The two of them, she was certain, could not have been better suited for one another. When he opened his door on that frigid December night three years earlier and wrapped her in his protective arms, she felt eternally grateful and in his debt. After the break-up when he stopped calling her at *The Globe*, Phil had vanished from her life, but not her thoughts. She had nagging regrets, and as with Jim, all she could do now was wonder what he was up to.

She knew where Phil lived and worked, and he knew all about her secret project, so if he was indeed connected to an FBI informant network, he would be the one still keeping tabs on her. It was why she had fled to Grammy's, knowing he would never cross that boundary. Over and over again she tried to make sense of his story about the dead army buddy. It was the first time he'd revealed anything meaningful about his time in the service, but then could not explain why, for starters, the Atlanta family didn't just give him a lump sum instead of installments? That's when her SDS training, or rather indoctrination about informants, kicked in. If she could trace that source, it might link up to the unexplained events in Chicago. The tugging heartbreak didn't seem to dissipate and until she had proof one way or another, she would stay depressed and stuck. She was desperate for a sounding board. Not only was she drowning in the holiday blues, but felt like she was losing her mind too.

Outside of the diner, the air temperature seemed to have dropped 10 degrees. Buttoning up her coat and tightening the scarf around her neck, she pulled down her ski hat so it rested just above her eyebrows. Despite the cold, last-minute shoppers weaved through the streets, in and out of stores, making their final purchases before the big day. The subway into Manhattan was a few blocks away; Jeannie decided on a whim to take the train all the way uptown to the 116th stop. She hadn't made that commute since she graduated two years ago.

As she approached the campus grounds, the scenery was just as she remembered. The same pathways winding through the columned buildings that she first navigated in the fall of 1967, full of giddy optimism. She wished her innocent vision of college life had lasted longer than the following spring, when it became clouded over by the raging protests and violent riots instigated by Jim and his friends amidst all the political turmoil. She slowed her pace as she headed toward her old dorm, hoping the sight of it would generate a happier wave of nostalgia. Instead, her icy toes were turning numb. In an about-face, Jeannie took a short cut through campus that put her on Broadway. Her body charged ahead until she reached the old Chock Full O' Nuts three blocks down. Pushing open the glass door, she headed for her old booth, relieved to find it empty. She ordered a hot chocolate and stared out the frosted windowpane. After the frothy mug was delivered, she pulled out the yellow pad from her canvas bag. Scanning her most recent notes, she bore down at the pages hoping to find something she'd missed. Could Phil actually be the real source of the envelope in Chicago? Would finding Jim somehow assuage her guilt for not telling him the truth about her arrest and release in Chicago? Would it even have even helped them in any way? Or was it really just her morbid curiosity to learn who had successfully escaped and who didn't make it? And then, the image of those colorful cashier checks; why a bank in Atlanta, did it mean anything?

The restaurant door opened, ushering in a gust of cold air. She looked up and saw a trim-looking man in an overcoat and hat heading in her direction. As he approached, Jeannie could feel her heart thumping through layers of clothing. Before the man claimed a stool at the adjacent counter, she caught the aging lines etched on his face. She wiped her palms with a napkin, then gazed back out the window. Would meeting Phil turn out to be just a fluke of fate or had he been recruited to follow her after she met Jim, at this very spot, six years earlier?

Phil was taking up all the space in her head; without any warning, she felt a tug of grief seep through her body. It came with a jittery feeling and a pins-and-needles sensation that crept up her arms. She had kept her coat over her shoulders, but now she was hot, beads of sweat heating up her neck, the room starting to spin. She gripped the sides of the table to keep from slumping over, and in the process knocked her bag to the floor, the pads and pens scattering in the aisle. The man at the counter seat popped up and crouched down to pick up her papers.

"No! I got it." But she couldn't move her head, much less lean down to retrieve her bag.

She heard the man ask for a glass of water from the waitress. "Can you drink this?" Jeannie accepted the glass from his hand and took baby sips of the tepid liquid. Then once again, he bent down, and this time picked up her stuff. "I'm no doctor, but you don't look so good, maybe you should get some air." His voice was kind and soothing. The water neutralized her dizziness.

"Thank you, yes, you're probably right." She reached for the check, but he picked it up first. "Let me get this, young lady, you go on home now."

She was too weak and shaky to argue. Gathering her things, she thanked him for his help. Outside, Jeannie inhaled the cold air and started to walk toward the subway. Halfway down the block, a wave of sadness hit her, first tears, then sniffles that turned into sobs. Keeping her head down, she wiped her nose on the sleeve of her coat. She was lost and needed help, but not from a random stranger. It had to be from someone who'd listen, not be skeptical, and understand that beyond this obsession with her secret projects, she was still so sad and bummed out about Phil. Who could she trust?

At the end of the block was a pharmacy that she remembered had a phone booth. She raced toward it, strength returning to her legs. Pushing open the heavy entrance door, she scooted down the aisle, closed herself inside the booth and sat down on the tiny stool. She hadn't put her gloves back on, so it took a few moments for her stiff fingers to extract a dime from her wallet and drop it in the coin slot. She dialed slowly.

After four rings, she answered. "Hello?"

"Hey Roz, it's Jeannie." Her voice was thick and nasally.

"What's the matter? Are you okay?" Roz's deep tone had a comforting quality.

"No, I'm not, I need to talk, I need to talk to *you.*"

"Of course. Where are you?"

Jeannie's breathing slowed down to a measured pace.

"Uptown, in Manhattan, but I will go anywhere we can talk alone, undisturbed."

"Okay, listen, I'm just wrapping presents and Jeffrey's out with his friends until dinnertime. Can you come here?"

"Okay, I'll be there in less than an hour." Jeannie hung up, feeling for the first time in six months that she had a friend. By the time she pressed the apartment buzzer, her nerves had settled down. As she went up the stairs, she told herself to be honest and not to stop until it was all out, everything. There was nothing to lose anymore.

Roz had cleared the dining room table and put out a bottle of red wine, two glasses and a plate of cheeses, sliced bread and a small bowl of olive oil.

After taking her coat, and giving her a long hug, Roz led Jeannie to the table, poured the wine, and put a little plate and napkin in front of each of them. "Okay, you're scaring me, what's going on?"

Jeannie took several small sips of wine and picked up a piece of cheese. She nibbled on it just to have something solid in her stomach. It was close to 4:00 and she hadn't eaten anything since breakfast. "Before I start, I'm going to ask you to please just listen first, hear me out. Then you can pick away."

"Got it." Roz leaned in, her eyebrows tightening.

Jeannie began with the Phil break-up. It was the story she assumed Roz, and everyone else had been dying for her to share. All of them already knew how they'd met, and how he'd been the one that convinced her to leave Jim. He was the 'gem, life-saver, nice guy'; and for all intents and purposes, her future husband.

Roz nodded and then poured them both another glass.

She told her every detail, from the search for scissors to the envelope with ten $500 cashier's checks, their blow-out fight, and finally how she packed a suitcase and took a taxi to her Grammy's house.

"What? Wait…are you saying he had over $5,000 lying around in some drawer?" Roz grabbed a piece of cheese, put it on bread and popped the bite into her mouth.

Jeannie nodded. "Yes, and from a bank in Atlanta!"

Roz tilted her head. "What's that got to do with anything?"

"I know, but remember, hear me out." Jeannie took a big sip of wine.

"Okay, okay, then what happened?"

"He told me some ludicrous story about getting the money as an act of kindness from the parents of an army buddy killed in 'Nam. He wouldn't reveal their names, said it was confidential. Who would I tell? I eliminated the possibility that he was some kind of bookie or drug dealer. Then it came to me; maybe *he* was the informant, it all made sense, the person who arranged my bail."

"Bail? Informant? What the heck are you talking about?"

The time had come. "I'm sure Jeffrey told you that I went to the Democratic Convention in Chicago in '68, and, well, I got arrested."

"Arrested? For what?" Roz's head titled to one side, her eyes straining at Jeannie's as if she were seeing her for the first time.

"Wait, let me explain. Even though I was arrested, I don't have a record because before I knew it, I was being escorted to the sergeant's desk where he not only let me go, but then gave me an envelope with a bus ticket back to New York and $200 in fifty-dollar bills. The oddest thing is the cop said something about it being a gift from my *pop*."

"I'm completely lost." Roz sighed, and Jeannie didn't blame her; she should have started from the beginning.

"The Black Panthers, SDS, Weather Underground, SNCC, any groups that had a political agenda were being watched and infiltrated by the FBI or other informants. This is a known fact. In Ann Arbor right before the Chicago convention, SDS leaders warned us about them. They told us to be really careful; maybe I wasn't careful enough."

Roz held up her hand. "Wait, wait, so you think that the money in Phil's desk means he's an FBI informant? Are you kidding me?"

Jeannie got up to pace. "Roz, listen, just listen. Phil just happens to show up at the coffee shop when I was getting deeper into the group. It took another year before I gave in to him, so why would he stay interested when we had only spoken three or four times in that whole year?"

"Maybe he liked you, felt sorry, whatever. But then, if I follow your logic, in the years you've been a couple, and in love I'm guessing, did he ever ask you if you knew where the SDS guys were hiding? Do you think he was keeping a file, sending reports to his superiors, and if so, why haven't you been brought in and questioned?" Roz shook her head and rolled her eyes, then poured herself more wine.

"Because I don't know where they are yet. But Phil knew I had been doing research since the bombing, to find out where Jim and the others could have gone." She lifted up her canvas bag and pulled out one of the yellow pads. "I've been searching everywhere and using my newsroom resources. I told Phil about it. Maybe he was just waiting until I got some concrete information."

"Stop, just stop!" Roz gestured to her to come back to the table and sit down. "Two things: Why hasn't he cashed those checks? And second, what did he say when you confronted him?"

"He couldn't, or wouldn't, tell me the truth. What he was saying didn't sound right. I told you, something about a dead army friend whose parents wanted to repay him for keeping a promise to their son. He *never* talks about Vietnam. Then out of nowhere, these people supposedly living in Atlanta send him these outrageous sums of money, and Phil, okay, doesn't want their money, but then just lets it lie in a desk drawer for years?"

Roz pounded her hands on the table. "So, you don't believe a pretty reasonable story and instead latch on to an impossible one, where Phil is a government agent? Jesus, Mary and Joseph!"

Jeannie hadn't expected Roz to believe her, not without substantial evidence, but had hoped she would be more understanding. She felt disappointed but also determined.

"I'm going to prove this to you, and everyone else in the family who has no idea why I broke it off with a "great guy" like Phil."

"How? By continuing on your wild goose chase, and yes, I agree, destroying the chance to be with Phil."

"No, it's not a waste of time, Roz; I'm a reporter, remember? It's not about finding Jim and the others anymore. I'm following the money to Atlanta, where coincidently my father had his car accident, and never came back."

Roz's twisted face told her she'd gone too far. "Your *father*? Oh my god, Jeannie, what's got into you?"

"Please promise me you won't tell Jeffrey, or anyone. I'm going to figure this out, one way or another, but being able to talk this out has been so helpful."

"Yeah, okay. That's all good for you, but what do I do with it?"

Jeannie moved closer and put her arms on Roz's shoulders, looking her straight in the eye. "Forget about it for now," she whispered.

# Chapter 11

## APRIL 1974

# *Grammy Helen*

"**N**EED ANY HELP, GRAMMY?" Jeannie yelled. "Go on, I'll be right there. And we're taking my car."

Helen scurried toward the door; yes, she was going deaf, but there was nothing wrong with her legs for heaven's sake. Her granddaughter seemed to be confusing the two lately.

"Pauley, we're leaving," she called up the stairway. "We'll be back before supper."

She didn't wait for his reply and wouldn't have been able to hear it anyway.

Jeannie was already behind the wheel of the Oldsmobile as Helen slid in, struggling a bit to pull the heavy door closed.

"It's like a studio apartment in here!" Jeannie said, waving her arm in a wide arc through the spacious interior. Her tone seemed lighter, more playful than sarcastic. A good sign for a change. "I would feel a lot better if we were going in my bug."

Helen gestured toward the snubbed nose vehicle parked in front of the house.

"I hope you're teasing. I've already told you many times over that I will not get in your cardboard box of a car, especially to Uncle Jack's. We'd never survive a fender bender in that." Jeannie had purchased that 'used death trap' a few months ago, causing friction with just about everyone in the family. Helen in particular didn't like the car one bit and was not reticent about expressing her concern.

"Alright already, Grammy, got it, let's just get going. I hate driving this boat any time, and it had to be a foggy morning to boot." She turned her head and spoke directly into Helen's face, a habit Jeannie adopted once she realized that the hearing aids only made sounds louder, not clearer.

Helen watched Jeannie tap a few buttons on the dashboard until she located the defroster, then adjusted the mirrors.

"Make sure you put these mirrors back to where you like them," Jeannie said as she shifted the steering wheel lever to reverse, and then cranked her head toward the street to back out of the short driveway.

Helen patted Jeannie's leg. "Oh, don't worry, dear, I only use the mirrors to see if my hair's in place."

"You'd better be joking."

A 90-minute trip normally would have been a welcome journey, but Helen was a little anxious about being alone with Jeannie for such a long stretch of time, a rare occurrence with her granddaughter's busy schedule. They had been living together for a year now and had established a routine. Helen would watch Jeannie hop between the bathroom and her bedroom, rushing to get ready in the mornings, and then she'd try to catch up with her for five minutes in the kitchen to hand her a cup of hot coffee, a piece of buttered toast and a banana to go. Jeannie would take a few gulps, throw the fruit in that canvas bag of hers, and finish the toast on the way out the door. When they did have a chance to talk, conversations would always begin and end with the weather, allowing Helen to offer some unsolicited advice. She'd remind Jeannie to grab a sweater for the air-conditioned buildings in the summer, to bundle up in the fall and winter months, and if there were any dark clouds overhead, to take one of the umbrellas from the foyer closet. When Jeannie returned in the evenings, often after 8:00 p.m., she'd set out a plate of leftovers sealed in foil. Many nights over the past year, Jeannie didn't come home until after 9:00 or much later. Dozing in front of the set, she'd do her best not to fully nod off. When it got too late, she'd get into bed, and shuffle through old Reader's Digests on her nightstand until she could no longer keep her eyes open. Her granddaughter had to know how it made her jumpy with worry. At her age, she never thought she'd be fretting about the comings and goings of children, and certainly not her 25-year-old granddaughter.

Then there was Pauley. She glanced back over her right shoulder as they pulled away from the curb. Would he be okay on his own for the whole day? She should have insisted on getting that old codger out of the house for a change of scenery and at least eating someone else's food besides her own, but he had pointed to his chest and shook his head. Helen knew he'd been unable to get rid of a lingering cough, and so wasn't surprised when he rejected the invitation. When her brother's mind was made up, she had no choice but to abide by his wishes. It had been that way since they were kids. She left him a hefty lunch plate, even if his appetite wasn't what it used to be. She had cause to worry. He'd gotten a terrible flu last October and all it took was a little draft to unsettle his lungs. With her hands full caring for him, she needed an afternoon break, and was looking forward to relaxing at her son and daughter-in-law's cozy Connecticut home. She let out an audible sigh and shifted her weight and attention toward Jeannie, whose auburn waves were pulled back in a ponytail, exposing her porcelain skin. It made Helen want to reach out and stroke her cheek. Jeannie shifted her eyes toward the radio, placed her hand on the dial, then looked over at Helen and stopped in mid-turn.

"Oops sorry, Grammy, forgot about the noise, it's been a while since we've driven anywhere together." Jeannie's words were indecipherable as the defroster flooded Helen's ears with whooshing static.

"What did you say? Wait until the windows have cleared up, dear, hard to hear you over all that." She pointed to the ducts blowing hot air onto into the huge dashboard.

They drove for about ten minutes in silence until they reached the highway. Helen had gone to the gas station the day before and not only had the tank filled but asked the young attendant to also check her tires and oil. Everything was "ship shape" the young man told her, which put her at ease. She only drove during the daytime and just short distances to the market, Bernice's, or the temple, and always on familiar streets. She'd take a cab to Jack and Cindy's place in Forest Hills, unable to bring herself to use the building's expensive valet service. Her son said he'd pay, pointing out so many times that the cab ride probably cost more than the parking; it didn't feel that way to her.

With her Bill so long gone, and Pauley in no condition to help, she had become friendly with the owners of the two local gas stations she'd patronized for years and both took good care of her car's maintenance. Even so, whenever Jack or Jeffrey were visiting, she'd ask them to check to see if all was well under the hood. She once asked Jeannie's Phil to see about her windshield wipers as they were making an awful scraping sound during a downpour. He drove to the auto parts store that very day and bought her a brand-new set and installed them too. He wouldn't accept her repayment either, no matter how much she insisted. While she didn't get that much time socializing with him, Helen saw him at enough family gatherings to believe his nice smile came from a solid place inside. Bernice had also shared that Phil never came to her house empty-handed, a box of cookies or a pie in his arms. But no matter how much she pried, her granddaughter's lips were sealed as to the reason she was now living under her roof, instead of his.

The dense fog sent a chill over the early spring morning. The defroster was slow to warm up the car, so Helen adjusted her coat collar more snuggly around her neck. "Can you see alright now, dear? I can't hear myself think with that thing going."

"Oh sure, Grammy, I can see fine. I thought you were cold." Jeannie punched the knob, allowing Helen to just make out the faint humming of tires against asphalt.

She darted her eyes from the road back to Jeannie. She saw that her shoulders had relaxed, and hoped they'd stay that way for the rest of the day.

"So, I guess you couldn't convince Uncle Pauley to come with us. Is he okay?" Jeannie had a perkier lilt to her voice.

"Well, yes and no. I'm not happy about it either. I called your brother before we left and asked him to check in on him later. I'm sure he'd rather hear from Jeffrey than me. He's a stubborn old man, refuses to see any more doctors, and lately, says morbid things like 'It'll get better, or it won't.' He's driving me crazy." Helen had not wanted to talk about her brother's decline; it only upset her and wasn't the point of today's escape.

"Yeah, he's not that talkative these days, it's so sad. He's been like a grandfather to me, and the rest of us."

"Now *you*? Okay, please stop, let's change the subject."

She watched Jeannie nod her head. It had been two weeks since Helen found the crumpled yellow note paper among used tissues, cotton balls and gum wrappers in Jeannie's waste-basket. She'd been emptying the bins throughout the house that morning into a larger garbage bag she'd take to the outside cans. Not even hesitating, she sat on the bed, pushed up her glasses and tried to decipher her granddaughter's chicken scratch. Among the arrows, diagrams, and question marks, she could make out the letters "SDS" with names in bubbles around it. Her eyes wandered down the page until she saw something that made her skip a breath. Jeannie had drawn a large triangle. On the top of it she had written "Phil," on the left were the words "cashier's checks," and on the right was the word "Atlanta," with an arrow pointing to two bubbles. Inside the left bubble were the words "army buddy" and in the right bubble, "Daddy." *Daddy*? What on earth could it mean? She needed to show Jack; maybe he could explain. She folded the paper into a small square which she tucked into the zipped pocket of her handbag. She phoned Cindy and arranged the day trip to Connecticut, not sharing her real reason for the family visit.

Helen wanted to have an honest conversation with Jeannie, and to get anything out of her, knew she needed to tread as lightly as possible.

"You're so busy at the paper. I know it's about Watergate, but what are your specific assignments?"

"I'm mostly doing fact checking, but you're right, at the moment, the grand jury decision is major news. Seven of Nixon's aides, or as we like to say at the paper, accomplices, were indicted. We think he's going down with the ship." Jeannie turned her head from Helen's face to the road, taking one hand off the wheel to animate her words. They came around a curve too fast causing Jeannie's bag to slip off the back seat onto the car's floor.

"Slow down, dear, we're not in a hurry." Helen turned her head, seeing that a bunch of pads had fallen out of Jeannie's bag, and without thinking, raised her arm over the seat back.

"*Leave it*, Grammy!" Jeannie shouted. "I'll pick it up when we get there."

Helen clearly couldn't reach it, and anyway, wasn't going to rifle through her papers, for goodness sake; she just hated messes and was wired to tidy and straighten.

"Please turn back around, it's dangerous." Jeannie patted the seat between them; the gesture made Helen feel as if she were being scolded.

Their heads went parallel, staring ahead, with a long awkward silence that followed. Jeannie flipped on the turn signal and moved into the slower lane. The low fog layer was now frayed by patches of muted sunlight giving the day more promise for blue skies. Helen was not going to let the tension between them linger; she was determined this day with her granddaughter would be a happy and peaceful one.

"Jeannie dear, I didn't mean to…"

"I'm sorry, Grammy…"

They looked at one another and laughed, then Helen reached out her hand to meet Jeannie's.

"I guess I'm just edgier with work than I thought. It's one breaking news story after another, and it's been going on for a year now. Most days, I don't have enough time to finish my own tasks, much less time to do my other stuff."

Helen let a few beats settle between them. "What other stuff? Is that what you bring home in your bag?" She glanced at the backseat. "It's like you never get a break; that can't be fair. I can talk to Uncle Jack you know."

Jeannie responded quickly. "No, don't do that. I like being busy, but truthfully, the Watergate stuff has doubled the workload." She reached toward the radio but again stopped herself. Helen waited a few more moments, then picked up the thread.

"You get home so late, honey, that's all, and you know how proud Uncle Pauley and I are when we see your stories, and not just because we love you." She looked at her profile again. "But even with all the extra time, there hasn't been an article, I think, for over a month. What is the story you're working on now?" Helen felt like she was inching her way in, and for the next 30 minutes, Jeannie was a captive traveler in her hulking car.

"I know, Grammy. I'm working hard to get another piece published. Like I said, it's all about Watergate. It's everyone's focus, and to be really honest, I've been doing more than any junior reporter and still haven't been tapped for the D.C. beat. Ernie and Uncle Jack know that a lot of my research has helped keep our stories almost as popular as *The Times*. I don't get it." Jeannie's voice was sharp, and Helen could feel her frustration.

"Maybe today you could talk to him about it. He'll listen, he always does." She took a breath. "C'mon now, why don't you give me a preview of your next piece?" She wasn't going to give up that easily.

Jeannie tapped her fingers on the steering wheel. Helen stayed quiet during the long pause.

"It's a political story, sort of human interest I guess, and may even turn out to be a series. Stories about the people who join liberation or radical groups and then go further, crossing dangerous lines." Jeannie took her eyes momentarily off the road to glance at her. "And you don't have to state the obvious. Yes, it's about people like me, but there's much more to it."

Helen let Jeannie's words sink in for a few minutes, and

then shifted her head slightly toward the back seat. It was all in that canvas bag, she thought, Jeannie's secrets and the things she didn't share with any of them. Something wasn't registering though. Didn't she need to find the people to interview?

Jeannie interrupted her thoughts. "What are you thinking?"

"Well, honey, I'm just wondering who have you lined up to talk with? It isn't that man from the group, what was his name?"

"Jim, and no. He's disappeared with the rest of my old roommates. Anyway, it's a work in progress, still in the formative stages." Jeannie pointed to a green turnpike sign showing a list of upcoming exits. "Hey, are we there?"

Helen quickly turned her head toward the road. "Yes, yes, it's three more exits. Be sure to move over to the exit lane in plenty of time." A defeated feeling ran down her neck. They had been getting somewhere but now Jack's home was just 15 minutes away.

"I can't believe I remembered the area. You know, I think I've only been to the Connecticut place twice. I must have just started college when they bought it, and we all went for their housewarming dinner, but I can't recall the second time."

Helen let out a sigh. "You went with your mother and Jeffrey. It was right after he got out of the draft, Labor Day weekend." Bernice hadn't included her in their getaway plans, and Helen was still miffed about it.

"Oh, yeah, sure." Jeannie kept her eyes straight ahead.

She opened her pocketbook and rummaged around for her lipstick. She felt like she had missed her opportunity to find out what Jeannie was hiding in that bag. It might be a challenge to ask the right questions on the way home. She would have to see how the day unfolded.

She spoke up again. "One more exit, sweetheart." It

reminded her of driving with Bill, how she'd always been his navigator in all ways, and as best as she could, had cheerfully helped him see the brighter side of life. It worked for a long stretch of time until it tragically didn't.

· · ·

IT WAS BILL WHO gave Helen the nickname Pollyanna, way before he knew it was her favorite childhood story. Who wouldn't be inspired by a brave orphan girl who always embraced a ray of hope no matter how dire her circumstances? She distinctly remembered the year the book was made into a movie, 1920, because Mary Pickford, her idol, played the role. That same year, she ran into Bill for the first time since losing touch six years earlier.

She and Bill had gone to the same high school in the Bronx, but he was two grades ahead and their paths never crossed. Years later, he told her that after he'd spotted her during a school pep rally, he was smitten. As was customary in their day, they communicated solely through letters. His were very formal with long sentences of humorless words crafted to show his best side, asking her to accept an invitation to share a beverage or to watch an afternoon picture show together. Helen, who was only 14, kept him at a distance, cordially responding to his entreaties in her beautiful penmanship, but stalling for time. Although she had been more than intrigued, "good" girls had to be careful not to be too forward. The flirtation went on for weeks, Bill's frustration building to bolder and more direct correspondences. In one letter, he expressed dismay at observing how she engaged with fellow classmates, particularly other young men. She responded immediately, defending both her actions and her honor. He quickly apologized, but her doubt had resurfaced. He didn't give up though, and after almost three months of exchanging letters, she agreed to have a cup of hot cocoa with him.

Bill turned out to quite handsome and friendlier in person, despite his stone-like gaze and the stern manner in which he spoke. It was a relief that they didn't have any trouble communicating face-to-face; the letters had created an intimacy she hadn't expected. After the hot chocolate, he offered to escort her home. It was only a 15-minute walk, so when he suggested they take another spin around the block, she happily agreed. They circled around and around until she felt blisters forming on her pinky toes. At the entryway to her family's apartment, Helen got her first kiss. It was just a quick brush of her lips, but the new sensation made her face flush. The following week she searched for him at school, but he had not shown up for any of his classes. She waited in vain for a letter, and after two weeks, Helen was baffled and worried. Finally, she learned from hallway chatter that his father had died suddenly from a burst appendix, forcing him to drop out of school and get a job. He had an older brother who was already in college, and a sister a year ahead of him, so at 16, it was up to him to become the family's breadwinner. She considered reaching out to him, finding out where he worked, or more boldly, going to his home, but dismissed it as way too forward and gave up.

Six years had passed when Helen spotted Bill as she was walking along Seventh Avenue in Manhattan on her way to a night class at City College. It was hard to be sure at first, but crossing over to his side of the street, she could see it was him—taller, more muscular, and just as handsome. She watched him push a rack of clothes into a side warehouse bay and noticed he was now sporting a thin mustache. She'd cut her hair in the flapper style and was wearing a bright red beret, angled to frame her face. Without a moment's hesitation, she called out his name, followed by, "It's me, Helen Goldman, from PS 61." Their reunion story would be told and retold for the next 35 years. She'd get almost all the way through, and then on cue Bill would finish, "How could I forget that face, those big green eyes? All I thought when I saw her crossing that street was, here comes my bride."

Helen should not have become a widow in her mid-50s. Bill should have been alive to see and enjoy his grandchildren. And Walter, her darling boy, should be gazing as she was now, at his beautiful daughter, so proud, but like everyone else in the family, also concerned at the sharp detours Jeannie had taken—that awful group of men, then leaving poor Phil, and now living under her roof with no end in sight.

Jeannie moved to the right lane in plenty of time and got off the exit.

"Make a right up here, it's about three or maybe four miles on this road, and then turn left at the big oak tree. I always forget the street name, but I'll recognize it."

Helen resumed her gaze out the window. There was nothing quite like the lush greenery of the country, wide tall leafy trees, many dotted with new buds. She loved the spring and the release of sweet fragrances breaking through the seal of winter. The fog had lifted leaving only blue skies, not a cloud for miles. Helen knew Bill would have loved Jack and Cindy's white-shingled home with its nautical navy blue shutters and wraparound porch. The bright promising day took her back to a cool April morning five decades earlier. After she and Bill were married, and he had moved up the clothing business ladder to become an assistant buyer, they finally had the finances to purchase a detached home in Queens. It was perfect for them, even if it needed coats of paint inside and out. She'd

gotten pregnant right away and nine months later, gave birth
to her precious Walter. It took another five years before their
rugged Jack was born, but who wouldn't see it all as a blessing? They'd weathered the Depression with two small kids,
Bill's business had a gradual resurgence, then Walter miracu-
lously escaped an army tour overseas in '44 and went on to
become a loving husband and father, and a doctor no less, on
the cusp of even greater things. A dense lump of grief lodged
in her chest. She untucked the tissue from her sleeve and wiped
the corners of her eyes; she worked so hard to keep busy, distracted, and overly involved with everyone's life, especially her
granddaughter's, to block the heaviness and pain that were
always fighting to get in.

Helen recognized the gas station and many other stores
in Jack's community. She tried to feel happy with herself for
arranging the adventure out of the city. She rarely left her
home now with Pauley pretty much housebound. She com-
plained about her brother's needs, but in her heart, she was
grateful for his presence.

It had been 17 years since Bill died in his sleep. He always
got up early to use the bathroom. But not that day. Only
slightly concerned, Helen flung her arm to his side and poked
at him. When he didn't move a muscle or open his eyes to
stop her incessant pleas to wake up, she clutched her heart,
knowing instantly he was gone.

Waiting for the ambulance's arrival, Helen paced up and
down the stairs, possessed by a voice inside, one she didn't
recognize, a deep guttural groan that echoed through the
empty hallways. With little time left to be alone with Bill,
she sat down on the edge of the bed, took hold of his hands,
and leaning over his inert body, kissed his cold lips for the
last time. Tears dropped onto his pale face as she stroked his

head and shifted her hands to rest on his chest imagining a still beating heart.

She turned away, her gaze falling on his night table; the book he'd been reading was closed, the water glass next to it half-full, his bifocals gently placed. She picked up the glasses and as she'd done every morning, opened the side drawer to store them for the day. Her blurry vision made it hard to focus, but there, lying in plain sight, was a pill container from the drug store. She pulled it out and felt her heart tighten when nothing rattled inside. Bill had stopped using the medication his doctor prescribed for sleep over a year ago. She pushed her glasses to the top of her head and read the label on the bottle. The prescription had been refilled two weeks ago! *What on earth?* It took a few agonizing moments to fully register the shock waves—her tingling ears blocking out sound, mouth so dry her tongue felt stuck in her throat, and her head rapidly shaking back and forth. They all knew Bill's spirit had been crushed when Walter didn't come home from Atlanta, but she hadn't truly comprehended the depth of his despair. She stared at his lifeless face, torn between rage for the selfishness of his decision—how *dare* he leave her all alone—and the fierce desire to hold him as tight as she could until someone would have to pry her away. The doorbell gave her a start. Without hesitation, she grabbed the pill container, stashed it in her robe pocket, ran down the stairs and threw the bottle into the kitchen bin. "A heart attack," she cried to the paramedics and that was the end of it. Never having a reason to keep a dark secret, Helen was in brand-new territory, but she learned to live with one after that fateful morning.

The heavy car trunk opening and closing jarred her out of the past. Jeannie opened the door for her. She wasn't carrying her canvas bag.

"You okay, Grammy?

"Yes dear, just a little carsick. Please, give me your hand." Helen stuffed the tissue into her bag and raised her arm for assistance.

Jeannie locked the door, and then handed her the keys. "Can you hold onto these? I'm not going to take my bag inside."

They walked together, arm in arm, along the curved pathway, passing the freshly mowed lawn and trimmed hedges. The front door swung open before they reached the porch.

"Hello Mom, Jeannie, welcome to Connecticut!" Cindy could have stepped out of the pages of *Town and Country* magazine. Her hair in soft curls bounced around her shoulders, a pair of gray slacks hugged her shapely legs, and a long-sleeved white sweater showed off her still slender waist.

Moving toward them, she held out her arms with a wide, toothy grin. She gave Helen the first embrace. They kissed cheeks and then Helen moved aside for Jeannie.

"Well, look who the Oldsmobile dragged in! Jeannie, my pet, it's been too long since I've seen that freckled nose. How's my favorite niece?" Cindy wrapped both arms around her. "Brrrr...let's get inside. Don't worry, Mom. I turned up the heat just the way you like it." Helen smiled as the three of them entered the house.

"Jack, kids, they're here," Cindy called out, as she took their coats. The large living room windows let the afternoon light in, filling the space with a warm ambiance.

Max was the first to emerge from the hallway. He looked as if he had just woken up; his dark, curly hair was flattened and stuck to both sides of his face. Helen glanced down at her watch and shook her head when she saw it was just a little past noon. Her tall, lanky 16-year-old grandson stooped down pulling her stout body into a clumsy embrace. Before they could talk, Scotty burst through the kitchen door into the living room, red-faced and breathing hard. He pushed up the flap of his navy blue Yankee cap, sweat dripping from his forehead.

"Hey! Did you guys just get here?"

While Scotty came to give her a welcome squeeze, Max lingered giving Helen a chance to see them both side by side. These two, she liked to tell her canasta friends, only looked like brothers. They couldn't have come from more opposite sides of the personality spectrum.

"Jeannie Beanie, what's shaking?" Scotty came up behind her and gently tapped the top of her head like a drum. At 19, he was six years younger and nearly a foot taller, but this had been his affectionate nickname for her since they were kids.

Jeannie reached up and grabbed his cap. "Okay, well now you lost your lucky charm. Can the Yankees win without it?" Helen watched Scotty chase Jeannie into the living room with a playful grin. She loved all of her grandchildren, no question, but Scotty had captured an extra slice of her heart. He embodied that same spit and vinegar energy as Walter during his teenage years, along with the easy charm, inviting blue eyes, and wonderful smile.

She trailed them into the adjoining space and saw a baseball game flickering on the television console.

Max sauntered behind and folded himself into the couch. Unlike his muscular brother, Max had a wiry frame. He was at that sullen adolescent boy phase where he'd only mumble one-syllable responses to any of her questions. Even as a little boy, Max had already resembled his stalwart father; their reserve and silence wasn't merely from shyness, it seemed more deliberate, as if they feared saying too much.

"Mom, hey, I didn't hear you come in." Appearing from

the opposite hallway, Jack gave Helen a start. He placed his
hands on her shoulders and bent down for his welcome kiss.
Then turned toward Jeannie and gave her a hug, "Long time,
no see." Helen saw Jeannie's mouth twist into a smirk and
responded, "Yeah, about 24 hours ago."

"You weren't working in there, were you?" Helen narrowed
her eyes and pointed toward the spare room that had been
turned into an office. The Connecticut retreat was supposed
to be just that, a refuge from the stress and constant demands
of his job. For the most part, according to Cindy, it succeeded,
but mainly because she was in charge, overseeing his diet, making sure they went out on regular walks in the afternoons, and
limiting his office time to answering truly urgent calls from
the weekend editor.

Jack rolled his eyes and put a finger to his lips. "Don't tell
you-know-who, but I had to make a few preemptive calls so I
can watch the games without any interruptions."

As if on cue, Cindy's voice sang out through the house
announcing that lunch was ready. Jack took Helen's arm
and escorted her to the dining table. Jeannie and Scotty were
already seated, passing platters and filling up their plates.
Unlike mealtimes in Forest Hills, where Cindy was insistent
that no one start eating until everyone was at the table, she
didn't stand on ceremony in Connecticut.

Max was the last to show up, having made himself slightly
more presentable in a Yankees T-shirt and a pair of faded jeans.
Helen slowly looked around the table, her eyes taking in each
family member, one at a time. Whatever was going on in their
lives, she loved them all so much and sent each a silent blessing.

"I've got a special surprise for you, Mom." Cindy emerged
from the kitchen with a plate holding two steaming, sil-
ver-foiled wrappers and placed them in front of her.

"Hey, that's not fair!" Scotty whined.

"Frankfurters?" Helen leaned over her plate, inhaling the grilled, seasoned aroma.

"Yes! And I have to confess, it was your son who suggested we at least have the smell of a baseball stadium in the house today." Cindy took a few steps away and stood behind Jack, laying her hands on his shoulders. "You know this guy must love you a lot to look and not touch."

"Oh, thank you dear, that was so thoughtful. I know it's not good for my digestion, but it is my favorite treat and once in a while it couldn't hurt, right?" Helen unwrapped the foil, still warm from the oven, thrilled to see both sauerkraut and dollops of mustard resting on top. Heavenly, she thought, as she took her first savory bite.

"Speaking of the game, turn it up, will you Max?" Scotty yelled louder than her hearing aids could handle. The dining area opened into the living room with a direct view of the television. She reached up to her right ear and pulled out the contraption. She folded it into her napkin and tucked it under her sleeve. It was the only way to reduce the volume, but the noisy eating, forks on plates, and cross talk made it hard for Helen to pick up full sentences with only one hearing aid in place. The boys seemed to be rattling on about Yankee statistics and prospects for the new season, there was reference to a double header in progress and something about the first game being nearly over, the Yankees losing badly. She glanced over at Jeannie and Cindy, sitting side by side, their noses practically touching in an animated conversation. Feeling as if she were in a wind tunnel, Helen had no choice but to ignore their chatter and enjoy her tasty hot dogs.

"Dear, do you have some coffee brewing?" Helen asked Cindy as she was clearing off plates from the table.

"Of course. I also have a box of bakery cookies and rugelach, I'll bring those out." She nodded over to Jeannie. "Come, sweetie, give me a hand in the kitchen."

The boys left the table as soon as they finished their last bites and splayed themselves out on either end of the big sofa, while Jack took his spot on the Barcalounger. It took less than a minute for the three of them to start shouting at the set like true fans. Helen enjoyed their exuberance and all the baseball jabber. At one time, she'd been a New York Giants fan. She especially liked Mel Ott and was crushed when the team moved to San Francisco in the fifties. If she squeezed her eyes into narrow slits, she could reset the scene in her own living room four decades earlier, Bill and her boys would huddle around a boxy transistor radio cheering wildly whenever Lou Gehrig came up to bat.

Family gatherings like these made it too easy for Helen to surrender to the waves of memory tossing about in her mind. It was a stronger force than a photograph on a mantle, or a familiar pattern of speech. A nostalgic odor or fragrance could quickly transport her out of the room, and back into a life so far past, and nearly forgotten, taking the wind out of her.

She stood up to see what was taking so long with her coffee. Helen had gotten into the habit of brewing a small pot in the early afternoons. Without that extra boost of energy, she'd find herself drawn to any sofa or even her bed and be asleep in minutes. She gathered up the remaining glasses on her way to the kitchen and pushed open the door with her hip. Cindy was setting up a tray with coffee cups, but her attention was focused on Jeannie.

"Tell me, please, I won't tell your uncle."

As Helen entered the room, they both looked at her as if they'd seen a ghost.

"What's going on in here? I thought we were on to dessert."
Helen felt awkward, aware that she had interrupted a private
conversation.

Cindy ignored the question. "Coffee's ready. Jeannie, please
hand me the bakery box, and a plate from the cabinet." Her
voice sounded too high.

"Are the Yankees still losing?" Jeannie asked.

"I don't know honey, I wasn't watching." She motioned to
her ears.

"We'll be right out," Cindy said, hurriedly placing a plate
of cookies on the tray. "I'm fixing it up so we can have dessert
in the living room."

"Can I help with…" Helen started, but Cindy cut her off.
"No Mom, really, we've got it, go on back in."

Disappointed, Helen turned around and left. Instead of the
living room though, she headed to the small guest bathroom
by the front door. She'd begun to feel a churning sensation
in her belly and forced up a burp that had a spicy aftertaste.
Why didn't she stop at one hot dog? She knew better than to
indulge like she had. Washing her hands, she looked up at
herself in the mirror. It wasn't only the meal that was upsetting
her stomach. She still hadn't figured out how to get Jack alone
to show him the note.

Jeannie knocked softy on the door "Grammy, are you
alright?" Helen's eyes grew wide in the mirror.

"Yes, fine, be out in a second."

"Okay. Aunt Cindy says your coffee is getting cold."

"Thank you, dear." Helen dried her hands, and then out of
habit, rearranged the curved strands of hair around her ears
to hide the hearing aids from view. As her finger touched the
piece in her left ear, she got an idea.

The noise in the living room had died down. Helen could see

from the boys' body language that the Yankees were moments from defeat. Cindy had made herself comfortable in the corner of the couch next to Max, who had picked up a book from the coffee table and was nervously turning it around in his hands. Scotty and Jack were saying something about the next game and a better pitcher. Jeannie sat quietly, staring out through the sliding glass door into the backyard. Helen reached for her coffee and took a sip; it had gone cold, but she didn't care.

Scotty piped up. "Okay, Dad, break between games, you said we could play some catch. And, Jeannie Beanie is going to join us."

"Who said?" Jeannie quickly replied. "No way, and not because I can't throw, but you know, Grammy and I should get going. I'm steering the boat today and I don't want to drive it the dark."

Helen agreed. Her body had begun to ache with fatigue and when that happened, all she wanted to do was take off her clothes and tight undergarments, slip into her housecoat and relax. She was also worried about Pauley; he likely wouldn't turn in until they were home safe.

Helen pushed herself off the couch.

"Jack dear, I have been struggling with these hearing aids all day; could you help me put in my new batteries? Let's do it in your office, I don't want those tiny things falling on the carpet."

"I can do it, Mom." Cindy answered before Jack had a chance.

'No, that's okay. You've been doing everything today." She walked over to Jack's chair and touched his arm. "Please honey, fix them for me, and we'll get out of your way before the next game starts."

Jack extended his arms out for a stretch and let out a loud yawn. "Okay, I'm coming."

She quickened her pace down the hallway, clutching her pocketbook in the crook of her arm. When they were both inside the room, she circled around him and closed the door.

"There's nothing wrong with my hearing aids. I wanted to get you alone for a minute." Helen looked hard into his eyes.

"What's the matter? Is it Uncle Pauley?"

"He's fine, for the time being, but no, it's about Jeannie. I realize you are very busy these days, sweetheart, but there's two things; one is troubling her, the other, me." Helen could hear herself talking louder; she glanced at the door to make sure there were no footsteps or a knock.

"I already know; she's upset about not getting the chance to go to D.C. I've wanted to send her several times, I'm just waiting for an opening. There are guys way ahead of her in seniority and experience." Jack sat down on the edge of his desk.

"Really Jack? She's working so hard. Can't you give her a break?"

He nodded. "Okay, got it. So what's the second thing?" Clearly, he didn't welcome her meddling.

"Do you know what else she's working on?"

"No, not specifically, that's Ernie's job. Why?"

"Well, I do, sort of. It's about finding those awful people from her SDS group; she wants to do a piece about them, and other subversive political types."

Jack stood up and folded his arms. "Is that what she told you?"

"Well, not word for word. She started to explain on the way here. It's all in that bag of hers, the one she guards with her life." Helen glanced at the door. "I'm really worried about her. With no warning, she breaks up with that sweet Phil, and moves in with me. That's fine, but I didn't think she'd still be living with me a year later. She's never home, always at the paper. Other than Jeffrey and Roz, she has no other friends or any social life to speak of. Something isn't right." Helen wrung her hands.

"Always at the paper? I'm not sure what would keep her there most days after 5:00 or 6:00 p.m. I'll ask Ernie to talk with her next week." Jack tried to sound neutral, but Helen could see by the way his eyebrows pinched that it didn't sit right with him either.

"There's something else." She opened up her pocketbook, took out the yellow paper folded into a square and gave it to him. "I found this in her waste bin."

She dropped her voice to a whisper. "It's been keeping me up at night. Please dear, can you explain it?" Helen tried not to sound so dramatic but couldn't help herself.

Jack slowly unfolded the paper. She watched his head move down the page.

"What is it, Jack?"

He looked into her eye, his face draining of color.

# Chapter 12

# MAY 1974

# *Jack*

WHEN HE FIRST EXPERIENCED the piercing stomach pains, Jack told Cindy he imagined it was like women's contractions during labor. Hearing this, Cindy shook her head and wagged her finger, admonishing him to come up with another description. "I'm sure it's really bad, honey, but I can tell you that pain isn't even in the same solar system." He visualized a sphere with tentacles in the center of his gut flailing about to escape confinement. Cindy had begged him for years to see a specialist, but he brushed her off, blaming stress of work and managing the symptoms with his chalky antacid tablets.

After the disturbing visit with his mother and Jeannie a few weekends back though, the sharp jabs became a daily occurrence. He restricted himself to one morning cup of coffee and switched from corned beef to turkey sandwiches, but was still going through a six-pack of antacids twice a week. The medicine brought temporary relief, and he was well aware that any added layer of anxiety could set him off. Having no clue what his niece was up to fit that bill. No matter how minor the story pitch, he'd always been on top of the reporter docket. With Ernie's daily briefings, and having Barbara's ear attuned to the pit's murmurings, he couldn't remember when he was ever out of the loop on assignments. But on her own, Jeannie was apparently investing time in speculative, time-consuming pieces. Reporters on the Lifestyle staff were required to pursue leads, then pitch them to Ernie. Why then hadn't Jeannie followed the rules? She definitely knew better. Then there was the note his mother gave him. What did her prospective story have to do with Phil, Atlanta and 'Daddy'? What in God's name was she up to?

The following week, without sharing his concerns, Jack asked Ernie to meet with Jeannie to go over her assignments. She mentioned only her work on Watergate, referring to notes on a bunch of yellow pads, saying nothing about searching for former SDS people or spending late nights at *The Globe* immersed in research. Jack would have to find a way to confront her as her boss, to get to the root of his worries as her uncle.

The spiking pains didn't let up on his commute home. Unable to raise the mashed potatoes from his dinner plate to his lips, he told Cindy he'd had a late lunch and wanted to get to bed early. Then restless sleep and a disjointed dream of some kind brawl that ended with a punch to his gut, jolted him awake. He rolled off the bed and tried to hobble to the bathroom, but never made it. Doubling over, he fell to the floor and let out an involuntary groan.

Cindy called his name, but her voice sounded far away. He felt her arm under his head yet couldn't answer when she kept asking if he was okay. Cindy positioned a pillow under his neck, then reached for the phone. Jack knew she was calling 911 and gasped, "No, don't, I'm okay," but she had already left the bedroom. She returned with a glass of water followed by Max, who Cindy must have woken up for help. Together they sat him up so he could take a sip from the glass.

"Jack, now listen to me. I called the paramedics; they'll be here in five minutes."

"No!" He shook his head, but then let a louder moan escape as they lowered his body back onto the pillow.

"Dad, it's going to be okay." His son's voice sounded tight and raspy.

Jack could see Cindy's fear, her head nodding back and forth in tiny movements, and her eyes boring into his as if they held some power to heal.

When the doorbell rang, she left him in Max's arms and ran to answer.

Two uniformed men rolled a stretcher into the room. Hearing the squawking of their radios, Jack's stomach seized up even more.

"Mr. Glazer, my name is Dan. Can you tell me what's going on?" He pointed a tiny flashlight into Jack's face.

"Not my heart, not stroke," Jack managed to say. Then pointed to his stomach.

Dan pulled his pajama top up and gently pressed his hand on Jack's abdomen.

"Ouch!"

Cindy piped in. "He's had this for years, but not like tonight."

"Mrs. Glazer, can you please get his medication for me?"

"He doesn't take anything, just antacids from the drug store."

"*Please*, just give me a shot, it'll stop spasms, be fine." Jack's halting speech wasn't helping his cause. "No ER, Cindy, begging, no hospital."

The other paramedic came over, and together they raised his body off the floor and put him on the gurney. "I'm sorry, Mr. Glazer, but we have to make absolutely sure that the doctor agrees with you."

Jack kept his eyes closed during the elevator ride and

through the lobby. He had a depressing vision of the night doorman on duty, he couldn't remember his name, spreading the news in the morning. He could hear the gossip about Jack Glazer's trip to Long Island Jewish Hospital in the dead of night. After the paramedics secured him in the back of the ambulance, they helped Cindy into the hull, and onto a small seat by Jack's head.

"Please honey, no siren, not dying."

Jack saw her turn to one of the paramedics to relay his request.

"I'm sorry ma'am, it's protocol." He slammed the door closed.

Jack heard the engine start up and, as they pulled away, he cringed when the wailing alarm alerted their sleeping neighbors that one of their own was in trouble.

Cindy held his hand, squeezing it tighter when she heard him call out in pain. As it worsened, Jack caught himself whimpering like a child. The ambulance's speed and sharp turns were not helping, so when it finally came to stop, Jack sighed in relief. As he was wheeled from the darkness into the bright lights of the ER, his body stiffened, and a shiver radiated from his neck to the inside of his thighs. A doctor appeared, about his age with a white cap tied around his head, wearing large black-framed glasses. Looking down at a clipboard held up to his face by a young nurse, the doctor pointed down the hallway. Jack heard Cindy's voice interrupt their exchange, saying something about *The Globe*. Oh no, he thought, and then their heads turned in his direction. The nurse put her hand on Cindy's shoulder and pointed to what Jack assumed was the waiting area. One of the EMT guys came over to his gurney and wheeled him into a small exam room.

"The doctor will be right in." He drew the privacy curtain as he left.

Jack held both arms around his gut, wishing his legs weren't strapped to the stretcher so he could pull them up to his chest to help control the pain.

"Hello, Mr. Glazer, I'm sorry we have to meet under these circumstances. I'm Dr. Peterson, and I might add, a loyal *Globe* reader. So, let's see what's going on with you tonight." As he spoke, he picked up Jack's wrist and felt his pulse while looking at his watch. After a few moments, he placed his other hand on his stomach, and pressed down.

"Ahhh!" Jack shrieked. "Please doc, just give me a shot of something, this needs to stop."

"Yes, that's the plan, but once you're out of immediate discomfort, we'll take a few x-rays to see if it's just a minor setback." The doctor spun around, opened the curtain and relayed instructions to someone in the hallway.

A few minutes later, a nurse returned with a tray. On it was a syringe and tiny bottles of a clear liquid. Jack's eyes tracked the doctor's hands as he first inserted the needle into the bottle, and then into his waiting arm.

"Okay now, this should start doing its job right away." He turned to the nurse and issued some more orders.

Jack knew it was morphine, the grand slam of painkillers and, as the doc promised, the steady vibrations soon began easing up, giving him a cloudy sense of calm. He closed his eyes.

In what seemed like seconds, the gurney was set in motion. He heard voices but was too dazed to understand. When the wheels stopped, he felt a rush of cold air sweep over his chest.

"Mr. Glazer, I'm Frank, the x-ray technician. I'm going to move you around just a bit to get some pictures. Will take about five minutes or so."

Jack didn't even bother to focus. His head was too muddled to think or care, and he must have passed out. Then he picked up a chorus of voices, one of them definitely his wife's. Even this groggy, he knew her lilting pitch. When he opened his eyes, he could make out the doctor, the nurse, and Cindy, who was gesturing and smiling.

"Mr. Glazer, welcome back. How are you feeling?" Dr. Peterson looked down, his head garb was gone, revealing wavy, salt-and-pepper hair.

"Better, good, can I go home?" He heard how sloshy he sounded.

"Yes, you actually can, but not until your son and nephew show up. With morphine in your system, you'll need a few guys to help your wife get you home safely. The good news, Chief, is that you'll live. The not-so-good news is that the x-rays show an active ulcer in your stomach lining, and while I understand the antacids you've been taking have helped with the flare-ups, it seems this time you developed an infection. I'm going to prescribe antibiotics that should get rid of it in 7-10 days. You'll start feeling better after the first few days of treatment."

Jack tried to smile. "That's a relief."

"One more thing though. Your wife says you know about the link between stress and the ulcer you've developed. It's easily triggered by certain habits, and in your case, that means pushing too hard, not slowing down, along with eating foods that don't agree with you. As I tell patients, this is something you're going to have to work harder to control. I also urge you to see your doctor on a regular basis."

Cindy spoke up. "Oh, don't worry about that, Doctor. Your patient will comply with orders from this higher up." She balled her hand into a fist and with her thumb extended, pointed to herself.

It took less than 20 minutes for Max to show up in cab and meet them in the waiting area. Jack had been transferred to a wheelchair—another protocol—and could be discharged only if wheeled to the hospital exit. His son came over to help, hair pointing in all directions, and while it was hard to read a 16-year-old boy's expression, his face showed unmistakable fear, the arched eyebrows telling all. Then came his nephew, Jeffrey who had to take the subway in from Brooklyn at four-something in the morning when trains ran in longer intervals.

"You didn't have to wake Jeffrey and ask him to come here. We could have managed." Jack knew that Jeffrey's involvement meant the whole extended family would know about the night's events before sun-up.

Cindy's droopy eyelids fluttered open. "Doctor's orders." She had been holding his hand since they wheeled him out of the ER. Max had stretched his skinny frame over three chairs, then shut his eyes, crossing his arms over his chest. That boy could sleep anywhere.

Jack felt terrible putting his family out, and Jeffrey too. He knew that Cindy didn't call Scotty; he was away at college and it wouldn't have done anyone any good. The morphine had cut the pain, but the fuzzy effects were fading. He wanted this drama to end already, and for things to go back to normal. He knew Cindy would not let him go into the office, and with no sleep and a debilitating fatigue overtaking him, he would not object. It would be the first time, with the exception of annual family vacations, that he wouldn't be at his desk at 7:00 a.m. on a workday.

The ER waiting area had a surprising level of activity for the ungodly hour; he didn't want to imagine patients with more serious conditions, those with blood wounds, or 'code blues'.

"Uncle Jack?" It was Jeffrey's voice calling out from down the hall.

Cindy straightened up and rose to meet her nephew.

"Are you trying to give us all heart attacks?" He knelt down and gave Jack a hug.

Jack was happy to see his much beloved nephew, even though he felt badly about ruining his night and probably the next day at work.

"Aunt Cindy said you needed a hand, so here I am."

"Yup, sorry for the late hour, truly. Let's get out of here."

Jeffrey went over to Max and wiggled his foot. It took several attempts to get him to stir. Max slowly unfolded himself and stood, nodded a greeting to Jeffrey, and then all of them, escorted him through the lobby and out into the dark night.

Cindy held the handles of the wheelchair, while Jeffrey and Max each grabbed one of his arms and helped him get free of the chair. A cab was waiting, and with more strength than he had expected, Jack was able to put sufficient weight on his legs and climb into the backseat. Max jumped into the front seat and gave the driver their address. Jack didn't feel like talking, he just wanted to get under the covers as quickly as possible. The aching had dulled, but he could barely put a coherent sentence together.

He shifted his gaze from the window to Cindy in the hump seat, her head turned toward Jeffrey. They were talking in a low whisper.

"You know, I'm right here." He mustered the energy to comment.

Cindy turned toward him. "Jeffrey was just asking if he could do anything, for Pete's sake."

"She told me I should stay over, in Scotty's room. Nice offer, but Roz doesn't sleep well if I'm out and about at 4:30 in the morning." He reached over and tapped Jack's knee. "You understand, don't you, Uncle Jack?"

"Yes, buddy, I do."

Jack certainly did. Wives, or in Jeffrey's case, fiancées, didn't appreciate being out of any communication loop, but particularly so in the middle of the night. He broke that rule too many times being stuck at the paper, and no matter how he'd try to explain to Cindy the next morning, she would dismiss him and shake her head, "You're not performing brain surgery, Jack." Besides, he didn't want Jeffrey to stay over. That would only extend the drama of the last three hours.

After the entourage got him through the lobby and up the elevator, Jack thanked Jeffrey for the third time, and threw an arm around his shoulders. "You did good."

Max would have to get up for school in three hours, and while Cindy assured him that he could take the day off, he said he couldn't afford to miss his morning classes with final exams only weeks away. He promised to come home early though, mumbling that he'd probably not make it past the lunch bell.

Hours later when he opened his eyes to the muted daylight coming through the curtains, Jack felt unattached to his body. Cindy's side of the bed was empty. He looked over at the clock and let his head flop back on the pillow when he saw it was almost 10:00.

"Cindy?" He rarely summoned her like this, but he needed her help.

"Coming..."

He sat up slowly and swung his legs to the floor.

She came in with a tray and set it down on her dresser. "Here, let me help you up, honey. How are you doing?"

"Need the bathroom, then I'll be able to report." As he

stood, he wrapped his arm around her shoulder then kissed the top of her head.

Dizzy and a bit nauseous, he used the toilet and then washed his face. As he came out, Cindy had already plumped up the pillows, and was waiting by the door to help him back to bed.

"You don't have to ask. I already called Barbara, everything's fine. I told her what happened; she'll tell Ernie, but then it's 'mum's the word' for the rest of the staff. It's a 'family matter' they'll say." Cindy had made a pot of tea with two pieces of toast and included the morning paper on the tray.

"I don't know what I would do without you, sweetie." He knew he was a lucky man.

"If you're okay for a while, I'm going to run to the pharmacy for your medication and then the market for some bland food items." She winked at him.

"I'll be fine. Although, not sure how I'll be able to handle all the solitude." He adjusted the tray on his lap and sipped the hot tea.

Cindy stopped her fussing about and sat down next to him on the bed. "Well, that's not going to be a problem. Your mother will be here any minute."

"Really Cin?" Jack shook his head. "Jeffrey, I knew it."

"It wasn't him. Don't be angry, but I had to tell her. She said she called the office this morning, and evidently, Barbara thought she already knew." She leaned over and gave him a kiss. "And honey, I'm going to leave the door open, so you don't have to get up. I told her that. I have a long list of errands, and so won't be back until she's gone."

Jack's mouth curved up into a smile. "Okay, go, escape while you can."

"I'll be back in a few hours, I promise."

Jack listened to Cindy's footsteps recede down the hallway.

He picked up the newspaper neatly folded on the tray. It had been a long while since he'd opened up *The Globe* and read it like a daily subscriber. It was hard to believe that less than 24 hours ago he had approved the final galleys for the 9:00 p.m. press run. Jack tried to read, but the anticipation of his overly dramatic mother bounding into his bedroom, shredded tissues in hand and embracing him with an urgent hug, made his sore stomach tighten and face wince with pain. There was no getting around this firestorm of a woman. She had become fiercer and more unrestrained as he and Walter had gotten older, doing whatever it took to protect her boys. While his father had naturally shared her love for them, it was his mother who did the lion's share. Thinking about his parents, Jack realized he had become just like his father, busy with work all week, reserving weekend time for chores and the kind of play kids learned to interpret as affection.

When Walter died, it had been his father who had collapsed internally, his grief turning into chronic sadness. As if sentenced to tread a desolate road alone, he became so withdrawn that he looked like a withering old man though only in his fifties. He died of a heart attack three years later, and his mother had yet another breakdown. She didn't want to leave the house, ate very little, had trouble sleeping, and refused any of Jack's help. He couldn't bear to watch his vibrant mother lose the color in her face and the will to keep going. So, he arranged a meeting with the rabbi, who convinced her to join a support group run by a professional grief counselor who donated one day a month to the temple. At the rabbi's suggestion, she volunteered with the local Hadassah chapter, wading in one tentative step at a time. While for decades she had assumed an active grandmother role with Bernice and the kids, she began to do the same with Jack's boys, attending most of their many sporting events. In a few years' time, she had regained some of, but not close to all the cheerfulness Jack experienced as a child.

The lobby called to announce his mother's arrival, and just as predicted, she followed the script. As soon as she walked in, she gave him a kiss on his cheek and a firm hug, then pulled Cindy's vanity chair to the side of the bed and sat, smoothing her dress over her knees.

"Tell me everything, start from last night." She reached over, encircling his hands in hers, leaned forward so she could hear every syllable.

"Mom, please, I'm fine, better. I'm sure Cindy told you, it's an ulcer that got infected. It'll take a few days for the medicine to work, but nothing to worry about. I'll live." Jack had swallowed the last painkillers he'd been discharged with right before she arrived, allowing him to converse without the twisted grimace.

"Oh, so you're taken to the hospital in an ambulance last night, and it's all okay?"

He sat up a little higher on the pillows. "That wasn't the fun part, no, but I've been able to deal with this chronic gut ache for years, guess it caught up with me. I've already gotten an earful from Cindy and the ER doc about avoiding another 2:00 a.m. siren ride to Long Island Jewish."

His mother lifted up her enormous, tortoise-shell glasses and rested them on her forehead, then dabbed the corners of her eyes with her tissue. "This isn't funny to me at all, Jack. You are the only one I have left, and I have every right to be frightened. You'd feel the same if it were Scotty or Max."

He reached out his arms, offering a reassuring hug. "I'm sorry Mom, I am. I will take better care of myself; I promise. No more scares."

She looked up at him, and touched the end of his nose, a gesture from his childhood. He needed to change the subject.

"How's Uncle Pauley?"

She straightened up and put her tissue back under the sleeve of her sweater. "About the same. The nice weather is helping though; I'm making him sit on the porch to get some fresh air into those lungs. We are good company for each other, when we're not arguing about my hearing or his stubbornness."

Jack smiled and reached for the teacup on his tray. It was cold.

"What can I get you, son?" His mother jumped up into an alert stance, always on the ready for caretaking duties.

"Okay, I could use hotter tea." He smiled as he watched her move to Cindy's side of the bed, pick up the tray and stride towards the kitchen.

He hadn't seen her since the Connecticut visit and knew she'd ask about Jeannie.

Within a few minutes, she returned to the room with the tray and set it back down on the bed. "Watch it now, it's piping hot."

As he slowly sipped, she returned to her chair. He waited for a few seconds, then indulged his mother's gift of gab by asking her about any upcoming Hadassah events, and of course, Bernice and the wedding plans. This got his mother on a roll where she went on about a recent dinner at Bernice's and Marty kept them all in stitches, and how happy she was that her daughter-in-law was finally in love again. She'd also had lunch a few days ago with Jeffrey and Roz at a lovely place near Jeffrey's job in the city where they talked the whole time about the final wedding preparations. Jack enjoyed the way she'd scrunch up her nose and gesture in sync with her animated stories. As he watched her, his chest began to swell, and he then unexpectedly choked up. His mother was just about the most unique human being he'd ever known. She could needle, enrage, frustrate, but those traits trailed far behind the mass of love and optimism that defined her. He felt himself blinking back tears.

"Okay, so dear, can we talk about Jeannie now? What did you find out?"

He put down the cup and leaned back against the pillows. "Not too much. Ernie did meet with her; all she showed him were her work pads with Watergate notes. Most of the research and fact checking has been hers, so Ernie's agreed that she earned her spot on the next bus to D.C. She didn't tell him anything else."

Helen nodded, and gave him a half smile. "That's good. She'll be thrilled. But what about the, you know, note I found?"

"Well, that's the rub. It's my job to find out why she decided to stay tight-lipped about the SDS piece. Even if it falls under the scoop category, reporters are allowed to keep their investigation secret until they can pounce on real facts, but not from me or Ernie. Jeannie might be close to reaching out to one of her underground guys, but it doesn't explain or excuse her subterfuge."

Helen's shoulders fell away from her ears, and her head tilted to one side. "Okay, okay, but Jack, what about all the other stuff she'd written in that diagram? How does it have anything to do with *Walter*? This has been bothering me for weeks."

"It doesn't. I can only speculate that maybe she thinks Phil is involved in some scheme or such with a veteran buddy from Atlanta. And scribbling "Daddy" might just be an association with Atlanta. Remember, Mom, you found it in her wastebasket. It was in there for a reason."

His mother gave him a stony look. Like him, she had probably spun herself around in dizzy scenarios for the past few weeks. He needed to get his mother off of the topic of Walter and Atlanta now.

"Jeannie has been working too hard, and too much. Look, I'm going to bump her ahead and let her go to D.C. next week. When she gets that trip out of her system, I'll sit down with her and get to the bottom of it. I promise." Jack patted the mattress space between them.

His mother was slow to nod her head. Jack could tell by the way she crossed her arms over her buxom chest and lowered her chin, that she wasn't satisfied at all. He didn't blame her; he'd want to cut through all the bull too.

She reached over and touched his arm. "Alright, sweetie, I'll let it go for the time being. Now I've been here way too long, getting you all tired out." She leaned over, put both hands on his face, and kissed his forehead. "Please don't do anything until you feel 100% better, and I mean it."

With a promise to call later, she left clutching a tissue as she waved from the bedroom door. She was right, the visit had exhausted him, and so he gently shifted his body flatter on the bed, closed his eyes and thought about that damn note his mother found. It still didn't make any sense. How could Jeannie make such a leap in logic? The silence of the empty apartment, along with the numbness from the last dose of medication, weakened his defenses, raising long-repressed memories of his 1952 Atlanta trip, at first hazy but then growing all too clear.

• • •

JACK TURNED 25 IN the spring of 1952. His tiny studio flat on the Lower East Side was just one subway stop from the paper. Working his way up from part-time mail sorter to junior cub reporter, he had spent two years at the City's rag of choice for New Yorkers who preferred headlines and sports pages to in-depth hard news. It had taken him five years to earn his bachelor's degree, delayed while returning GIs got the first crack at college admittance. After Walter graduated from Hunter College in May of 1944, he enlisted in the army and was stationed at Fort Dix. Thankfully his flat feet kept him from overseas combat, doing desk duty instead as a private first-class at the New Jersey base. His parents, despite being deeply patriotic, were quietly thrilled by Walter's foot problem.

"So close to home." His mother would clutch her hands over her heart and knock on any piece of wood within arms' reach. Not a day went by in which she didn't peer through the living room curtain watching the mailman on his daily rounds and call out to no one in particular, "There goes the angel of death." She got into the habit of spewing random prayers asking God to do 'His job' and put a stop to this hellish war. When Jack's 18th birthday was just a year away, his mother began a ritual pacing. It was hard to watch her positive attitude fraying day-by-day, just like the tattered tissues she carried under her sleeve to wipe her eyes and nose. Jack would never forget the moment news of the invasion of Normandy was announced on the radio. Windows of light flickered from every home, his mother pranced about singing and touching his face with her soft hands whenever he was within reach, always with some note of gratitude for the Lord's intervention.

Nevertheless, life didn't snap back into an idyllic calm afterwards, not by any means. Reentry for returning GIs had been brutal; the broken bodies and lost souls filled the dark spaces in their town left by nearly four years of war. His family, temple congregants and church members, housewives who hadn't joined factory lines, all pitched in to help the war effort. His mother volunteered at the local hospital, his father sorted mail at the USO office, and he'd hop on his bike after school or on the weekends, helping neighbors who needed a few things at the store, new ration books or mail delivered, saving them precious gasoline coupons. They all felt useful and told themselves it all added up to small victories. But had anyone really been prepared to absorb the vacant stares of returning soldiers? Even in the small confines of Kew Gardens, Jack would see faces warped with fatigue, hollowed eyes searching for relief from what he imagined had been horrible images of death.

This was not the case for Walter. He came roaring back to New York and declared his new-found career direction. "I'm going to be a doctor!" Their proud mother happily would have erected a blinking billboard on Metropolitan Avenue to share the good news; instead she rushed about announcing his decision to her Hadassah chapter and canasta group.

Walter had no trouble getting into medical school; he studied hard that summer and did well on his entrance exams. Jack had started City College in the fall; he couldn't even consider applying to a fancy private school. Walter, however, had the GI bill and when accepted to Temple University's medical school, he was gone again by the following January.

•  •  •

JACK WOULD ALWAYS REMEMBER the exact time, 7:25 a.m. on June 14, 1952. A beautiful Saturday, the first one in months where he didn't have to get up and go to work. Before collapsing into bed the night before, he had promised himself he would just let the day unfold. But then the call came.

It had been the accent, the thick, undecipherable drawl of the sheriff's greeting that made his sleepy lids pop open. He couldn't comprehend his introduction, or keep up with the context, only managing to piece together a string of words: "accident, Walter Glazer, and then, didn't make it." It made no sense. He wanted the conversation to end, to rewind the tape, return to a faded dream, ignore the sun through the slatted blinds, and make it dark again. He saw again how he had tumbled to the floor, crouching in pain, holding his stomach, the previous night's dinner rising up in his throat, and the dash to the toilet, nearly missing the bowl.

The next 48 hours had required him either to assume Superman powers, where like the great comic book hero, he could pick up cars to save small children trapped underneath, or stay in shock mode where he'd confine the pain to the edges of his heart until it could no longer be held back. After splashing water on his face, he dialed the sheriff back. He remembered having to ask him to keep repeating the directions to the town and station. Then it came, the cause of death. Jack reacted by dropping the receiver, crying out "no, no, no." Thirty minutes later, when he caught the subway to his parents' home in Queens, his eyes blurry and burning from tears, he couldn't stop his brain from uttering 'suicide' over and over again in beat with the train's motion. Staring through the windows at each stop, he focused on the faces of people waiting on platforms, going about their business, the world rotating just like the day before. Not for him though, and never again would it be the same, everything had been changed in an instant, by one horrific and senseless phone call. It was impossible, not Walter. If Bernice and his parents were told the real story, they would never recover. And so, when he emerged from the subway into the warm June air that morning, he'd begun to convince himself that Walter had died tragically in a car accident. This was the story he'd tell.

Jack tried to rush his mind through the traumatic scene where after crossing the threshold of his childhood home, he dropped the huge boulder of sudden loss into the still waters of his parents' living room: creating a violent wave that crashed chaotically through the house, knocking over their family memories, the three of them gasping for breath, drowning in sorrow. He and his father had to react quickly to lift his mother from the floor where she collapsed. They stood there, arms around her wailing body, until his rattled father could break free and get a sedative from the medicine cabinet. All that sobbing and moaning; somehow, he managed to insist on being the one to drive alone to Atlanta to retrieve Walter's body. Holding the steering wheel of his father's car, tears streaming down his face, he drove interminable stretches of highway, stopping only for coffee and Coca-Colas to stay alert. He remembered filling up at a gas station somewhere in the Carolinas. Using the bathroom, the dirty, cheap mirror above the sink showing a distorted reflection, the pain around his mouth and red-rimmed eyes made him appear ghoulishly disfigured.

He didn't make it to Braselton that day; fatigue and an empty stomach forced him into a roadside motel where he passed out. It was early the next day when he reached the nondescript southern town ninety miles outside of Atlanta. There were two men in uniform to greet him. The first was the pear-shaped Sheriff Dixon, appearing to be in his forties, the gun belt riding under his ample waist; the other guy was older and his uniform more decorated, a gray moustache covering his top lip. They sat him down in a room with no windows while Dixon, in a voice Jack would never forget, told him what had happened.

It was at some tavern, there had been a wooded area near the parking lot, Walter was drunk. The senior officer tapped Dixon's shoulder, and took over. Saying something about a breach in protocol, admitting that his deputy allowed Walter to enter the cell with his belt. Papers were brought out, an official document exonerating their department's negligence in exchange for contractual silence about Walter's arrest. All they needed was his signature. Ironically, it was also their idea to change the cause of death to a car accident, broken neck on impact, they'd take care of the hospital records as well. Jack signed quickly, trying to steady his shaking hand so his signature would be legible. After that, he was treated like visiting royalty, chauffeured to the morgue, where two sympathetic nurses were by his side during the horror of identifying his brother's lifeless body, and then back to the sheriff's station where he signed over the title of Walter's car, agreeing to the arrangements to transport the body by train back to New York. The older officer said the station would pay for all expenses. By the time the sun went down on that sticky day in June, Jack was back on the road with Walter's suitcase, and a large manila envelope that held his wallet, rings, and the napkin from Ray's Tavern.

• • •

JACK'S BREATH SHORTENED TO spurts, and then suddenly, he cried out, not with a few tears, but with loud wracking sobs that poured out of him. Unable to resist, he surrendered to the images: he and Walter playing baseball in the streets, the family dinners, Yankee games, the teasing, fighting, Walter's Fort Dix homecoming, the wedding to Bernice, his medical school graduation, Jeffrey, Jeannie, and then...the morgue. Jack felt the mucus from his nose seep into his mouth but didn't care. He finally reached over to Cindy's bedside table and grabbed the tissue box. Before he could wipe his face, he heard the front door open and close. There was nowhere to hide. Would this be the moment where he would share his secret with Cindy? Would she forgive him for keeping the truth from her for two decades?

# Chapter 13

## MAY 1974

# *Jeannie*

JEANNIE WOKE EVEN EARLIER than her grandmother, and quietly slipped out the front door. She'd been waiting for the right day to beg her uncle for a spot on the D.C. press bus, and after getting an encouraging nod from Ernie, she knew it was now or never. It wouldn't be an easy sell though; Uncle Jack would ask about her other work, and she'd have to come clean about looking for her former SDS comrades or anyone who knew them. She wanted to find out if they were safe, of course, but the article, she'd explain, would focus on what drew them and other young people into risky activism, and where they were now. She'd work hard on the pitch, why it would appeal to their readership; she'd show him preliminary story outlines and the list of grassroots organizations she planned on contacting. She had every intention of completing the piece if her uncle approved. The main priority, however, was to convince him to let her on that bus, giving her a chance to slip away to Atlanta for the weekend to dig deeper into Phil's army buddy story.

Feeling fairly confident that she'd make the cut soon, Jeannie had spent a few lunch hours over the past week making phone calls to Vietnam Veterans Associations in and around Atlanta. She felt particularly encouraged after a friendly chat with the administrator of the downtown chapter. The man explained that they did indeed keep thorough lists and conducted weekly meetings with vets and their families. While Jeannie didn't know the name of Phil's deceased army buddy, she would try and narrow down her search to Phil's time in Vietnam. The administrator provided his name and direct extension, and said he'd help her out in any way he could. The lead gave her the added courage to make a direct plea to her uncle. Twenty-two years as her surrogate father, and two more as her boss, but Jeannie still had to tread carefully with Uncle Jack. No matter how serious the calamity or joyful the occasion, he'd grown quite adept at stoic facial expressions and keeping his feelings to himself.

Tiptoeing out the front door, she moved quickly to the tranquil street, gazing up at the billows of clouds edged in blue against the morning sky. The neighborhood foliage had reached the mid-spring peak with cherry blossom trees forming a canopy overhead. Walking the blocks toward the subway station, she inhaled the bloomy scent and a smile spread across her face. For the first time in months, she was optimistic. Maybe it was living with Grammy and hearing the repeated catch phrases she'd share when told of any problem, "This too shall pass, sweetheart," or "Things could be a lot worse, you've got your health, right?" If Grammy only knew what went on with SDS and its reincarnation to the Weather Underground with the drugs, bomb-making discussions, and the ugly, shameful times with Jim, she'd stop questioning her desire to refocus her energies on the stories she was assigned by Ernie. This was precisely why she had to guard her privacy; her good-natured grandmother, she was finding out, could also be nosey and a bit of a snoop.

Most nights before bed, Jeannie would sink into the pillow and review her work pad for new leads. Scribbling notes or crafting diagrams, she'd ruminate about how Phil might have been recruited as an FBI informant, or if there was a link between the Atlanta bank that issued Phil's checks and her father's accident 22 years earlier. Sure, it was a long shot. She'd circle or underline the viable adds to the storyline, but soon she'd hit a wall and toss the notes in the trash. She'd shut off her night lamp and close her eyes with a gnawing fear she was going mad, and then relive nightmares set in pungent marijuana smoke with unwashed men plotting deadly scenes. Her eyes would pop open, and in the darkness, she'd blink herself back into the safety of Grammy's house. If she couldn't fall back to sleep, she'd turn the lamp back on, pick up a trashy novel and read until her mind turned to mush. The mornings were a welcome relief, and with them, a renewed sense of purpose. By the time she'd ascend the subway a few blocks from *The Globe's* midtown office building, she would have planned out a way to squeeze in her extracurricular research time.

Jeannie contrived the earlier arrival so that she could have a few minutes with her uncle before the newsroom's flurry of bodies made it impossible to focus on anything but deadlines. Advocating for a D.C. spot was the main sport of reporters envious of the guys who'd gotten the chance to rub elbows with renowned journalists from all over the world. The only way to be part of the club was to be given that same opportunity. If she got it, she'd be able to fluff up her feathers in the pit too and finally achieve some degree of respect from those who still saw her desk space as a reward for being related to the Editor-in-Chief.

Uncle Jack's office door was closed, lights out, venetian blinds flat against the large glass window that gave him a wide view of the pit. He always arrived at 7:00 a.m. sharp, preceding the day shift by a good hour. The array of wall clocks with five different time zones confirmed 7:30 a.m. in New York. He was late; so unlike him. In fact, the saying around the pit was that all the wall clocks were set by Jack Glazer. He never called in sick. Maybe it was Max, or Cindy. Or, she shook her head, just a simple traffic jam. She went to her desk, laid down her bag, and quickly scanned memos and scattered piles of notes she'd left the night before. Mailroom and office staff, reporters, typesetters, and secretaries would begin the march into *The Globe* in a half hour, and by mid-day, the printing press underneath them would begin to vibrate through the floorboards.

Heading into the lunchroom, Jeannie measured grounds and water for two pots into the coffeemaker, then waited for the ready light to go from red to green. She poured herself a large cup and returned to her desk. Her eyes darted from her papers to the main entrance. *Where was he?*

When the minute-hand clicked into the 8:00 a.m. position, the front entrance doors opened and in they came, a chaotic swarm of worker bees buzzing into action. She glanced at the colorful flow; there seemed to be more chatter, smiles, a buoyancy. Springtime, she guessed. When it ebbed to a trickle, Jeannie glanced back to her uncle's office but it remained dark. Something was clearly wrong. Glancing toward Barbara's desk to the left of Uncle Jack's, she could see the white patent-leathered pocketbook resting on the surface along with a Dunkin' Donuts bag. Barbara would know what's up; after 10 years by the Chief's side, she could finish his sentences, anticipate decisions, and straddle the delicate line of managing his professional and personal business. Jeannie needed to find her. She tried to navigate through the bedlam of staff engaged in morning banter but became impatient and took a detour to Ernie's office. She shook off thoughts of Uncle Pauley and his failing condition and shuddered a "God forbid" in the back of her throat if it were about her grandmother. That left her

Uncle Jack's chronic stomach thing, which they all knew he'd been masking for years. Picking up Barbara's voice drifting out of Ernie's office, Jeannie allowed her last thought to go in a selfish direction. Why wasn't he here today? Of all days, when she had finally pumped herself up to have the talk with him.

The back of Barbara's small frame was blocking Ernie's line of sight, so neither of them saw her standing at the threshold. "Okay, got it, not to worry, I'll take care of it." Her words were clipped.

Not wanting to be discovered eavesdropping, Jeannie made her presence known. "Oh hi, good morning, sorry to bother you, Ernie, I was just wondering..."

"Chief's not coming in today, took a bit of a turn, but let's keep that between us. And I mean it." He stood and turned his attention to the piles on his desk. "Staff meeting's still at 8:30 sharp."

Jeannie felt a twinge of panic in her throat. *What kind of turn?* She needed more details, but that wasn't going to come from Ernie. He'd been an army sergeant stationed in Europe during the war, so everyone knew that his words were the last ones issued. She backed out into the hallway. With her tightly wound gray bun exposing her small head, Barbara did an about face, showing a frown of worry that made her middle-aged skin go even more slack.

Dark scenarios raced through her head. She had to call Aunt Cindy, but where and how? She had a phone on her desk, but everyone would hear her conversation. The giant clock read 8:25; she'd never make it to a street phone booth and be back in time for the staff meeting. She picked up her receiver anyway and dialed, her head curved away from the guys. Her aunt answered on the second ring. Jeannie didn't let her say more than hello.

"Aunt Cindy, I'm rushing to a staff meeting. Tell me quick, please, is he okay?" Jeannie cupped her mouth over the receiver.

"Who told you? It wasn't supposed to be common knowledge..."

Jeannie cut her off. "It isn't. I asked Ernie. Please tell me."

"Your uncle is fine, recovering. His stomach thing turns out to be an ulcer; he needs to stay put for the rest of the week."

Jeannie no longer had to worry about being overheard as her pod-mates had all headed to the conference room. "Got to go, but I'm coming over to check for myself. See you after work." She hung up without getting her aunt's okay. She grabbed a fresh yellow pad from her drawer and scooted around the office perimeter and into the smoky room. She was the last to her seat.

By lunch time, she'd heard bits and pieces of the story from her grandmother. "He'll live," she assured her. Still worried, Jeannie broke her regular routine and left with the rest of the crew at five and splurged on a cab to Queens to avoid the crowded rush hour trains. The tradeoff was enduring the maniacal taxi driver's sprint through narrow lanes and bumper-to-bumper tailgating to the last second. When the cab came to an abrupt halt at her uncle's apartment building, she felt like she'd been on the Cyclone ride at Coney Island, relieved that her wits and limbs were still intact.

Hector, the doorman on duty, knew her by sight and gave her a sympathetic nod.

"You're here to see your uncle? Mrs. G says he's doing better. We are all very glad to hear that." His voice was gravelly, but kind.

"Me too. And thank you, Hector." She quickened her pace to the elevators.

She and Aunt Cindy hugged as if they hadn't seen each other in years.

"Go on inside, he's expecting you. You'll stay for dinner?" She called after her as she headed to the bedroom.

"Uh, not sure. Let me see the patient first."

Jeannie could hear the television blaring as she entered the room.

"So, this is where you've been hiding out all day?" She glided over, bent down and gave him a kiss on his cheek.

Jack smiled and reached for her hand. She took his, and then stared into his face, which was as white as the sheet he was lying on, his hair matted against his forehead, his eyes puffy with a redness around the rims. It frightened her, but she tried to maintain a poker face.

"Do I look *that* bad?"

"Well, maybe a little worn around the edges. I heard about your night. Did you get any sleep today?"

He tried to sit up straighter but winced in the process. "Turn off the set, will you? I've had enough." She did as he instructed, and then sat on the vanity seat next to the nightstand.

"So, was it your grandmother or Cindy who broke the story?"

She smiled. "Guess."

"Okay, so that's why you rushed over after work. I'm fine, just not up for a jog around the park, but maybe tomorrow." Just like her uncle to downplay. He'd either refuse to talk about his health issues, or would dismiss them with a corny joke.

"So, now you tell me, what happened today? Is the building still standing?"

Jeannie sighed. He was impossible.

"Yes, the presses rolled on, and as you probably know, more Judiciary Committee tussling. But it's a sinking ship, the old Nixon upper lip is going limp. You know that also means it's getting more cutthroat in the pit. Almost everyone has gone to D.C. on the bus, except for a handful of us." She looked him squarely in his face.

"Okay, well, if Ernie can spare you, I'll check the list and see if we can squeeze you in next week."

Jeannie practically jumped off her seat. It wasn't a definite yes, but close enough.

"Thank you so much, *Chief.*" She had his ear now. "And while we are on the subject of trips, I was hoping to get a few days off the following week. I mean, I do have some vacation time. I just want to, well, go somewhere close by." She heard herself pausing more than she wanted.

"Where to?" He didn't show any concern, but she couldn't be sure. He also didn't ask about her other work, so she decided to just ease into the Phil break-up story link.

"Okay, now hear me out. It would be to Atlanta. I know I never told you, but the reason I left Phil is because I don't believe he is the guy I thought he was." She felt her neck muscles tense up.

"Go on." The crease between his eyebrows grew a little deeper.

She hesitated. *Would he be even more skeptical than Roz?* A stab of regret pressed against her throat. Too late to turn back though, so she went for it.

"Okay, so I found a stack of $500 checks totaling $5,000 in his desk drawer from a bank in Atlanta. When I asked about it, he hemmed and hawed, then talked about a lost army buddy in 'Nam and how he went to Atlanta to see the parents, to keep a promise he made before he was killed. To show their gratitude, these people sent Phil money they had saved for their son. I don't know why, for his friendship, he said. But even if that were true, why send installments? Why not a lump sum? If he didn't cash the first check or two, why did they keep on sending more? And why *didn't* he cash them? It's not like he doesn't need the money. Naturally, he said he couldn't take their money, but the family allegedly insisted. And then, they just collect dust in his drawer? Does this make sense to you?" The words poured out of her like a pitcher of water knocked on its side.

"Hold on, you're all over the place. I don't know, Jeannie, sounds more yes than no. If you don't believe him, then you must have considered an alternative theory?" His jaw jutted forward.

"Yes, well, sort of. The first thing I need to do is go to Atlanta to see if I can corroborate his account." She took a deep breath.

"Okay, for argument's sake, let's say this needle-in-a-haystack effort pans out, what then? This would burn any remaining bridge with Phil, or more than likely, if you get nowhere, it puts you right back where you started." He paused. "What else is there, sweetheart?"

She hoped she wouldn't have had to go this far.

"Okay, let me explain. I was always a little skeptical about the timing of Phil showing up in my life. Everything had been unraveling with school and Jim. I was in a desperate place. We connected so easily, it was as if he knew me, could read my mind, saying what I needed to hear, and always trying to convince me to leave the group. We'd met a few times, and only talked over the phone on three other occasions and not for long either. Yet, he hung in there for almost a year. I believed it was love at first sight. But, again, too many things weren't adding up."

"Hang on a minute..." Jack put up his hand and shook his head.

"Wait, *please* just listen." She cut him off, stood up and then after a quick pace around the room, returned to her chair. "I think Phil might have been involved in a surveillance operation, assigned to SDS, and that," she turned her head toward the window; the waning sun had cast a pinkish light through the room, "he could be an FBI informant. Maybe the money is from the feds."

Her uncle didn't move for a few seconds, then reached for the water glass on his tray.

"That's quite a huge leap. Even a cub reporter knows when he, or rather she, is on a bumpy road to a dead end. Unless you've got something else to support your theory, a trip to Atlanta is a waste of time and money." His voice was severe, boss and uncle having merged into a tower of authority.

"I *do* have something else. I didn't tell you, or anyone in the family, and maybe I should have a long time ago. In Chicago, I got arrested, lots of us did. But I only spent maybe two hours in a jail cell with eleven other girls before my name was called. I thought it was Jim bailing me out, with what money I didn't know or think about back then. Instead, I was escorted to the desk sergeant who handed me an envelope. Inside was $200 in fifty-dollar bills and a bus ticket back to New York."

"What?" Her uncle sat up too quickly and cried out in pain. "*Why didn't you tell me?*"

"Uncle Jack, please, relax, lie back down. We were warned over and over again about informants; clearly, it had to be one who paid my bail. I first thought it was you. Do you remember when I got back to New York that summer? I thought you might have had reporters in Chicago watching out for me. Well anyway, I was terrified. I wanted to tell Jim, but I was afraid of the repercussions. So, I stayed with the group for more years than I should have, and then suddenly, Phil comes along."

Cindy's voice sung down the hallway. "Dinner in five minutes."

Jeannie had forgotten one last thing. "Oh, and when the cop gave me the envelope, I remember his exact words, "Tell your pop we appreciate the tip." That really freaked me out. Someone must have paid off the sergeant, but who? Phil's checks were from an Atlanta bank. If his story is a lie, then yes, I know it's really a long shot, but could any of it be linked with Daddy's accident?"

She had let it all out, no more secrets. Her uncle had grown even paler.

"Stop it now, Jeannie. If there was an informant that paid your bail, the odds that it was Phil are pretty low. Going to Atlanta, a connection to Walter, or rather, your father, is simply ludicrous. You need to put away all this nonsense and concentrate on the real work on your plate." He was plainly issuing an order and chewing her out too. She saw his face contorting with pain and felt badly about making his condition even worse. She didn't want to come across as insensitive, but she also didn't appreciate him immediately rejecting her story, even if it hadn't quite jelled yet. Why didn't he want her to go with her instincts? Something wasn't right with him, and she needed to figure it out.

She stood up just as Cindy bounced in with a tray. "Chicken broth for you dear, and Jeannie, you can join Max and me at the table."

"No thank you, I've got to run. She leaned over and gave her uncle a perfunctory kiss on his forehead. Picking up her bag, she turned toward the hallway.

"Wait," her uncle called out in a strained voice, "don't waste any more time, Jeannie, I mean it. When I get back to work, I'll check it out with my contacts at the FBI, okay?" She didn't respond, pretending not to hear him. "Focus on D.C."

At the bedroom doorway, her aunt reached out to hug her, "Is everything okay here?" Jeannie nodded and left the apartment without saying goodbye to her cousin.

Out on the street, she felt guilty for rattling her uncle when he had just spent the night at the ER; it wasn't like her. But as she walked toward the avenues, her mind was riddled with questions. Why hadn't he reacted more about the jail money and bus ticket? It was a legitimate red flag. Why didn't she ask *him* for an alternative theory? Who else could have arranged her bail other than someone who'd been watching the group, then planned to trail her back to New York? But she didn't use the ticket, and didn't leave SDS, not for another year. Then Phil shows up at her favorite coffee shop just when she's about to flunk out of school. Her theory wasn't that far-fetched, and her uncle, of all people, who for decades had trained dozens of reporters to search under every rock, follow the hunches, and keep sniffing until the clues formed a pattern, should have been more curious, not cut her off and order her to stop. His whole demeanor had been out of character. It had to be the health scare; he must have been distracted by his condition, not being at the paper, but then, she knew, hell, everyone knew that Uncle Jack was a journalist at heart, so something else seemed to be preventing him from thinking like one. By the time she caught a cab home, she was more determined than ever to pursue the link between Atlanta and Phil.

Ernie started Monday morning's staff meeting sharing the news about the Chief's illness, minimizing it so it barely registered as a problem, and reassuring everyone that although not physically present, he's being kept in the loop.

Howie, the veteran reporter raised his pen. "So, do you foresee any delays in the next D.C. bus trip?"

"Not really; tomorrow at the latest. We may be drawing straws at this point." Ernie was trying to be light, but like all the remaining reporters, who hadn't been selected yet, Jeannie was not amused. For the rest of the day, she kept a low profile and a steady beat on the typewriter, occasionally piping up to join the guys' routine banter. She knew the second her name was called, she'd get the nepotism glares, but decided not to let it get to her. The promised memo was passed out just before 4:00 p.m. on Tuesday afternoon, and there in the middle of the list was her name. At last. She was glad Howie was put in charge. He had already been to D.C. twice, and out of all the veteran reporters, he was the one she liked and trusted the most. But he still couldn't resist ribbing her.

"So, Miss Glazer, what a surprise, huh?" His meaning wasn't lost on her, or the other reporters in the pod, their smirks unmistakable. One of only two women reporters at the paper, Jeannie knew the guys didn't see either of them as equals. All the other women were secretaries or clerks, and were either married or soon to be. The other reporter, Ginny, a skinny graduate of NYU's Journalism school, was junior to Jeannie. She had done a brief internship at a small New Jersey paper, and was ecstatic when Ernie hired her on at *The Globe* a few months back. As a probationary cub, she was not going to D.C.; she worked the local beat, doing everything by the book. Ginny didn't appear to socialize with anyone outside of the building; Jeannie had talked with her only a few times in the lunchroom, when their breaks overlapped. She spoke in a whisper and ate like a bird, pecking at her salads with frugal bites.

Howie was in his late 30s and had just celebrated his 10-year anniversary at *The Globe* in February. He'd been her unofficial mentor and assumed the role primarily in deference to her uncle. On the rare occasions when she'd join the staff for drinks after work, Howie would try to make her feel a part of the inner circle, until they'd finished the rundown of the day's drama, then he'd drift away to engage with the other men. Jeannie's co-workers had not become her friends.

It had been only a few days since the unnerving exchange with her uncle, and rather than talk to him again, she got the updates on his recovery from her grandmother. Jeannie thought her uncle's odd behavior meant he was hiding something, and she decided to look for clues in his office. Now that her seat on the D.C. bus was confirmed, Jeannie put her plan into gear the following morning.

Step one was monitoring Barbara, Uncle Jack's stalwart secretary. Even though her boss was out of the office, she stayed busy firing away at her typewriter and answering a steady stream of phone calls. Barbara left her desk only for short stretches, sometimes entering Ernie's office, but more often her uncle's, where she'd open the door, march in with file folders, and come out with loose papers tucked under her arm. Each time, she turned on the lights and then snapped them off when she left. She didn't bother to open the blinds. This went on all day long Jeannie until 5:00 p.m. when Barbara, preparing to leave, tidied up her desk and tucked her pocketbook into the crook of her arm. Jeannie held her breath as Barbara checked that the door to Uncle Jack's office was closed. But the door wasn't locked, or at least she didn't see Barbara fuss with the knob or use a key. That was a huge relief. She didn't have a back-up plan if she couldn't get into his office.

Jeannie glanced around the pit. As if in a choreographed dance, at five o'clock sharp, everyone began to put their plastic coverlets over typewriters, return pencils to holders, and arrange office paraphernalia to the edges of their green blotters. Jeannie pretended to follow, getting swept into the flock of bodies heading for the exit. In the stuffy crowded elevator, she picked up chatter about weekend plans, even though it was only Thursday, baseball games, bike rides in the park, bands playing. From her spot in the back corner, she overheard a few guys talking about meeting for a drink at Chase's Bar, *The Globe's* hangout. They knew she could hear them, but didn't ask her to come along.

Jeannie decided to kill time by doing a bit of shopping for the D.C. trip, then getting some dinner. When the coast was clear, she'd return to *The Globe* to have a quiet look around.

Armed with a Macy's bag and her hunger abated, Jeannie walked back to the building. It was an old structure built in the 1920s, and while somewhat refurbished, it retained its quaint, stately appearance. Between two elevator banks stood a long console where a team of uniformed guards sat on high-backed stools and directing visitors to their desired floors. She recognized the faces of all the regular day-shift guys, but had never become too chummy, a smile here and there. She wasn't familiar with any of the night-shift men, so she intentionally slowed her gait as she veered toward the elevator on the left side. As casually as possible, she spoke up.

"Good evening, I'm with *The Globe*." She held up her I.D. with a key attached. "I forgot something."

The guard barely nodded, motioning her to pass while he reached down to lower the volume of his transistor radio. As soon as she pressed the UP button, the elevator door creaked open and she scooted inside. The lift was a true relic. Glancing at the tiny flip seat in the front corner from its operator-run era with a shudder of claustrophobia, she couldn't imagine spending eight hours a day in an airless contraption surrounded by anxious riders constantly in motion.

On her floor, she navigated the hallways, glancing behind her, until she arrived at *The Globe's* frosted glass pane doors. Uncle Jack, Ernie, and of course Barbara, had keys, as well as all the reporters who, like her, rarely kept eight-to-five hours. She timed her return for 8:30 p.m. to avoid any lingering eleventh-hour guys finishing up final edits before the 9:00 p.m. press run.

Jeannie flipped the switch to the right of the entry doors and watched rows of florescent lights along the 12-foot ceiling flicker on. Too bright for her snooping, she quickly shut them off. Hurrying to her uncle's office, she opened the door and slipped inside.

She didn't turn on the overhead light, and instead tip-toed across the room, clicking on the long-necked desk lamp. Mostly sealed up for the past week, the office had a musty tobacco smell. Uncle Jack wasn't a smoker, but kept ashtrays, now emptied but still reeking, on his desk and meeting table for Ernie and the many others who couldn't be without their cigarettes. She felt her courage flagging and needed to move fast. Easing into the enormous desk chair, she began rummaging through every drawer in the desk. After 10 minutes of flipping through folders and wiping her sweaty palms on her dress, still unsure what she was hoping to find, she pushed away from the desk and switched over to the credenza under the window. Two big drawers, each tightly packed with manila files dating back to the 1950s, *Letters to the Editor* in the first drawer and accolades and significant historical events in the second. Nothing out of the ordinary. She carefully closed the drawers and stared out the window into the night sky. Every second in her uncle's office put her in jeopardy of being discovered. Time to get out of there. Reaching down to pick up her bag, her eye caught a small drawer at the bottom of the credenza. She pulled the handle, but it didn't budge.

The floor she kneeled on suddenly shook with a whirring crescendo of sound "Oh shit," she blurted out, "the presses!" It was already 9:00 p.m.; she'd been snooping too long. Why was this tiny drawer the only one locked? Shining the desk lamp on the drawer, she felt a keyhole under the handle. She needed to find that key. Ransacking the center drawer of his desk produced only a jumble of pens, pencils, paper clips, small notepads, coins and sticky lifesavers. She had to switch on the overhead light, despite the risk. Scanning the room, Jeannie saw trophies, awards and knickknacks randomly placed in and on top of bookshelves, with papers and binders covering the other flat surfaces. Looking again, she zeroed in on a bank of Yankee championship mugs, almost hidden on a top shelf in the farthest corner of the room. She stepped closer. Stretching her arms and straining on her tiptoes, she moved each one slightly, dislodging a heavy film of dust that clung to her hand. Pushing the third mug a few inches to the right, she heard a slight rattle and carefully pulled it off the shelf. She gasped. A small, gold-colored key lay at the bottom. Fearing discovery, she barely stopped herself from crying "Yes!" She rushed back to the credenza, inserted the key, and turned it to the right. The drawer opened, revealing one 8"x 10" manila envelope, wrinkled and worn. No addressee, but in the left-hand corner, was a faded, return address with an unidentifiable law enforcement logo. She sat down and held the envelope closer to the lamp. Her hands shook as she opened the metal clasp. Reaching in, she pulled out a plastic bag—something was inside. She carefully extracted what looked like a cocktail napkin, on the bottom it read, *Ray's Tavern, Braselton, Georgia*, in black lettering. Holding the napkin up to the light, Jeannie focused on the blue-inked shaky handwriting. "J—forgive me, never tell, take care of kids, so sorry, love you."

Jeannie squinted at the napkin, trying to comprehend what she was looking at. She read the words again, praying they weren't what she thought. "Never tell?" Who? "So sorry?" When she reread "take care of kids," the realization came at her like a tidal wave, making her throw the napkin onto the floor. "*NO!*" she cried, followed by a succession of "no's" and "oh my gods," her head shaking back and forth. She picked up the napkin, resisting the temptation to rip it to shreds. Panicked, she jumped to her feet, began pacing around the office, and stubbed her toe, unable this time to suppress a loud moan. "Shit!" She fell forward onto her knees and gently clasped her injured foot. The press drums continued to roar; she crisscrossed her arms around her legs to hold herself together. She tried to fight the shaming word that began to pound her head in rhythm with the machines. The drums stopped abruptly, and a faint tapping sound of heels on the linoleum floor emerged in the sudden silence. She would take it all with her. Hurriedly putting the napkin into the plastic bag and stuffing it back into the manila envelope, she closed the drawer, relocked it, and threw the key and the envelope into her canvas bag. Just before turning off the desk lamp, she saw her Macy's bag in the corner and grabbed it. Moving to the interior window, she separated a few window blinds to survey the open space, terrified that a security guard had been sent up to find her. Seeing no one, she crept out, closing the door; it barely made a sound. The time under the New York clock read 9:45 p.m. She limped over to the exit, relieved to make it to the elevator without being yanked by the collar.

Waiting for the elevator, Jeannie started to tremble. Her teeth chattered and the hallway seemed to be rocking from side-to-side. Dizzy, she leaned back against the wall for balance and slowly, sank to the floor. Was this really her father's suicide note? Her head began to tap, then bang into the wall, *Why, why, why, and forgive him for what?* Hearing the elevator arrive, she stood up too quickly, nausea dimming her vision. She shuffled like a drunk into the small space, and right before the doors closed, Jeannie saw a moving shadow. Standing there, an arm reached out toward her, was Skinny Ginny. Their gazes met, but Jeannie didn't even flinch as the heavy doors began to close between them. After pressing "L", she managed a muted hello to Ginny; the doors sealed shut, and then, she began to silently cry.

Clutching her bag, she kept her head down. The lobby doorman called out to her, "Night, miss." She lifted one hand in a feeble wave, then slipped into the revolving doors. Out into the dark night, tears streaming down her face, Jeannie wished she had somewhere else to go, somewhere she could be alone to think. Or rather to scream, and freely break down.

It was too late to wander the empty streets, plus her toe had swelled up making it hard to walk without wincing. She wanted to call Jeffrey, but Roz already thought she was crazy, and just admitting how she found the napkin was too awful to confess. So many violations of trust by her own family, and now, she finally knew, by Uncle Jack. With no one else to turn to, Jeannie decided to take the longer subway commute back to Grammy's. The thundering train would give her the background noise needed to try to unravel a 22-year-old secret.

In the long tunnel out of the station, Jeannie managed to condense the revelation to two devastating points. Uncle Jack had told the family that her father died in a car accident but lied because it was evidently an even more horrible event that caused him to end his life. Who knew the truth besides Uncle

Jack? Aunt Cindy? It couldn't be anyone else. How could she look into the eyes of her grandmother, mother, brother, and most of all Uncle Jack, now that she knew? D.C. was two days away. She wouldn't be running into Uncle Jack at work, but she'd have to avoid Grammy's gaze at all costs. She'd spend the weekend at the public library searching through as many Georgia phone books as it took to find "Ray's Tavern" in a town called Braselton.

• • •

THE ONLY FEMALE ON THE trip, Jeannie had her own hotel room in D.C., and threw herself headfirst into doing a great job. She didn't exactly rub elbows with the big names at *The Washington Post* or the slew of other famous journalists but got an earful from the other assistants like herself. Between waking up at dawn, fighting for space in press briefings and following around veteran reporters, congressmen and their staff, Jeannie was run ragged, yet her adrenalin had not stopped pumping all week. Being so close to national breaking news, she kept her focus and energy on proving to be such a valuable asset that Howie would recommend her for another trip.

She had not forgotten about the note and snuck away during lunch breaks to make long distance calls to Atlanta's Better Business Bureau and the Chamber of Commerce. No "Ray's Tavern" in Braselton, but the helpful operator with a thick southern drawl, provided five restaurant names in the same zip code. It was on the fourth call, to a place called "Junior's" in Braselton, that she caught a break when a man answered after nine rings.

"Howdy, Junior's, can I help ya?"

Jeannie swallowed and paused too long.

"Hello, anyone there?" She heard men's voices in the background.

"Oh, sorry, hello, good evening, I was, hmmm, did your restaurant change its name? I was actually looking for a place called *Ray's Tavern*."

"Why, yesiree, that was over 10 years ago, I reckon. I'm Ray Jr. Everyone round here started calling the place Junior's after pop retired. He didn't mind much." This guy could not have fit the down-home mold any better.

"Oh great, just wondering, is Ray Sr., uh, still around?"

"Sure is, stronger than an ox, with a bull head to match. He just left. Still comes here every day to check up on me." His voice had dropped to an even folksier gravel.

Jeannie fell into character. "I'll be coming in from Atlanta tomorrow around one or so, and I'd like to talk with him if he's around, about the old days of the Tavern, for a story I'm writing. I'm a reporter doing a piece on southern places like yours. Could you give me directions?"

"Sure, I'll let Pop know, any publicity is welcome. And you'll get more than an earful; I promise you that." He chuckled.

"Thank you so much. See you tomorrow."

Jeannie had booked the flight the previous Saturday, despite her uncle's forceful rebuke. *The Globe* guys knew she was taking the weekend off, but she had told them she was meeting college friends in Miami. Knowing the news of her plans would soon reach the Chief, she wanted him to believe she'd taken his advice, even though deep down, she knew he wouldn't buy that subterfuge for a minute.

The flight was short, and the car rental process was much easier than she expected. By the time she navigated out of the city and reached the highway, the Georgia day had heated up and she turned up the air conditioning. She nearly missed the exit, but luckily caught the tavern sign, a picture of a wagon wheel with 'JR's' in the center. More arrows pointed the way into the gravel lot. Older cars and trucks, maybe a dozen all together, were bunched close to the front entrance. She chose the far end of the lot. The tavern exterior was painted pale yellow with brown trim; definitely going for the western theme.

As she locked the car door, a strong breeze came up, making the leaves flutter on the oak trees surrounding the place. She smoothed down her dress and kept her sunglasses on until she entered the dark interior. Her eyes blinked into focus. One table had diners, but the rest of the patrons were men who were all hunched around the huge bar. The aroma of savory chicken nearly knocked her over. She had eaten a good breakfast but could have been convinced to hang around for a tasty lunch. Every head turned in her direction. She took in another deep breath, looked around for a hostess, but no one approached her.

A man behind the bar finished his conversation and waved her forward. She put her sunglasses in her bag and followed his lead.

"You must be the writer gal—called yesterday?" Junior's thick, black moustache completely covered his lips. He had a beefy frame and a wide neck.

"Yes, I'm Jeannie. Nice to meet you."

"Pop's over there." He pointed to the end of the bar. Breaking away from a lively conversation with two other men, an older version of Junior acknowledged her entrance. "Told him you was coming, been sitting there like an old fool, waiting for y'all since the doors opened."

Ray Sr. got up, grabbed his beer, and extended his arm toward a booth by the window. Junior asked her if she wanted something to eat or drink.

"Just a coke, thanks."

When they were seated, Ray was the first to speak up. "Hard to believe someone would write about this place, guess there's a first for everything." His accent was even thicker than his son's.

Jeannie nodded, took out her notebook and pen, then began asking standard background questions. Was Ray a Braselton native? Why had he decided to open the place? Did he mostly service local customers, or out-of-towners? The kind of get comfortable questions she'd asked many times before.

Ray told her about buying the tavern a month after the war ended and turning it from a shanty with slop for food to a popular pit stop with the "best chicken-fried steak in a hundred miles."

"Smells like it." She smiled while scribbling down notes, hoping for a way to cut to the chase. She didn't feel right lying to him.

When he began talking about travelers from all parts of the country seeing the sign and coming in for a meal before reaching Atlanta, she stopped him.

"Hey Ray, I have something to confess here. While I am a reporter, I'm not here to do a story on the bar. The real reason I'm here...well, I'd like to ask you a few questions that might sound totally crazy. It turns out my own father was one of those travelers, like you said, who had passed through this town, stopping over for a meal, also on his way to Atlanta."

Ray looked at her squarely and smiled. "I knew it."

"I'm truly sorry for not saying so right away, but I had my reasons. Up until a week ago, my family and I had been told that my father died in a car accident outside of Atlanta, but then I found something that brought me here, all the way from New York."

Ray leaned back and put both hands flat on the table. "Whaddya find?"

"It was a note on a napkin from this place that had been locked away in a drawer for 22 years. Turns out to be the last words my father ever wrote."

Ray tilted his head toward the window and rubbed his index finger and thumb along his jawline. She sensed a shift in his demeanor. He knew something.

She took out a photo of her father standing against a fence in front of their home, bare-chested, wearing shorts and squinting into the camera.

"Do you recognize this man? He was 30 at the time, apparently stopped here to eat, on June 14, 1952 to be precise." Jeannie handed him the photo.

Ray reached for a pair of glasses in his shirt pocket, adjusted them on his nose, and held the photo at arm's length. It didn't take more than a few moments before he nodded in slow motion. "Yes, Miss, I do." He gave the photo back to her, looked down at his hands, and finally, after a long pause, began to speak.

"He was a jittery feller until a few drinks settled him down. Then a regular come in, a real talker and drinker from a big real estate family, salesmen, the whole lot of them. Those two talked and drank until closing time. Your daddy couldn't keep up with Hank's guzzle, that was his name, and so Hank kindly helped him to his car." Ray took a sip of his beer but turned his face away from hers.

"That was all, until I seen a car out yonder with New York plates when I was locking up." Ray pointed to where her rental car was parked. "I got worried and called the sheriff.

I'd done that many times before, can't have no one leaving my place too drunk to drive. Next thing I see is flashing red lights, and then your daddy getting shoved into the sheriff's vehicle. Don't know what happened to Hank, likely he'd already driven off. Recalled being glad, least that feller would sleep it off in jail. Ain't the first who'd done that and won't be the last."

"So, you're saying he was arrested?" Jeannie's mind leaped to the faded star logo on the manila envelope.

"Yep. Next day, they come to pick up his car, but your daddy's not with them, they got a tow truck, and that fat Sheriff Dixon comes on in here telling me to follow him outside. Something happened, he said, an accident, and did I know who your daddy had been talking with the night before. I didn't see any point in telling him, don't like the guy, and Hank had been a solid customer for years. Dixon told me to forget what I saw, and that if I talked to anyone about it, he'd shut me down. I'd never been threatened like that by the law or nobody else. Never saw Hank again neither. Heard he'd gone up to Atlanta, but that was too many years ago to be sure."

Jeannie took a sip of her coke; it was warm and flat.

"Do you by any chance know Hank's last name?"

"Well 'course, everyone in town knew Carlton Realty. Hank's short for Henry."

Jeannie wrote it down, and then put the photo back in her bag.

She got up and thanked him, and as she shook his big rough hand, he wished her good luck, and added, "You be careful now. Hank seemed like a real private guy, friendly, but always kept to himself, probably wouldn't like people poking around his business, or at least that's how I remember him."

On her way out, she waved goodbye to Junior. Sitting in the rental car, she thought about paying a visit to the sheriff's office but knew it would be a waste of time. That case was closed two decades ago. Instead, she'd make the sunset drive back to Atlanta and devote the next day to finding Hank.

# Chapter 14

# MAY 1974

# *Hank*

HANK ROLLED TO HIS left side away from the bedside clock and tried to empty his mind of cluttered thoughts. Some nights he could get five, sometimes six relatively peaceful hours of sleep, but it was the length of time required to slip into unconsciousness that unsettled him. He'd read all about insomnia and followed the advice of experts. He'd get ready for bed by 9:00, making sure it was lights out by 10:00. He stopped having coffee after 3:00, and didn't eat anything too spicy for supper. Hank knew when he stopped drinking, he no longer had a reliable drug to wipe out the demons hovering above his head at night. He had started watching Jack LaLanne's fitness program a few years back, so in addition to swimming laps, he'd bought some hand weights and even changed his diet—less steak and fried food, more vegetables. His regimen did make a big difference in his body, energy and disposition, for the most part. Though no diet or exercise routine could erase the feeling of isolation he lived with his whole life. When his dark thoughts couldn't be suppressed, despite whatever breathing techniques he'd employ, Hank's last resort was the bottle of Valium within arm's reach of the nightstand.

Rolling over to his right side, he pushed himself up. He had long ago installed blackout curtains in the east-facing bedroom and if not for the light from his bedside clock, he wouldn't have been able to see his own hand reaching for the bottle. It was nearly 4:30 a.m.—too close to dawn to take the pill—but what the hell. He'd pay tomorrow at work with more cups of coffee than his stomach could handle, but it was better than no sleep at all.

Jarred from a deep sleep by a full bladder, he turned to read the clock: 10:35. For a few confusing seconds he thought it was the night before. He never slept this late, especially on a workday. He rose too quickly, dizzy like the old hangover mornings. He hadn't heard the phone but Tammy had most certainly called him. His rare lapse from punctuality would cause her alarm. He needed to call the office right away.

He lifted himself off the bed. Shaking his head to clear the fog, he stumbled to the bathroom, relieved himself, then went into the kitchen to make the call. He picked up the receiver and instead of a dial tone, he heard Tammy's voice.

"Hello? Mr. C? It's Tammy, I didn't hear it ring on my end."

"Guess we're on the same wavelength, I was just about to call you. I overslept and will be there in an hour." Not particularly sheepish about the delay, Hank knew he didn't have any specific appointments until later on in the afternoon.

"Okay, yes, except, you see, there's someone already here. She wasn't on the calendar, but is insisting on seeing you today, whenever you get in." Tammy didn't sound like herself, more tentative and high-pitched.

"Who is it?" Hank raked a hand through his lacquered hair.

"A young lady, she wouldn't give me her name, says she needs to talk with you directly."

Just barely awake and still disoriented from the valium, Hank struggled to process what was happening. His first reaction was foreboding, then anger. How dare someone just show up to his office unscheduled, withhold her name, and then make demands on his time. He didn't even know any 'young ladies' except for his daughters. Hank had no intention of rushing into the office now unless it was really urgent.

"Put her on the phone."

He heard Tammy's muffled voice in the background, some shuffling, and then, "Mr. Carlton, I'm sorry to bother you like this, but my name is Jeannie Glazer, and sir, I'm not in town for long, in fact this is really my only day here, and I was hoping to talk with you. It's important."

Hank's knees buckled. He grabbed the counter for balance, felt his throat close up.

"Mr. Carlton, sir, are you still there?"

Too many thoughts made it hard to response. He gulped in some air and pushed out the words.

"Why don't you get the directions from Tammy. Come on over, we can talk here." If they met in the office, his curious secretary would ask questions.

"Oh, well sure, if you wouldn't mind, yes, that would be great." He had imagined her voice to be perky but appreciated that she also sounded sincere.

"See you in a bit." He hung up first. *How in tarnation did she find me?* He had less than a half-hour to figure it out.

Dashing back to his bedroom, he stripped off his boxers, jumped into the shower and let the hot water beat down on his head. *How was this possible?* His contract with Tony had ended over four years ago, six months after the bombing, and Tony hadn't contacted him since. After Phil and Jeannie broke it off, and she moved in with her granny, Hank didn't see the point of continuing his relationship with Tony. The job was done, case closed. He even stopped his subscription to that New York paper, *The Globe*, putting an official end to his investment with the Glazers.

It could only be Phil then; Hank couldn't see any other way she'd have found him. No point calling Tony now—there was nothing his private eye could find out in a half-hour even if he picked up. He did not want Jeannie to see him frazzled and was never comfortable unless well groomed. He shaved, managing to steady the razor between his fingers. After a splash of aftershave, he brushed his teeth, combed and applied a tiny squeeze of goop to the sides of his hair. He picked out navy slacks and a coral golf shirt from the closet, then slipped his bare feet into a pair of soft brown loafers. Taking long strides to the kitchen, he prepared a pot of coffee and turned on the oven. Out of habit, Hank always kept a package of cinnamon buns tucked away in his freezer. Infusing the house with that particular scent of buttery sweetness was an old real estate trick, intended to treat buyers to a tasty snack so they'd overlook a prospective home's imperfections. When the oven reached baking temperature, Hank removed the foil and popped them in. Though definitely not on his diet, the cinnamon buns and coffee would help him stay sharp and get through the next hour.

Hank set two coasters on the coffee table, and then cracked open the sliding glass door facing the pool just a sliver. Looking up at the gray brooding sky, he pondered the significance of finally meeting Jeannie in the flesh. The stove timer rang. He returned to the kitchen, took the buns out of the oven, poured himself a cup of coffee, and went outside. He sat on the bench underneath the folded umbrella. Dread and fear pumped through his body, but as he sipped his coffee, and looked around the desolate patio, he felt a giddy charge of anticipation. However bizarrely, he had become intimately involved with Jeannie's journey into adulthood, and although he'd never met her, somehow felt as if she were his own child.

His ex-wife and kids had moved to Florida a year ago when their oldest started college in Miami, leaving visits fewer and farther between, and only scheduled around milestone events or holidays. The youngest was graduating from high school next month; he'd written to tell her he'd be there, but he didn't hear back. They hadn't spoken in two, maybe three months. Hank decided he'd call her later; he was the grown up after all.

He had no way to contact Phil to get an explanation, at least not before Jeannie arrived. Why had Phil never even cashed his checks? According to Tony, he was a broken man when Jeannie left him. Tony stayed close with Phil's father and knew that Phil hadn't found anyone to replace her. Hank shook his head, none of this was making any sense. Whatever brought her to his doorstep, Hank was certain of one thing: he would not reveal his identity and would stick to his plan. He had no choice.

The doorbell chimed out with its four-beat musical scale, familiar to Hank only from occasional home deliveries.

He straightened up, took a deep breath, slipped back through the glass door and headed for the foyer. The framed rectangular mirror next to the entrance allowed him one last look at his reflection. He'd always been a vain man, and now in his mid-fifties, Hank spent even more time maintaining his appearance. After smoothing his shirt down his taut waist, he pulled open the sculpted wood door.

She was wearing a pale yellow sun dress with tiny white polka dots, a matching belt cinched at the waist and a white sweater capped her shoulders. The word 'waif' came into his mind. Her curly reddish hair was pulled off her face by clips on either side. She had indeed transformed from the photos of a ragged college hippie into a refined beauty.

She spoke first. "Hello, Mr. Carlton, I'm Jeannie. Well, of

course you know that. Thank you again for agreeing to see me on, uh, no notice at all."

He almost reached in for a hug. "Good morning, please come inside." As she passed over the threshold, Hank detected an herbal scent.

"My, it smells yummy in here."

"Not sure if y'all had some breakfast, got some coffee brewed, or maybe you'd like some tea to go with the pastries." He pointed toward the sunken living room, and without any hesitation, she went straight for the couch.

"Coffee for sure, please."

"Cream and sugar?" He asked, turning toward the kitchen.

"You really didn't have to go to this much trouble, Mr. Carlton. I'm just barging in on you..."

Hank interrupted. "Not a problem at all, don't get many visitors up here. And please call me Hank, my father's Mr. Carlton."

"Okay, and just cream, Hank."

Something about her innocence, but also a casual forthrightness, soothed him a bit. He refilled his own cup and poured one for her, then arranged the warm buns from the cooling rack onto a round platter. He opened the fridge and took out the cream. After laying it all on a decorative tray, a treasured souvenir from a long-ago European vacation, he carefully walked back in and set it on the coffee table.

"You have a lovely place, Hank. I kind of figured it would be; the drive up these hills was so picturesque."

"Thank you for saying so, Miss Glazer."

"Oh now, fair's fair, please call me Jeannie." She was quick. Her clipped New York accent wasn't something he'd heard for years.

She reached over for her mug, poured in some cream, and

put one of the buns on a small plate, then smiled before taking a bite. When she rolled her eyes and sighed, Hank imagined her as a little girl, enjoying a happy moment.

"These are too good." She picked up a napkin and wiped her mouth.

"Yesiree, no treat works better on all the senses." He'd keep up the small talk until she was ready to explain her visit.

He took a bun from the serving plate and bit off a small nibble; his nerves were outranking his empty stomach. After another swallow of the tepid coffee, he propped up the pillow behind him and sat back.

Jeannie finished up the bun, drained her cup and looked up at him for a brief moment. She then picked up the bag she came in with and placed it on her lap.

"I'm thinking you may have recognized my last name, or maybe not, it's been over 20 years now, and, well, it had only been that one night. But then I figured you must have had some inkling, or you wouldn't have let a stranger into your private residence." Her eyes looked into his. Maybe it was her reporter training, or some such thing, but he felt she had rehearsed her introduction, and was now trying to catch a revealing twitch in his face.

"I'm not sure what you're implying, Miss Jeannie. Not unusual for out-of-town folks to inquire about properties in Atlanta, and we're one of the bigger firms, been around for going on four decades." Hank's palms felt wet and so did the back of his neck.

"Okay, got it. I'm not looking for real estate, and don't want to take up too much of your time, so I'll get right to the point."

Refolding his legs, Hank shifted his eyes from her face to the bag.

"It turns out, coincidentally, that you spent an evening

chatting with my father, Walter Glazer, some 22 years ago in a tavern in Braselton. It was called 'Ray's back then, but his son took over and now it's 'Junior's.'"

A fist to the belly. He'd only gotten a real one once, wobbling home from a bar in an underground pocket of downtown Atlanta. Hank knew she registered his concern as he involuntarily arched his eyelids and brows in reaction.

"That's what you came down here to talk about?" He'd keep up the cat-and-mouse game for as long as possible.

"It's more complicated than that, you see..."

He cut her off, and then blamed his fraying nerves for jumping in too quickly, "Guessing you can't ask your daddy directly."

"No, I can't. He was arrested that night, but I'm guessing you know that. He didn't make it out of his jail cell, though. My uncle told the family it was a car accident. Who'd question the story, especially if the sheriff made it look like one? But then I found this." She removed a plastic bag from an envelope she pulled out from her bag. "Been locked away in my uncle's drawer all this time." She held it out, offering him to take it.

Hank's hands went numb; he felt paralyzed.

"Are you okay, Mr. Carl...or I mean, Hank?"

He opened and closed his fingers to stimulate some circulation. "Damn arthritis. Hold on a second." Buying a few more seconds, Hank then reached over and took the plastic bag.

Gently pulling out the napkin, Hank squinted down at the string of blue lettering, and then saw the faded tavern logo. *So that's how she found me!* Pretty impressive, he thought, that she'd gone all the way to Braselton to see if that shanty shack along the highway was still there frying up breaded chicken steaks. He held his breath knowing it was Walter's last words.

"Go on, read it, but please be careful."

He let the fragile napkin flutter between his fingers, then surrendering to the awful truth, Walter's last scribbled words. His stomach ached again for this innocent man who, because of him, had decided to kill himself to save his family an eternity of shame. Now he knew for sure that she had been spared the bigger, uglier reality.

He struggled to swallow. "I'm so sorry, Miss Jeannie, truly."

Rain began to pound on Hank's roof, accelerating loudly for a few moments as they remained silent.

She stood and walked over to the glass door. "Why would he do it?" She turned her slender body back toward him. "What, for heaven's sake, should my uncle 'never tell' and then 'forgive him for?' What could he possibly have done that was so horrific? You were the last one who talked to him, did he happen to tell you?" She was clearly worked up and started to pace around the room. "Even if he was too drunk to drive, and that bartender thought calling the sheriff was for his own protection, what could have happened on the way to jail that..." She raised the volume of her voice over the rain, but then it cracked. She took baby steps back to the couch and sat down, her eyes searching for answers.

Four years of sobriety but all he wanted now was a large tumbler of scotch. No question, he had to keep denying the truth, to protect them both.

"But why ask me? Why didn't you make it easier on yourself and ask your uncle?" Hank was stalling, and although an accomplished liar, he felt pressured, his heart thumping in his chest. She was upsetting his plan; he'd have to hold on tighter to keep up the charade.

"Like I said earlier, it's more complicated; it's not going to make sense to anyone."

"Try me." Thinking he'd gotten her off track, he felt his pulse slow down.

She leaned back against the couch to let her head rest. The rain eased into a dull hum; more light entered through the glass door.

"It's connected to a sharp left turn I'd taken in college. I don't know why I'm telling you this. It's kind of like when I interview strangers—oh, I didn't mention this, but I'm a reporter for *The Globe* in New York. I write feature stories, and just spent a week in D.C. with Watergate stuff. Anyway, if you ask in the right way, people will tell you anything, and many, I've come to find out, have been waiting for years to tell all. I'm the pin in their balloon. It's all just wild speculation, and according to my uncle, a road to a dead end." She shifted her head and looked at him. "I'm blabbering, aren't I?"

"No, you go on now." Hank wanted her to stop and leave before more revelations were shared. But still, he just couldn't grasp that Walter's daughter was here sitting in his home on a cool, soggy afternoon. Her defeated posture made him ache with empathy.

"I'm on this trip to verify something important about an old boyfriend, a project I've been working on for years."

Oh no, Hank thought, here we go.

"I was in a group called SDS, have you heard of them?"

"I think so. Weren't they the kids protesting the war?"

"At first, yes, but then things got out of control. I was at the Columbia scene in '68 when those riots broke out and got involved with a guy from the group. Before I knew it, I was at the Chicago convention that summer, an even crazier fiasco, and got arrested." She paused, fumbling with the straps of her bag.

This conversation had to end. How to respond, could he

disguise his rising panic? He decided to keep his face as stony as possible.

"The arrest was bad, I can't lie, not a place I ever imagined myself landing, but it helped that there were other girls like me, scared and clueless." Hank watched her mouth turn up in a wry grin. She was even lovelier when she smiled.

"The night wore on, we were all hungry, hot and tired. I thought someone from SDS would have come looking for me. I did get bailed out before the others, but not from my so-called boyfriend like I expected. And on top of that mystery, I was also given an envelope of cash, $200 to be exact, the most money I'd ever seen at one time, plus a bus ticket back to New York."

Hank didn't move a muscle.

"The sergeant said something about it being a gift from my father. I didn't know what to do or think. I somehow made it back to the motel and never said a word to anyone. It had to be an FBI informant; we were warned about them. Someone was watching us, or me, and so rather than come clean with the guys, I dove in deeper, way over my head." She took a breath. "I must be boring you."

"No, please, go on, I'm all ears." Hank found himself reliving it all, the story more real, more riveting with her telling it, despite seeing the head-on collision coming around the curve.

"I got trapped, in a sense, and spent too long with SDS, sucked into its militancy. I will spare you the details. But by coincidence or design, I don't know anymore, a man named Phil shows up at a coffee shop I always went to near school, and this is going to sound dramatic, but he may have saved my life. I got away from the group, escaped really, and started living with him. We fell in love, it was magical, but maybe a too-good-to-be-true thing. One morning I found something in his desk I shouldn't have, a bunch of uncashed checks from here, a bank in Atlanta. When I asked him to explain, I could tell he was lying; something about a dead army buddy, and the parents so grateful for his friendship that they decided to send him money. Does that make any sense? And even if it were true, why didn't Phil cash those checks? I've been obsessed for years about someone keeping tabs on me and now believe Phil may have been that informant all along."

Hank swallowed too fast and felt a pocket of air go down his windpipe, causing a full-blown coughing fit. He stood up and hacked his way to the kitchen for a glass of water.

"Mr., uh, Hank, are you alright?" He heard her call out.

Sipping slowly to soothe his throat, Hank waved and nodded.

He filled up another glass for her and returned to the living room. Not at all prepared for what would come next, his plan shattered, Hank knew he couldn't do this anymore. Christ, hadn't he held this secret long enough, becoming sick with guilt? She was owed the truth, and besides, with her astute investigative skills, she'd eventually find out, someway, somehow. It certainly wasn't fair to torture this poor girl a moment longer.

He sat down next to her on the couch giving her an adequate amount of personal space. He didn't have the courage to look directly into her eyes.

"Jeannie," he paused before heading over the cliff, "I know about Phil because, well because, I was the one who hired him."

She abruptly faced him. "What did you just say?"

He glanced over; her brows were practically touching.

"There were no coincidences or informants. It was me. I have been the one watching out for you, and your brother a bit too, but he managed to do alright without my help. I heard about you two from your daddy, yes, on that night at the tavern; he even showed me a picture of y'all."

Jeannie put her hand over her mouth and stared at him wide-eyed, like someone who'd seen a ghost. "I don't understand!" She lurched to her feet. "Why on earth would you do that? You lied; you've been lying since I walked in this door. I want the whole truth, right now! Why'd you let me go on and on when you already knew about Phil?" She put her face so close to his that Hank flinched backwards.

"Please sit back down; I'm fixing to tell you." His southern drawl became more pronounced when he got nervous.

Her body spoke two languages, one completely closed off, not wanting to spend another second in his company, and the other, he knew, was curious as hell.

"I've never uttered a word to anyone about the night I spent with your father, so please let me get it all out, at my own pace."

She took her time easing back to the couch but didn't look at him.

Hank began back in Braselton with his nightly jaunts to Ray's, a bar close enough for him to walk along a wooded path to and from his home. No way, he told her, could he ever get behind a wheel with the amount of alcohol he consumed in those days.

"Your daddy was at the bar when I came in. Out-of-towners were rare, and I was sick of the locals, so I sat down next to him. He'd already had a strong one from Ray, so we didn't have much trouble getting acquainted."

Hank explained that he was good at holding his liquor and remembered a lot of their conversation. Walter already had himself a meal, but even so, they'd spent hours on those bar stools and lost count of Ray's refills.

"Been around a lot of folks who, when they pass a certain

line, either get real quiet or talk up a blue streak. Your daddy was in the second category. He told me about being a new doctor, reason for his trip to Atlanta, and then, like I mentioned, spent the rest of the time talking about you and your brother. When I asked him about your mother, he, well, I shouldn't be saying this…"

Jeannie's eyes then turned toward him. "Don't stop, I want to hear it all."

He stood up and went to the patio door. He couldn't sit for the next part of the story.

"He didn't seem to be happy, with her. Well maybe unsettled, not himself, in a way I could understand. That's what my instincts were telling me. I didn't press on, but then there was a change in the air between us. I took it as a sign. No one was left in the place but us. Ray took away our empty glasses and said he was closing up. I helped your daddy to his car but driving 90 miles to Atlanta in his condition was out of the question. I told him I lived close by, that he could sleep it off and get a fresh start in the morning."

Hank opened up the glass door. The rain had tapered off, leaving a damp breeze in the air. He stuck his head out and inhaled, searching for courage.

"He insisted he could drive, and as he struggled to insert his key into the door lock, I took hold of his arm and tried to stop him. I managed to get him away from the car, and onto the wooded path to my home. His legs had no power; I had to hold him up. And then it happened."

Jeannie had been holding her arms around her chest. Her back arched. "Go on, Hank."

"I don't feel right in sharing the details, but you get the drift."

Jeannie dropped her head into her lap. Hank waited it out; he'd said enough.

A long minute passed between them before she raised her head and looked at him. "So, the secret you kept was that my father was a homosexual, like you. Is that it?" Her mouth turned into a sneer; it gave her a cruel appearance.

Hank came back to the couch, but this time sat on the recliner facing her. He'd never heard anyone assign that label to him out loud.

"For me, yes, but your daddy, not sure if the arrest or the truth, made him decide to..."

She stared straight ahead. He watched her unwrap her arms and squeeze her fists together. Then in an instant, she bolted off the couch and came at him. "You! You raped him and then left him there, alone..." Her arms came down hard on his shoulders, she pushed him back against the chair. Then, the tears.

He deserved all of her anger, and hurt, but not the accusation.

"I didn't take advantage, *I swear to you*, but yes, when I saw the red spinning light on the Sheriff's car come into Ray's parking lot, I ran. I have regretted that decision every day for the past 22 years."

She fled outside to the patio.

He had to finish, she had to know the rest, he wanted to make it right, at least with Phil. Standing at the far end of the pool, Jeannie's gaze was fixed on the panoramic view. Only wisps of low clouds remained, the sun struggling to break through.

He went to the cabana storage, pulled out a towel and dried off two picnic table chairs, then beckoned her over. She weaved her arms through her sweater and slowly crossed the deck.

"Please sit, let me get to the end."

He returned to that tragic night, his dash home, rushing inside, securing the chain behind him, and before drinking himself into unconsciousness, going over every possible way to get Walter out. "It could have been me too, so yeah, I escaped like a frightened rat. But at sun-up, I took a heap of cash with me, deciding I'd grease that fat Dixon's palm; everyone in town knew his pockets were always open for bribes." Hank hadn't expected to get so far into the story, but at this point, he had a more than captive audience, and nothing left to lose.

"It wasn't yet 7:00 a.m., but the air was already hot and thick. I took the fastest route to the business side of town, no one was out except a few paper boys. I parked across from the station and as I was running through my script, about being a colleague of your daddy's tracking him down when he didn't show up in Atlanta, it was a long shot for sure, but then I see an ambulance, no lights, pull up and park at the side door. I don't know why, but I jumped out of my car, and hid behind the fender. The guys get out, take a gurney from the back, and five minutes later, they're wheeling it back outside, but now it's got a body underneath a white sheet. I fell to the ground, looked straight into the hot sun, and begged God to forgive me."

A breeze rustled the leaves from the magnolia trees, the few that had fallen in the downpour moved to the edge of the pool.

"By the following weekend, I had packed up my things and left town for good. Found a place in downtown Atlanta, married the first woman I met, bought a ranch house, had two daughters, and tried to forget that night with a steady diet of liquor, cigarettes and sleeping pills. The divorce came when the kids were still in elementary school, and with it, a descent into such profound despair, that well, I needed some reason or purpose to get out of bed in the morning."

Jeannie kept her gaze on the horizon above the bank of trees. He looked at her profile, not a line out of place, down to her long graceful neck. A few birds flew overhead; one of them left the flock and skimmed the pool's surface. He wondered how much more of his soul-bearing she'd tolerate, and decided her silence meant he had a yellow light to proceed.

"With the booze, I'd gotten into the habit of flipping on the television for any kind of distracting noise. Some detective program caught my attention, and in a month's time, I'd hired a private eye to find out what happened to y'all. I had no notions of doing anything, truly, but when I learned your momma was still a widow, I thought, well, maybe I could help out with your college tuitions."

She turned her head sharply. "Wait, you're the one who paid our tuitions? Geez, I thought I'd actually earned a scholarship."

"You might have anyway, but don't right believe that matters anymore. And I know I should have closed the book right then and there, but like with that TV program, I kept wanting to see the next episode. And then all hell broke loose with those riots, so I decided to keep an eye out. When you got arrested, I couldn't sit on my hands, not again. I don't know why that sergeant said the envelope was from 'your father'; it must have been his assumption, that's all I can say."

He wanted those to be his last words of the story, but Jeannie seemed to be revving up. She swerved her body toward him and plunked both hands on the table.

"My uncle also lied to all of us, but now I understand why. You, on the other hand," she raised one arm and pointed her index finger into his face, "have put us all in an impossible situation, me in particular, you know that, right? You got me out of jail, yes, but if you hadn't, would I have called my family for help? Would I have stayed with SDS despite the jail trauma, or returned to New York and broken away? I want the last four years back, the ones that had me spinning in circles, blindly following leads that were never going to pan out. You're right about it not mattering anymore, but that's because you didn't let me have that choice!" She raised her hands and pounded them down on the table; droplets of water from the rain's residue splashed between them.

He didn't know what to say. She didn't give him an opportunity and began again. "And of course, there's the reality that, without Phil, I could be either dead from an exploded bomb or on the lam from the FBI like Jim and the other Weather folks, who are literally looking over their shoulders 24 hours a day. That I know is true." She shook her head and took a deep breath.

"But I've left the most disturbing elephant in the room for last, my father, the one I was prevented from knowing at all. The man who supposedly had a secret life, like you, and would rather take his own life than face it, and that's only if that scene in the woods, as you say, had been consensual. Why didn't he believe his family who loved him would understand the mistake?"

He'd let her stray too far. She was still so young, naïve, even if she did work for a big newspaper and was exposed to daily strife and injustice, her last comment raised a flag of ignorance that he would not let fly any longer.

"I'll say it again, Miss Jeannie, there are no more words or deeds to express my regret and sympathy for what happened to your daddy. But you have no idea what you're talking about when it comes to who I am and what people like me have endured and will continue to go through. You graduated from a fancy college, fought against the war, marched for civil rights, and know, I assume, about what happened at the Stonewall bar five years ago. Moral outcasts, pariahs, descendants from the devil...I've been a member of that concealed world for as long as I can remember. About 95% of us stay hidden, and we get good at living the lie, we get married and keep pretending we're happy with our choices. But there's a huge trade off, no one must figure it out, not parents, brothers or sisters, or God forbid, co-workers, because no one can be trusted. It's endless miles of obstacles to navigate around, no stopping to rest either, or the folks with pitchforks will catch up with you. If you make it round the barriers, you end up scooting through each day like a hated rodent, avoiding either a whack from the nearest shovel, or much worse, doing it to yourself, with alcohol, drugs, and existing forever in the narrow spaces between invisible bars. Some don't make it."

He was spewing thoughts that had been buried for years but didn't care anymore.

"None of the laws have changed, especially in places like Georgia. You can still get ten years for engaging in those acts, but being arrested for it? That's the tip of the iceberg. Sheriffs can sit back because the vigilantes do a good job keeping sinners like me in their crawl spaces. I'm betting your daddy got a scolding of the worse kind, all those Christians parading around like they got the rights on God. Where was he going to run? Even if your family got him out, he'd still be locked in a jail cell with no window of hope. I've put myself in his shoes too many times. Replayed the last scene in his head. Unlike someone disfigured in a horrible accident, your daddy would not be pitied or get a shred of sympathy. No, he'd be seeing faces frozen in disbelief, disgust, you kids traumatized, confused, having to grow up with a family secret too shameful to reveal, endless lies he and his kin would have to tell." Hank shook his head. "No, it was over, he reckoned his life was over."

The silence between them wore on for several minutes. He

folded his hands in his lap and kept his head down.

The patio went still, no breeze or birds overhead, and to Hank, it also felt like they were both holding their breath. She spoke up. "So, I was right to come to Atlanta," her voice softened, "and to this pristine cul-de-sac, not a dead-end street." She looked up at the sky. "I don't know who my heart is breaking for more, my poor father, a stranger to me, or my uncle, the man who took over for him. I don't want to think about my mother, or Jeffrey, but as much as you might disagree, my grandmother would have accepted her son no matter what."

He nodded. "What will you do?"

She turned back toward the pool. "Talk it out with Uncle Jack, hoping he'll see me as an ally. Not sure how he'll react to you though."

When she stood, he did too. She led the way back through the glass door and stopped at the couch to retrieve her bag. He kept a safe distance behind.

"Can I use your bathroom before I go?"

"Of course." He pointed to the half-bath in the foyer.

He didn't budge until she came out. As she headed toward the front door, he scooted in front of her and opened it wide enough for both of them to stand together in the threshold.

"I guess in a bizarre way I don't understand yet, or maybe never will, I should thank you."

He knew it was a gamble, but went with his gut, "Forgive your daddy, and folks like me, and if you can find it in your heart, Phil too."

Jeannie looked up at him, her eyes squinting into his face one last time. He wished he could read her mind. She then adjusted the bag on her shoulder and without another word, walked to the rental car. He waited until she got in, started the engine, and drove off.

The sun had warmed up the dewy air. He stepped out to the end of the flagstone path inhaling the freesia plants along the way. He felt his chest tighten. That familiar wave of loss again, a sensation he'd experienced too many times in his life, but then a tiny surge of relief followed. He crouched down, picked up the morning paper, and shuffled back inside to safety.

Chapter 15

# JUNE 1974

# *Jack*

H IS FACE TOWARD THE window, Jack propped his legs up on the credenza and rested his elbows on the worn arms of his leather chair. The twilight hours were his favorite and although brief in a city of skyscrapers, Jack took a few moments to enjoy the transition from day to night. He liked to look out at the office building across the street, dotted with patterns of desk lamps and overhead light banks, and watch the recurring figures in their square frames who, like him, were working well past the five o'clock hour.

Now in his third week of recovery and faithful to his bland diet, he was back at the helm. *The Globe* had never been just a job and he returned even more grateful to steer the second largest news organization in the city. Over the years, he'd been invited to sit on dozens of panels, industry events where newspaper and magazine insiders offer up their experiences and best practices to budding journalists, management types, and writers. He routinely declined; he never felt comfortable talking into a microphone to any kind of audience, but mostly, he didn't feel right sharing *The Globe's* trade secrets, particularly how his reporters approached challenging assignments, and definitely not how they secured their sources. He'd send Ernie as his stand-in, who'd utter short, generic responses, nothing significant to mull over or take away. He couldn't, however, skip the annual United Press International conference when it had been conveniently held at New York's Waldorf Astoria in March; the editors-in-chief session was slated as the keynote event. Sitting next to his cohorts from *The Post*, *Times* and *Daily News*, and heavily perspiring under the bright lights, he'd stayed with the pack, until they were all asked to list the most meaningful news events covered under their watch. He was first up, and without having to pause, blurted out Nixon and Watergate. He surprisingly found his voice and told the crowd that the scandal had transformed his investigative journalists into indispensable warriors. His entire impromptu speech was recorded and printed the next day in several papers, including his own. "If not for committed reporters surfacing vital sources, Congress might not have been pushed to the edge by the public's rage over the cover-up. As a result, the House and Senate, like Roman gladiators, were suited up and ready to confront the President of the United States. They'd entered truly unprecedented territory." Jack didn't like all the attention, but the paper did sell out that day. He made friendly bets with the other editors after the conference that Nixon wouldn't make it past the summer. *The Globe* got a boost, remaining competitive with its Watergate reporting. He was proud of the quality of work his staff was churning out, and it kept paying off with a two-fold increase in circulation despite extended television coverage. He raised his arms out in a long stretch, let out a quiet sigh, and turned off his desk lamp.

Exiting the building, Jack thought about Jeannie, the only reporter it seemed who was not on the same footing as the others. After D.C., she had lied to the other reporters, telling them she was visiting a college friend in Miami, but instead, ignored his warning and snuck away to Atlanta. She returned to work on Monday morning with puffy eyes, according to Ernie, as if she hadn't slept in weeks. Yesterday, she managed to evade Jack on his first full day back at work and today she called in sick.

Against his better judgement, when he got home, he called his mother to ask about Jeannie's health.

"Why, is she sick?" His mother sounded surprised.

"She's not home?" Jack was equally confused.

"No, I thought she was still at work. That's her regular schedule, but we haven't seen her much at all since she came back from D.C. And you know how busy we've all been with the wedding plans. Should I be worried?"

"No, it's fine, but I've got to run. Cindy and I are going to a movie tonight. I'm getting the cut off sign from her right now. Love you Mom."

"Okay, okay have fun dear."

He hung up the receiver feeling a little guilty for his white lie. Jack couldn't remember the last time he'd sat in a dark movie theater. Cindy and boys loved the movies, but even a whiff of their buttered popcorn made him queasy.

It was not like Jeannie to go AWOL. What was going on? While he didn't know her day-to-day whereabouts, she wasn't one to play hooky. Did she have any copy to finish today? He could check with Ernie, but that would raise suspicions. She'd been secretive about what she was working on, maybe she left clues on her desk. Jack wondered if she would come back to the paper tonight; no one would see or stop her if she did. He stood up and turned off the TV. Even at low volume, it was a distraction. He needed to be alone to think.

"Cin?" He called out as he headed into the bedroom.

"What is it? I'm with Max."

Before replying, he quickly changed into a pair of sneakers and grabbed a long-sleeved shirt from his closet.

"Going out for a walk." Avoiding Cindy, he glided down the

hallway and out the front door. He had planned on finally telling her the truth about Walter during his recovery. But before he could, Jeannie revealed her Chicago arrest and the mysteries surrounding her bail, the $200 in cash she was handed, and the uncashed checks totaling $5,000 drawn on an Atlanta bank she'd found in Phil's drawer, all of which somehow convinced her that Phil had been an informant and betrayed her. He knew she travelled to Atlanta to investigate, but what did she find? Before revealing what he himself knew, he needed to know what she had learned.

Was his niece avoiding him? Maybe she was too embarrassed to admit that she had found nothing on her southern trek, or been wrong about Phil, and was now back to square one. He'd torn up that menacing note his mother had fished out of Jeannie's trash. Were there other scraps of paper with additional speculations? Jack didn't want to think about Walter. As far as he knew, Walter's death had nothing to do with Chicago or Phil. Besides, there were no records to find in Atlanta, and she'd have no clue where to start.

The balmy Friday night had brought the crowds onto the streets; happy couples and families were perched on park benches or dining at outside tables of bustling restaurants. Jack felt regret as he heard the laughter and music float out of every establishment. It had been months since he'd taken out his wife and son, and was always derailing Cindy's plans, complaining that he was too tied up at work, then too tired to make the effort. And why spend the money, now that his strict diet meant he couldn't enjoy a rich plate of pasta or a glass of wine. It wasn't fair to either Cindy or Max, and he was denying himself the pleasure of their company. At least they all had the weekend in Connecticut last month, some quality family time where his mother, Jeannie, and even Scotty made the two-hour trip from Emerson to round out the festivities.

But then his mother pulled him into the guest room and showed him Jeannie's twisted scrawl. He suddenly realized that it was seeing Walter's name and the diagonal arrow drawn to the word "Atlanta," that had panicked him, sent his always precarious gut reeling, and led to his collapse and the ER trip. While the diagnosis was just an ulcer, it was now official, like a collar around his neck, it gave his watchdog family too much power to tug him back at the slightest hint of discomfort. He hated it all, particularly the carte blanche intrusion into the privacy of his pain, something he had jealously guarded the last 22 years.

Reaching the end of the block, Jack watched a couple get out of a cab. "Hold on," he called out waving to the driver.

He slid into the back seat.

"Where to?" The bearded cabbie eyed him from the rear-view mirror; the car reeked of tobacco.

"*The Globe*, 45th and..." The driver cut him off. "I know where it is."

It would take 30 minutes without traffic, an hour round trip. He hadn't told Cindy how long he'd be walking, but an hour was pushing it. He would call her from the office and explain he'd forgotten important papers.

Cracking the taxi window for some fresh air, he sat back and watched the lights of the city sail by. He didn't remember the last time he returned to the office at night; any press break-downs were Ernie's responsibility, who, along with his capable print staff, got the machines running again. The blizzards, massive protest marches and bloody riots that kept whoever was still in the building captive until order was restored all seemed to occur after his normal 6:00 p.m. quitting time. He would have been there for the blackout in '65 that caught the evening staffers and press room guys in a 13-hour power grid shutdown, but he had left early for Scotty's basketball game, a rare event for him that he promised both Cindy and Scotty he'd attend. He did have three overnighters at the office that he would never forget: the assassinations of JFK, MLK, and, then RFK. He recalled that for many hours there was hope that RFK would survive, and he had the staff prepare two outcome galleys; weary eyes glued to the AP feed to see which one went to press.

At 8:45 p.m., he arrived at the building's entrance. Once through the revolving doors, he waved to the same guard he'd passed while exiting the lobby two hours earlier.

A young man, clean-shaven with glasses, stepped around his podium, smoothing down his uniform jacket.

"Oh, hello again, Mr. Glazer. You forget something too?"

"Uh, yes, I did. Be just a few." He wondered what the odd "too" meant but too rushed to ask, he headed straight for the elevator banks.

After unlocking the glass entrance doors, Jack went to his office. There was a faint spotlight through his window blinds. He frowned, feeling confused. He was sure he had turned off the desk lamp when he left for the evening. He twisted the knob and pushed open the door. His niece bolted up from behind his desk and let out a shriek. He spontaneously responded in a deep scolding voice that had not passed his lips since the boys were in grammar school.

"Jeannie! *What are doing in here?*"

Her eyelids popped. Clutching her bag with both arms, and after a few sniffling breaths, she began to cry, her lips quivering. "I'm so sorry, Uncle Jack, it's so bad of me, please, let me explain." Her words were labored, the tears dotting her cheeks. Jack didn't offer her a tissue.

"Why are you here and in my office? And, you don't seem very sick." He felt himself grinding his teeth.

She slipped around the desk and sat down at the small conference table. "I'll tell you, okay, but just sit down, and please don't shout at me."

He watched her wipe her nose on the sleeve of her sweater, shoulders drooped.

He didn't want to sit just yet. "Start talking."

She inhaled and exhaled loudly, then spread her hands out on the table. "I know about Daddy, and the man he was with that night. I found him in Atlanta."

His secret revealed, Jack hesitated. Then, the desk phone rang, piercing the silence.

Staring at her, Jack went to the phone, and picked it up on the second ring. "Hey, yes, sorry Cindy, I forgot I had to do something here." He listened to her berate him but then cut her off. "It was important, I'll be home soon, yes, yes, I'm fine." He hung up. One more item for Cindy's list of his transgressions.

Returning to the table, he pulled out a chair and sat down. Jeannie hadn't moved an inch. "How on earth…"

She interrupted him; eyes still glassy. "I did go to Atlanta, but not to investigate Phil's army buddy story and the uncashed checks. I heard you when you said it was ludicrous, but then you wouldn't even listen or consider the bail mystery and totally shut me down. That wasn't like you. There was something you weren't saying, or maybe, hiding." He watched her do a quick scan around his office.

Jack's leg started to jiggle, an annoying tic he and Walter had inherited from their Dad. He recalled his mother at the dinner table, imploring them to stop, as the silverware hopped along the Formica surface. He casually dropped one arm in his lap and pressed down on his right leg. "Go on."

"I thought, well, I believed maybe you weren't being honest, it was a strong hunch, one I was trained to follow, and so a few days later, I came in here and did an unforgivable thing. I went through your file drawers, but I swear I didn't have any idea what I was searching for and then, I found the, well, the napkin."

He couldn't believe what he was hearing. A whirring sound tunneled through his head, like when a few years back, his doctor had to pump several large syringes full of water into his ear canals to remove wax. Between her violation of his inner sanctum and how she managed to put all the pieces together, Jack vacillated between blind outrage and awe.

"I could call a security guard right now and get you escorted out of the building for what you did, you know that?"

"Yes, in handcuffs too."

His shoulders eased up a bit at her attempt to break the tension between them. "Don't be glib with me young lady, this is serious."

She nodded then began again. "No, no, I understand, but the ends did kind of justify the means. It was a stroke of luck that I even found the key." She reached into her bag, felt around, and then handed it to him. "I was here to put it all back." She pointed at his Yankee mug.

He didn't take it from her, so she placed it on the table.

"It was so shocking, horrible to read, and then the pounding *whys* made me crazy trying to figure it all out. You saw the tavern address on the bottom of the napkin too, weren't you curious, I mean, to find out what might have happened there?"

Jack shook his head, determined not to answer any questions. "Tell me who you found."

Jeannie sat up straighter and leaned in. He hadn't meant

to soften his tone and speak to her like a colleague. He was still furious, but also impressed. "I checked the yellow pages as far back as I could, nothing there, then decided to try the Atlanta Chamber of Commerce, but no *Ray's Tavern*. They gave me a list of a dozen or so eating establishments in a hundred-mile radius of Atlanta and I called them all until I learned that Ray had turned the place over to his son, who renamed it *Junior's*. His father still hangs around the place and so I got to talk to him."

"How did you accomplish that?

The corners of her mouth turned up a little. "I told Junior I was doing a story about roadside taverns outside of big cities, he bought it and so did his father, well, at first. I came clean pretty quickly. He seemed like a man who held a lot of secrets."

In his role as editor-in-chief, he'd have praised Jeannie's dogged persistence to locate her sources; it was the foundation of solid, crafty journalism, and she learned fast how to traverse the terrain.

"What did he tell you?" Jack didn't want this to drag out any longer.

She went into her bag again and pulled out an envelope. "I showed him this picture." She took the photo from the envelope and placed in on the table. "I asked if he recognized him, knowing it could be, as you say, a long shot. But then, he handed it back and told me he did. And then went into a story about Daddy talking to a guy at the bar until closing time. They both had too much to drink. Ray called the sheriff when he saw a car still in the lot. He'd done it before, he said he didn't want any drunk driving accidents leaving his bar. When he saw Daddy get arrested, he figured he'd sleep it off overnight, but then the sheriff came back the next day, had the car towed and ordered him to forget the incident altogether.

He said that had never happened before. He wasn't likely to forget it."

Jack leaned in and folded his hands on the table, his right leg now in full jiggle mode.

Jeannie went on. "He told me the guy's name was Hank Carlton, he'd been a regular customer, some real estate broker, very friendly. Ray said he didn't tell the sheriff who Daddy was drinking with, shouldn't have mattered and besides, like he explained, just a harmless regular. But then Hank never came back. Ray heard he'd gone up to Atlanta."

Not bad, Jack muttered to himself. If he wasn't so angry and unnerved, he'd tell her so.

She stopped. "Before I tell you about Hank, don't you have something to tell me?"

"What are you talking about?"

"C'mon Uncle Jack, you know why he got arrested."

He stood and wrapped his arms around his chest, then walked toward the door.

"Where are you going?"

He opened the door and looked both ways, closed it, then came back inside, but didn't sit. More than two decades later, he thought he'd be telling the truth to Cindy, instead of his niece. He wasn't sure if he'd feel relieved or sorry. He was exactly her age when it all happened.

"It took a day with an overnight stop at a motel to get down there," he said. "Two law enforcement men were waiting. They had papers ready for me to sign. I didn't understand. The fatter one spoke first, while the more official one went further and explained that the perpetrator had been put into the cell with his belt. A major procedural violation, afraid I might sue them over it. The fatter one said I should let it go, it wasn't a case that would get any public sympathy and would cause me and the family more shame. They took care of all the expenses. Records were adjusted and I was sent on my way. I never wanted to see, hear or think about Braselton again. So, to answer your question, no, I didn't do a thing but get back home in one piece, and then, well, I spent the next 22 years staying quiet and looking after you all."

They stared into one another's eyes. Jeannie got up and moved closer to him, but he held up his hand to stop her.

"Tell me about the guy."

She stopped like a gangly little girl unable to control her awkward body.

"He seemed to recognize my last name and at first, I couldn't understand how. One dinner, one night, and two decades in the past. I had the note and just wanted to talk to the last person to see Daddy alive, I wanted clues, you know, about his mental state. I don't know what happened next, but I ended up telling him about me, SDS, the arrest, Phil, all of it. Then, he gets all jumpy, coughing and getting a drink of water, sits back down, and after some long pauses, reveals that he was the one who paid my bail in Chicago, bought the ticket back to New York and hired Phil!"

Jack returned to the conference table and banged his hands on the surface. "*What?*"

"I had the same reaction, but much worse. He starts telling me his life story and then about being in the woods with Daddy, and how the sheriff found them. Hank had run away but went to the station at dawn the next morning just as an ambulance arrived. He left town, but the guilt, he said, stayed with him like unhealed fracture. He hired a private eye to find us. He was the one who arranged the scholarships that paid for our college tuitions and then when I got in trouble, he took care of it. Phil was sworn to secrecy."

Jack could not stop shaking his head back and forth. "This is unbelievable, how dare he!"

Jeannie looked surprised. "How dare he what? Tell me the truth?"

"Yes, to all of it. It wasn't his place. Who the hell does he think he is and what gave him the right to get involved in our family's business? He was the one who violated your father, not the other way around, it was all a big, tragic mistake, don't you get that? Walter, your father, was *not* like Hank." He'd never spoken his thoughts out loud, but he was too riled up to stop himself. He'd kept the secret pent up for years and years, and now, here he was, uttering his truth, and as far as he was concerned, the only truth.

The press drums began to rumble through the floorboards. Neither of them reacted. Jack looked at his watch, 9:15, the presses were 15 minutes off schedule.

Jeannie spoke up. "If it wasn't true, or somewhat true, why would Daddy take his own life? That makes no sense. It could have been sorted out if it was a mistake. But then the note, he pleaded with you not to tell. What more do you need?"

Jack raised his voice over the machines much louder than he needed. "I'm not having this discussion with you. It's been over for too long and while you succeeded in digging up his remains, I'm telling you to bury them again, do you hear me?"

She stood up. "Yes, I hear you, but no, that's not fair. Hank had no reason now to lie, and certainly no obligation to reach into his own pocket and pay for our college education. If it weren't for his guilty conscience, I probably would have been blown up on 11th Street!"

Jack clawed back at her words. "And if he hadn't done what *he* did, your father would have been alive to take care of you all."

"You can't say that! Neither of us knows the whole truth, but you're the one who needs to accept some of it. This can't be a secret anymore. You don't think it was a shock to find out? I could barely get food down my throat and forget about a full night's sleep since I found that napkin, it's all been interrupted by awful dreams. Like a film reel looping over and over again, it was the sequence as Hank described, but I'm the one catching the two of them, my own father, for god's sake with another man."

She took a deep breath. "Don't you see? I had to keep trying to sort it out, and realized the real tragedy is that people like Hank or Daddy have had to live a dreadful secret their whole lives, hoping and praying no one finds out. It's bad enough today, but in 1952, being arrested in Georgia, what were his options?"

Jack's stomach began to growl at him. "I'm going to say this one more time, and you need to listen very carefully." He didn't want to argue anymore, but she was treading on razor thin ice, too close to bringing down the entire family. "This investigation is over, you found your answers, you know who paid your bail, you know why Phil showed up just when he did, and most importantly, why he didn't cash those checks. He fell in love with you, and you, I suppose with him. Go back to him, tell *him* the truth and get on with your life."

The air was thick between them, neither moving for a few moments. Then, she leaned over the table, picked up the envelope with Walter's photo and stuffed it into her bag, leaving a wide berth between them as she headed for the door. Before closing it after her, she turned to him. "I'm sorry again for what I did, it was wrong. But unlike you, I cannot forget, and I won't forget." She left his door ajar.

He sat motionless until the press drums rolled to a stop.

The phone rang again, but he didn't pick it up. He wasn't accustomed to losing battles, and certainly not to sons, nieces or nephews. He didn't know what to think anymore, he didn't have the reserves to process this new turn of events on his own. As much as he hated to admit it, he needed help. It was time to tell Cindy.

"What happened to you?" She popped up from the couch and turned off the TV before accosting him at the door. He couldn't blame her for being both livid and anxious. It was late, after 10:00.

He saw her empty wine glass on the coffee table. He could use something stronger.

"I know it's not on the approved list, but I need a scotch."

Softening, she met him on the landing and put her hands on his face. "What's the matter? You look terrible."

Jack put his arms around her shoulders and pulled her in. She was in her night dress and robe, hair pins in little wheels along her cheeks, and no make-up, but he could still smell the residue of perfume along her neck. Cindy was, without a doubt, the best thing that ever happened to him. How could he have shut her out all these years? Either way, he was in the doghouse.

He pulled away. "Jeannie was at the office. Actually, I found her in my office snooping around. Let's sit down, we need to talk."

Cindy's eyes widened. "You're scaring me."

"Please, can you fix me that drink? Just one." She nodded slowly and went into the kitchen.

Jack took off his shoes and fell into his lounger. His body throbbed with fatigue, but unfortunately his mind was still racing through various scripts he had begun to play out on the cab ride home. He wanted to make the story less painful for her, but then confronted with the truth: the pain was his and his alone to bear.

She came back with a glass of scotch filled with more ice than alcohol and handed it to him. He took a decent sip, letting the liquid coat his throat.

"Why was she in your office? I thought you said she was sick."

He finished off the glass, and in seconds, felt a numbing fatigue. He really was exhausted, longing to get into bed and close his eyes. "It's a complicated story, and it's late. Can we talk in the morning?"

"Not a chance." Cindy settled into her spot on the corner of the couch adjacent to him. "We don't have any plans tomorrow and neither does Max. We have all night."

He'd have to count on the liquor to make the confession go down smoother.

"It's about Walter. He didn't die in a car accident; he took his own life." He knew that the shock of what he just said was like a slap her in her face, but he needed to get right to it.

Cindy reacted in slow motion. "Suicide? Your brother, oh my god, why? What happened, I'm not understanding..."

He reached out and took her hand. "He stopped at a tavern outside of Atlanta and had dinner, sat next to a local man, they both had too much to drink. Then something happened after they left the bar together. Walter got caught and arrested."

Jack knew he was being vague, but the details had lodged in the back of his throat.

Cindy could see his obvious discomfort. "For what?" She put her hand over her mouth, "What are you saying, that he and the guy...?"

He nodded without looking at her. "The crime and sentencing were the same then as it is now, a felony with up to ten years in prison. We could have fought it, but I guess he didn't believe he had a chance. All I got was this." He pulled the plastic bag out of his pants pocket and waved it toward her. He was moments from breaking down, they could both hear it in his voice.

Her hands were trembling as she took it from him. Cindy was now the napkin's fourth reader when it had been meant for his eyes only. She didn't need a reminder to be gentle. He watched her strain to absorb the faded words. When she looked back at him, there were tears in her eyes.

"This is unbelievable, I don't know what to say, it's too sad to imagine how he could have become that hopeless. How did he even do it, wasn't he in jail?" Her voice had gone shallow. Cindy had never met Walter; her only knowledge of him came from his mother, and briefly from his dad before he died. Bernice barely spoke about him, remaining in her martyr bubble. Jack channeled all his grief, resentment and pain inward. No surprise he developed an ulcer.

"Yes, that's the $64,000 question, isn't it?" He went into more detail to describe the creepy station and sleazy sheriffs, the deal he was conned into making and his excruciating 15-hour drive back to New York where he cried, screamed and then rehearsed the story he'd share with the family over and over until he started to believe it himself.

She got up and curled her body onto his lap. "Oh sweetheart, I'm so sorry. I wish you would have told me. I could have been a shoulder to lean on. You know that." She kissed his forehead and then his lips.

He was an idiot, but could he really be blamed for honoring his brother's last request? And for God's sake, he had only been 25 years old.

They sat for a while, then she tentatively looked into his

eyes. "What does this have to do with Jeannie being in your office?"

He then began her story, but Cindy stopped him before he got to the Chicago arrest.

"The guy paid for their college tuitions?" Cindy raised herself off of his lap and moved back to her perch on the couch.

"That's just the tip of it." He shared how Hank arranged the set-up with Phil and the uncashed checks, causing Jeannie to construct a ridiculous informant theory, until she finally learned that Hank was the one who'd pulled the strings.

Cindy got up and began to pace around the living room.

"I don't know what to think. I'm sure you've given it more thought, but now that Jeannie knows, will you or she, together, tell Bernice and Jeffrey? Your mother?"

Jack brought both hands to his head and massaged his scalp. "Tell them what? That Walter was supposedly a homo, had sex in the woods, was arrested and then killed himself? Oh, and that I kept it a secret for 22 years, until Jeannie, my ace reporter, broke the story."

Cindy looked at him with an expression he'd never seen before, squinty eyes and pursed lips, revulsion and disgust.

"Jack, please, you're being heartless and cruel."

"But I'm right. No matter how it's said, those are the facts, except about it being Walter's choice to go into those woods. I don't believe it and won't ever change my mind." He got up slowly from the recliner and went back into the kitchen. He needed another scotch, just a small shot, if he hoped to get any amount of sleep tonight.

Cindy didn't stop him or speak. Her gaze remained on the night sky.

He poured and drank the scotch while standing at the counter, and then returned to the living room. He walked over to his wife and lightly touched her arm.

She turned toward him. "I get that, Jack, but we'll never really know the truth. It shouldn't change, I sincerely hope, the caring big brother he was to you. Don't you think Jeannie has a right to her feelings too?"

"No, of course the Walter I grew up with will always be my Walter, but that's the whole point. You see, don't you? I had to tell Jeannie in no uncertain terms to keep her mouth shut, she's so sure her version, the one from Hank, is the truth. No, this needs to be the end of the line. She'd found what she was searching for, so enough is enough."

"What did she say to that?"

"What do you think?" Jack closed his eyes in defeat. "I'm terrified. She's like a bloodhound on the chase, and if she wants to take this story further, how can I stop her? I could fire her, but let's face it, between Bernice and my mother, I don't know who'd torture me more. It's a simmering pot at the moment, and if I, or we, can somehow prevent the full boil, then maybe she'll let it die out on its own accord."

Cindy piped in. "We? No, honey, I can't do this with you. If she comes to me and wants to talk, I will be there for her. I don't want to see her follow in your footsteps and get sick over it. But don't worry, I won't breathe a word of our conversation outside of this room."

Jack knew Cindy would stay silent. She was raised like him, during the Depression where they shared similar beliefs about family business, struggles or personal tragedies staying private and hidden if necessary. If Jack was given the choice, he never would have broken his brother's confidence. But for their offspring growing up in an age of conflict and rapid change, the landscape had shifted. Jack understood that for Jeannie's generation, there were no assurances of a better outcome if they just stayed quiet and waited it out, and the more they fought the status quo, the more obvious it was that a fight was necessary. He might have come with a different set of sensibilities, but he wasn't naïve about what the next generation had inherited.

He put his arm around Cindy's and together they stared out at the starry night.

"Will you ever forgive him?" Cindy kept her gaze at the window.

"For taking his life?"

"No, for the reason he did." She tilted her head up toward his eyes.

Jack didn't know how to respond. She didn't know Walter at all, there was no point taking it any further, at least, not tonight. His biggest concern was what his niece might do next. He let a few moments pass between them, then wrapped her up in his arms, and whispered into her ear.

"Not going to be able to put the Jeannie back in the bottle, am I?"

She shook her head. "Not a chance."

## Chapter 16

# JUNE – AUGUST 1974

# *Jeannie*

URING THE PLANE TRIP back from Atlanta, she knew she had to find another place to live. It was shamefully overdue. Grammy and Uncle Pauley had immediately taken her in—like a stray dog begging for shelter—over a year ago, and would never admit how she disrupted their lives. Her coming and going at all hours of the day and night, eating their food and believing if she stayed on the fringes of their routines, all would be fine. It was meant to be temporary, a refuge where she could pull herself together, she had assured them, but Grammy's house became a protective bunker where she could plan and strategize with virtually no limitations. She had offered to pay rent, buy food, help around the house, but her grandmother wouldn't budge. Instead, she slept in a cozy clean room, nibbled whatever her grandmother kept stocked for her, and could count on leftovers just in case. In return for their kindness and generosity, Jeannie only occasionally joined them for dinner and some weekend breakfast chats. Grammy and Uncle Pauley remained patient with her evasive responses to their questions, and no matter how hard they pried, Jeannie could become abrupt and testy when they crossed boundaries about work projects or Phil. How they put up with her for so long was beyond belief. Guilt had been a by-product, but she understood their help was automatic because they loved her. Even so, she should have spent

more time in their company, not less. She had to leave. It was
hard enough to avoid Grammy's eyes those few days after
she found the heartbreaking napkin, but now that she knew
about Hank, it would be impossible to remain in such close
proximity. At least not until she could sort it out with her
uncle. Without having to shell out rent money, Jeannie saved
enough to feel financially secure to finally be on her own, and
spent two oddly enjoyable weeks scouring the rental markets,
selecting a handful of promising apartments to check out.
She called in sick to devote a full day to visiting the different
properties. It was a tight schedule, requiring multiple points
of coordination with owners and managers and lots of fretting if a subway train took more than five minutes to appear.
Because Fridays were less hectic at the paper, she chose that
day for her search, believing no one would miss her.

The last apartment she visited, a small one-bedroom in
Chelsea hadn't been the best, but it was nestled in what seemed
like a safe neighborhood. She walked in and out of trendy
shops, navigated to convenient subway stations, and observed
friendly body language on the streets. *Victory*, she told herself,
as she finished a slice of pizza at a busy Italian place a few
blocks from the prospective apartment. Before catching the
subway back to *The Globe*, she called the building manager
from a phone booth and told him she'd take it. When he
confirmed that she could have the keys the following week,
Jeannie felt her feet float off the ground, relieved not giddy, a
burden lifted. When was the last time she was this hopeful?
She could be settled into her first apartment with no roommates as soon as next week.

Before heading back to her grandmother's, Jeannie needed
to make one more critical stop. She arrived at *The Globe* lobby
20 minutes before the 9:00 p.m. press run, giving her time to

get in and out of the building before the drums rolled.

She had never known her uncle to return to the office in the evening. He'd work late, but once exiting the lobby doors, he didn't come back. Maybe if the massive press drums exploded and the building caught fire, then yes. Otherwise, not likely.

So, when his office door flew open and there he was, a snorting bull ready to charge, her heart nearly stopped beating. Red-handed and ashamed of sneaking into his office, she tried to hold it together, but his raised voice and clenched jaw frightened her into tears. If she hadn't stopped for the pizza, she could have returned the napkin and key an hour earlier.

Full disclosure was the only route out of the mess; besides, Jeannie knew he would assert the pressure until she had nothing left to hide. Jeannie expected to be scolded, chastised and even punished for her indiscretion, but to threaten to escort her out of the building? No other time in their relationship had he been so unrestrained in his anger and disappointment. She'd also never given him a reason, even when she went to Ann Arbor with SDS, and all that went so completely awry afterwards. He'd kept his disapproval to a minimum and gave her a second chance with a job at the paper.

For the first ten minutes of his interrogation, she felt like he'd never look at her the same way again, that she'd broken his trust and he wouldn't love her so much anymore. She'd observed this man her whole life and courage under fire was what he demanded of himself and expected of others. Anxious for his approval and feeling lucky to be in his world, his reporters all strove to crank out well-researched work under heavy time pressure. Earning his loyalty and acceptance was a dream for any upcoming journalist. She had taken an enormous risk without considering that if caught, she could lose her job and worse, his respect, and maybe, his love. Being the Chief's niece naturally gave her a leg up over any candidate and a reserved chair in the pit, but she didn't want favoritism. No room for slip-ups; maintain a high bar just like her seasoned co-workers; long hours, nights and weekends. But she knew that had Uncle Jack walked in on another reporter, there would be no calls to the police or the building's security guard. Instead, the offender would be on his knees begging for mercy or submitting a resignation right on the spot.

She started by asking for mercy, but he was too mad to soften up. She didn't blame him; she'd done the unthinkable. But there was another side to it. Nervously sputtering through her story, she detected a flicker in his eyes when she got to the part about finding the bar, then Ray and finally, Hank. There had been lucky breaks at each juncture, but still, she had demonstrated unwavering grit and determination, qualities he could take credit for. She didn't expect Uncle Jack to praise her efforts, but neither did she expect to be commanded into silence and then cut off. She'd only had a vague idea of her father, gathered from a few faded photos of him holding her tiny body. Still, she had to vigorously push away the image of him in that cell, scribbling his last words and doing what he did. Everything she had discovered: his outing in the woods, the note requesting Uncle Jack's silence, a cover-up by a careless sheriff, and an astounding intervention by a stranger named Hank, was all distressingly true.

Yet her uncle was telling her to let it go, and even worse, shove it all back into the same unmarked grave.

"Don't test me young lady, this isn't up for negotiation."

"But you can't mean this!" She pleaded with him.

It was like ordering his reporters to put the brakes on their 18-month Watergate investigation in the final lap of the race. They would fight like hell to convince him otherwise and that's what she'd have to do, but in what form and how, would take time to plan.

The next morning, she sat with Grammy and Uncle Pauley at the breakfast table. A moment before she was about to break the news, Grammy spoke up.

"Where were you yesterday, sweetheart? Uncle Jack said you were sick." She poured Uncle Pauley another cup of coffee, and then topped hers off.

Jeannie nibbled at her toast. "Yeah, well that's all been straightened out with him. I did call in sick, but I spent the day looking at apartment rentals. I found one in Manhattan, much closer to the paper and can move in anytime. It'll take a week or so to get the basic furnishings, like a bed, dresser, not too much to haul in." She paused and shifted her gaze between them. "You both know I overstayed my welcome by a year or so."

Uncle Pauley spoke up, "It's good news for you, honey, no young woman should be living with old coots like us."

Jeannie leaned over and gently touched his wrinkled hand.

"You didn't overstay, darling," Grammy added. "We loved having you here." More prone to tearing up at the any hint of sentimentality, Grammy pulled her trusty tissue from the sleeve of her robe and wiped the corners of her eyes.

"Where in Manhattan?" Uncle Pauley looked over his glasses as he sipped his coffee.

"Chelsea, it's small, but cozy. I know it was a quick decision, but I walked around the neighborhood browsing shops and restaurants. The residents look like people my age and well, I guess I could use some new friends."

Grammy faced her head on. "But not before the wedding, I mean that would be too much, don't you think?"

No, Jeannie thought to herself, it's precisely what she

needed to do. Her nerves were already on high alert and if she had to endure one more nitpicking detail about her brother's wedding, she was afraid she'd lose it. Whatever it took, even if she had to sleep on the floor, she'd be in her new place by next week. She needed to be alone and get her wits together before the big event. Roz had asked her first cousin to be the maid of honor and told, rather than asked, Jeannie to be one of her bridesmaids. She had been fitted a few months ago for the dress, a hideous design appealing to no one else except Grace Vincie, who loved lavender taffeta and puffy sleeves. To Jeannie, it felt like everyone would be joyously celebrating the wedding except her. She had reentered another version of her private universe and sadly would get no help from her uncle, the only person who could empathize.

"Well, not really, I only have a few suitcases for clothes. I'll look for a bed today at Macy's and I think mom can part with my old dresser and a bunch of hangers. Dishes, silverware and bedding are easy enough to pick up too."

Grammy got up and took her plate to the sink. "I can come with you today, sweetheart, it's good to have another opinion, you don't want to rush into purchases you'll later regret."

Jeannie would have enjoyed her company too. But unlike the other confidences held back from her grandmother, she had to be extra vigilant about hiding the trip to Atlanta. Grammy would ask for more details about D.C., then also the supposed weekend in Miami, and the lies would keep piling up. Jeannie wasn't strong enough yet to deflect them.

"Thanks for the offer, but I've got to meet the apartment manager, and then run around to a bunch of stores. If I see you turn up your nose at any of my purchases, I will return them. Okay?"

Drying her hands on a dishrag, Grammy gave her a sideways

look. "Fine, I have a list of errands around town too. Then will we be seeing you later for dinner?"

Jeannie picked up her plate and Uncle Pauley's, whose face was hidden behind the morning paper, and walked them to the sink. She leaned down and kissed the top of her grandmother's head. "Not sure, depends on my productivity, remember I need to go over to mom's and see what she's willing to part with. That could cause delays."

"Yes, of course, alright, we will hope to see you later tonight."

Jeannie took two steps at a time up the stairs and grabbed the yellow pad on her nightstand. After her stressful encounter with Uncle Jack, it had taken hours to fall asleep, and when she did, her sleep was dreamless and fitful. She had tried to read, but couldn't absorb more than a paragraph, so she had retrieved her pad and jotted down the weekend to do list. She'd call the manager and arrange to get the key, sign papers, and pay the deposit and first month's rent on Monday after work. This would free up the day to stop at her mother's and then drive around Queens looking for deals.

She showered quickly, threw on a light-weight shift and sandals and braced herself for a sweaty day in and out of her old funky VW bug. Jeannie knew she should have called first, but her mother has been so on edge with the wedding that it seemed better to just surprise her.

The car's interior was stuffy but had retained a little of the overnight chill. She only drove her beat up car on the weekends and hoped Grammy would agree to keep it out front after the move. She didn't need or could afford to keep the car in the Manhattan, but it would be nice to have it around just in case.

Both her mother and Marty's cars were parked in the narrow driveway. Before walking up the familiar path, Jeannie balled her hands into a fist, opening and closing them several times for circulation. Now that her mom had a boyfriend, Jeannie had to knock on her childhood front door and wait for a response before turning the knob.

"Coming, just a minute." She heard her mother's feet tapping down the hallway.

"Jeannie! What are you doing here?" She was still in her robe. "Come in, honey."

"Hey Mom, sorry I didn't call first." They hugged; the smell of bacon clung to her hair.

"That's fine, we were just finishing up breakfast, I can make you a plate."

She followed her mother into the kitchen. "No already ate, thanks." Marty was standing by the sink in sweatpants and a t-shirt. "Hey Jeannie, to what do we owe this pleasure?" He gave her a hug too.

"Let's all sit, and I'll tell you."

Her mother poured her a cup of coffee and sat down. "Is something wrong?"

"No, no, actually, it's good news." She went into the details about the new apartment and kept her tone upbeat. Marty thought it was exciting, but her mother seemed less enthusiastic.

"Why so sudden, and couldn't you have waited until after the wedding?" It wasn't that uncanny that her grandmother had expressed the exact sentiment, they were practically joined at the hip these days, especially about the wedding.

She assured them it would be fine, then went right into her plan for getting the apartment essentials over the weekend.

"I was hoping you could donate to the cause and let me take my old dresser?" She asked as if it was an afterthought, not wanting her mother to believe the only purpose of her visit was to get the furniture.

"Oh, alright dear, but the drawers aren't empty. I've been storing things in them, mostly papers. Let me see if there's any room left in Jeffrey's wardrobe."

Marty piped in. "Got movers?"

Jeannie figured she'd need a small U-Haul but hadn't gotten that far in corralling the extra bodies to help her carry the big stuff.

"I'll rent a truck, and maybe see if some of the guys at the gas station want to make a few bucks." Not a bad idea once it came out of her mouth.

"I can help too, so put me on the list." He winked at her.

"You're on, Mr. Cohen. Okay, I gotta get going."

Her mother followed her down the hallway. "Keep me informed on the move, you know, it's such a busy time for me right now."

Jeannie got the hint. "So yeah, how are you holding up with the wedding stuff? Hard to be the mother of the groom, huh?"

"You have no idea what that woman is like. Grace Vincie might have just about the worst taste in everything. I gave in to all her demands to make sure that Jeffrey and Roz would be married under a chuppah with the traditional glass breaking. All about compromises, and I've got Marty to thank for that."

Jeannie gave her a parting squeeze. "You should be happy you get to wear your own dress. Remember I'm in the purple lace bridesmaid disaster!" Her mother smiled and pinched her cheek.

"Good luck today, sweetie."

It did turn out to be a lucky day, from parking spots to great sales to no humidity. She didn't want to return to Grammy's for dinner and so decided to stop at Sal's Pizzeria for a bite.

She arrived during the height of the Saturday night dinner rush, but thankfully managed to find an empty spot at the counter. The waitress appeared in moments and took Jeannie's order with a friendly bounce to her step.

Her glass of red wine came first and by the time the spaghetti arrived, she had less than a sip left, so she ordered another glass. She was glad the alcohol buzz had drowned out most of the background table bantering, leaving only faint melodies from the jukebox. She didn't see Sal at the ovens, which was a relief. She wanted to be alone to think. The food absorbed some of her second glass of wine, but still left a lightness around her head and down her spine. If she hadn't been living under her grandmother's roof for the past year, Jeannie wondered whether a nightly bottle of wine would have become the routine escape from stress, and loneliness. With Phil, and his bartender job, he rarely drank at all, and if he did, it was to be polite and share a glass with her. She still thought about him almost every day, but particularly when she had had a few too many. The image was visceral and always the same; Phil's mouth exploring hers, the gentle stroke of his hands on her neck, along her waist and beyond. She wished she could go back to the way it was, rewind to the moments before she opened his drawer and found those god-damned checks.

Hank had come to Phil's rescue, and rightly so, but when her uncle chided her after her return from Atlanta to call Phil, implying that she owed him the apology, it felt too late to circle back. Clichés danced around her muddled brain, *water under the bridge, crying over spilt milk,* or the most depressing one, *that ship has sailed.* Being wrong about Phil's ties to the FBI was humbling, but then to learn he'd been hired by the man who had been with her father that night and all that came next, had been too much to absorb. On the other hand, Hank also revealed that Phil had still not cashed his checks.

She glanced at her watch, only nine; Grammy and Uncle

Pauley would still be up watching television. Jeannie needed somewhere else to go, but her choices were pitifully limited. Roz and Jeffrey popped up first, but it would take 25 minutes or so to make the drive, and her slightly blurred vision put the kibosh on that. It was a long shot, too. They'd probably be out with friends or more likely, wrapping over a hundred wedding favors. She could just see Jeffrey tying tiny bows on boxes filled with hard-shelled Jordan almonds or whatever Mrs. Vincie had decided on. If her cousin Scotty was in town, she'd have phoned him, not to confide, but to be entertained. Jeannie looked forward to seeing him at the wedding, but he was the only one. With the exception of Roz, how had she ended up with no real friends at 25 years old? Meeting Jim so early on, she hadn't formed any solid attachments at Barnard, not even her roommate, and the SDS folks were never really friends. She'd spent almost two years with Phil and his cohorts; but they were all gone now and whether it was her doing or not, she was never invited into the inner circle at the paper.

She paid her bill and wobbled a bit out on the crowded street. Her car was somewhere on the next block; she'd have to concentrate to remember exactly where or on what side of the street she had parked. Each step felt heavier, fatigue coming over her so fast she almost curled into a little ball and passed out on the sidewalk. "Keep moving," she muttered to herself just as a tall guy in front of her turned her way with a nasty look. "Take it easy, bitch." Even though it was very dark, she told herself that he was just a teenager acting tough to impress his friends. Moving away from him, she weaved through the bodies lining the sidewalk and leaned her back against a storefront, close to tears. Directly in front of her was a phone booth. She hurried to it, and closed herself in. She pulled out the bar's business card Phil gave her the first time they met, then fumbled for a coin in her wallet, dropped it into the slot, and dialed the number. After four rings, a gruff voice picked up, shouting "Frankie's" over the background roar. Not Phil. "Oh hi, is Phil Reeder working tonight?"

"No, hasn't worked here in a year." And then he hung up.

She should have figured that he wouldn't be bartending forever. The call producesd a jolt of adrenaline. She turned the card over, tracing her finger over his nearly illegible letters, bringing her back to their bench looking out over the Hudson River along 72nd street, where he'd written his apartment address and home phone number. She couldn't bring herself to call that number, wanting so much to hear his voice but unable to bear the disappointment if the robotic message "the number has been disconnected" came on, eliminating her last link to Phil. She left the booth and walked to her car as briskly as her tired legs could manage. Glancing around at the familiar landmarks of her family neighborhood, Jeannie knew she didn't belong there anymore. She was glad she had found the new apartment.

There were glitches all week with department store deliveries and securing both the U-Haul and helpers. She enlisted Jeffrey who said he'd help Marty load up her things from Grammy's as well as the dresser from her mother the following Saturday. She left work early on three consecutive days to meet the manager and be at the apartment for deliveries. She didn't make any excuses for her absences. Her uncle noticed her unusual activity and on Friday morning, asked her to come see him in his office.

"Were you going to tell me about the move?" The morning light from his window outlined his head and torso.

"Yeah, sure. I've just been juggling a lot."

"I guess so. I am happy for you, that's all. Can we call a truce here?"

She didn't know how to react. A conciliatory gesture, maybe, but far short of an apology or a revocation of his gag order.

"Are we in a battle of some kind?"

He leaned back in his chair, crossed his hands with his index fingers touching, like the church in the steeple gesture. "No, in fact, we are on the same side."

She looked into his eyes. "If you mean to go on as if nothing has happened, then no, we're not."

He wheeled his chair forward. "Don't do anything rash, please. I'm asking you to consider the serious costs to our family."

She stood up. "I need to get back to work. Ernie's piled it on today."

Thankfully the Saturday logistics worked out as the family rallied around her. Jeffrey and Marty arrived at Grammy's front door at 9:00 a.m. sharp, delighted to find that she had prepared a huge tray of bagels and lox for the movers. Her mother came along, bringing a bag full of extra linen and towels, then helped with last minute packing. And Cindy called, offering to lend Max's muscle. She thanked Cindy—it was nice of her to offer—but told her they already had plenty of help and got off the phone. Jeannie wondered how much Cindy knew about her father's death, or for that matter, what had transpired between her and her uncle over the past few weeks. When she got settled into her new place, she'd ask her aunt to come over to help decorate so she could test the waters.

By late afternoon, Jeannie's new apartment was littered with boxes, suitcases and furniture. Jeffrey, Marty and her mother had insisted on helping get the big stuff squared away and then, exhausted and hungry, they left together to explore the neighborhood, following their noses to a steak restaurant several blocks away.

They ate heartily, with several bottles of wine and toasts to her new life. Jeffrey got looser and gossiped about the wedding, making them all laugh with harmless stories of his future mother-in-law's antics, all told in her nasally Italian accent. Marty kept the giggles going with his jokes and her mother's eyes dazzled with profound contentment. Jeannie had rarely seen her mother this happy. It would have been idyllic if only she had remained as blissfully ignorant as her family.

The next five days sailed by. She actually looked forward to her new commute—just ten minutes on the train—and enjoyed setting up the apartment and even shopping for her own food. She just needed to get through the wedding Saturday evening without falling apart.

It took more time than she allotted to get the scratchy purple gown over her head and settled in the right places on her body. Afraid she was cutting it too close, she hurried out of the door of her apartment and threw her hand up to hail a cab to Queens, as a few passers-by stared at her god-awful bridesmaid outfit. By the time she arrived, the balmy day had given way to a less humid, and pleasant, late afternoon. Roz would be relieved as the ceremony was taking place in an expansive garden area outside the Knights of Columbus reception hall. They didn't want it to be religious, so avoided the fraught choice between a rabbi or priest. It was to be a civil ceremony with a justice of the peace. Her mother got her way with the chuppah, but the rest of the reception decor, including the food, band and order of events was all Grace and her Italian clan.

Jeannie finished a glass of champagne during the formal photo session and then downed another one just before the ceremony began. Besides distracting herself from the binding dress and stiff satin heels, the buzz would help her manage the onslaught of pitiful looks for not having a plus-one, and laugh off any conversations about the paper, or how 'your Uncle Jack is treating you.' She wanted a break from thinking about their secret.

Roz's gown was lovely, the bustier showing off ample cleavage against her flawless olive skin. Jeffrey looked smart and formal in his tuxedo and tails, like a concert pianist ready to enthrall an audience at Carnegie Hall. Both her mother and grandmother wore tasteful shades of blue and lavender to match the wedding theme, and Aunt Cindy subtly outdid everyone in a brightly flowered sleeveless dress that narrowed at her waist and knees. The lacy shawl over her shoulders matched to a tee. The groomsmen wore dark blue suits and looked as if they couldn't wait to change back into their jeans and t-shirts. She scanned the room one last time before the wedding march: couples, all ages, matching up, smiling and anticipating the happy event. Why couldn't Phil be here too, holding her hand and sharing the moment. Where was he? What was he up to? He wasn't at Frankie's Pub anymore, and he never talked about future plans. He could be anywhere doing anything.

Tears of joy, then a burst of cheers followed Jeffrey's stomp on the napkin-covered wine glass, making their union official. From that moment on, Jeannie, drinking steadily, became a distant observer flitting from one person to another, smiling and clicking glasses. When asked about herself, she gave a prepared answer: "All good, moved into a place in Chelsea, work has been very busy with the Watergate stuff." If pressed, she'd add a few lines about going to D.C. Then she was off before anyone had a chance to ask about her own love life and make her feel even sadder that she didn't have one, or had one, and lost it. As the night wore on, her reflexes grew slower, and she found herself trapped in a conversation with her mother's librarian friend.

"Hold on there, Missy. What about you? Got a fella?" She winked at her.

"Not at the moment, but if you let me go, I promise to look for one here." She smiled and danced away in tune to the band's melody. She then did the requisite spin around the floor with her brother, then Uncle Pauley, and finally Uncle Jack.

"Everything went off well, don't you think?" He spoke over the music.

Jeannie avoided his eyes and pretended to be happy. "Yes, so far so good."

After the toasts, the cake and last song, the scattered guests waited their turn for a final congratulatory hug from Jeffrey and Roz. All the liquor she had consumed was making her head spin and stomach flip; somehow, she made it to the bathroom and splashed water on her face. The next thing she clearly remembered was being back at her apartment the following morning when she woke up with dress marks embedded into her skin, but thankfully her aching feet had been freed from the painful heels. She found her cousin Scotty's note explaining that he had found her in the garden lying under the chuppah after she got sick, cleaned her up and, with Max's help, drove her back into the city, carrying her inert body into the apartment.

Terribly hungover and mortified by her behavior, Jeannie stayed holed up in her apartment on Sunday, letting the answering machine absorb the stream of family calls. It had been coming for a while, but between Atlanta and the wedding hoopla, she felt like she was drowning and struggling to keep going. Phil would have understood. She missed his affection, of course, but his friendship and loyalty most of all. The pounding headache and queasy stomach lasted all day. It hurt even to lift her head off the pillow.

Aunt Cindy was the one who showed up that evening with a care package. Jeannie thought she didn't want the company, but when her aunt wrapped her willowy arms around her at the door, she hugged her back and sniffled into her shoulder.

"Oh, there now, honey. It's okay, let's get something soothing in your stomach and relax a bit." She picked up her shopping bags and followed Jeannie inside.

"Well now, you're practically moved in. It's so darling, really."

She set the bags down on the kitchen counter. "You have room for a little table and two chairs in this corner. I'll keep poking around. We want to get you a few housewarming gifts."

Aunt Cindy got busy arranging a plate of take-out roasted chicken, mashed potatoes and a tossed salad. She grabbed a fork from Jeannie's new silverware set, tore off a piece of paper towel and took her plate into the living room, setting it down on a packing box that was serving as a temporary coffee table.

"I love the couch too; the rust color will be easy to find matching pillows. Is it comfy?"

"You tell me, you're the first guest to sit on it."

Jeannie sat on one of the folding chairs that Marty had donated from his basement and picked up her plate. With the first bite, she realized she was hungrier than she thought, and tried not to eat too fast.

"This is really delicious, thank you so much." She chewed through the sentence.

Her aunt leaned back, slipped off her shoes and curled her legs underneath her. "Our pleasure. It was your uncle's idea."

Aunt Cindy didn't beat around the bush. "Can we have a heart-to-heart talk sweetie? I have been meaning to get in touch since you returned from your trip. And then, with the wedding and all, well, anyway it seems like the dust has settled a bit."

Jeannie cleaned her plate, got up and went into the kitchen. "I'm making myself some tea; would you like a cup?"

"Yes, thank you. And look inside the bag, there's some dessert."

She boiled the water, got out two cups and put the bakery cookies her aunt had brought on a small plate. Cindy had gotten up to browse around the place, making encouraging comments and suggestions. "Here's where the bookshelf should be, and you'll be needing a small desk, I assume. Not at Macy's, I know some great little second-hand stores; we can go to together."

Jeannie carefully set down the mugs and plate on the cardboard box. "I think I'll be needing a coffee table or dining room set before anything else."

They sat back down and sipped their tea. Jeannie popped a chocolate shortbread cookie into her mouth. "Yum, I'm feeling like a person again."

Aunt Cindy smiled, and then paused for a few moments before speaking up.

"I didn't know about your father. Your uncle just told me after he found you in his office. It's been keeping me up at night, too. If you hadn't found that note, none of us would have learned it from your uncle. Jack also told me about Hank, what he did for you and his theory about your father's disposition, or whatever we want to call it."

Jeannie interrupted. "Homosexual. And it wasn't a theory."

"Jeannie, please, you don't know that for certain."

She sat up on her knees. "The evidence speaks for itself. He took his own life, for god's sake, and left a note that held

Uncle Jack captive his whole life."

Her aunt reached for her tea and took a sip. "Okay, okay. I get it. But what now? We can't change the past. And for the rest of your family, do you believe it would help them to know the truth?"

Jeannie had thought of little else. "I'm not sure, but can you now say you wished you didn't know the truth? I felt so incredibly sad at first and like Uncle Jack, blamed Hank. Then I shifted into rage at those sheriffs, the fat one who probably told him that what he'd done was unforgivable. Being different like that was, as Hank said, considered a crime against nature, and in the south, a life sentence. He said they will always be labeled the worst kind of deviant, forcing people like him to settle for a lonely life. In his case, it meant hiding out in his big house on an isolated hill." Jeannie watched her aunt unfold her legs and place them on the floor.

"Look, I've gone over it and tried to discount Hank's story too, but even if my father got too drunk, and had been taken against his will, why had he lost hope for a resolution? Innocent people are arrested every day, but for *this* crime, this act, there will never be a fair trial. This is the story that needs to be told." Jeannie had raised herself up onto the couch and stared into her aunt's eyes.

"So, what are you saying? You want to write something about what happened to your father? Not in your uncle's paper? You can't be serious, Jeannie."

"I am, but it will take time, good research and live sources. I'm going to pitch a column theme to Ernie tomorrow. He's had me doing local fluff pieces for a month, which have just been fillers to get people's eyes on something else besides Nixon's descent into hell."

She shook her head. "What's your idea?"

Jeannie jumped up and got her yellow pad. "I've been thinking about it for the past two months." She sat right next to
her aunt so they could look at her notes together.

"It's about injustice, but also the courage and perseverance
it takes to make things right. I know a little about this as, well,
you know, I've been an insider. It's about young people like
me who have had enough and started organizing to stop and
change a system that keeps us all scared, powerless and hidden.
It will document the people who step up, keep on fighting,
while others surrender, or worse, look away. Papers devote
70% of copy on breaking news, finances and sports, along
with human-interest pieces that I and a few others toss in,
and then there's the editorial guys who write opinions about
anything topical and juicy. But since I've been at *The Globe*,
there hasn't been an engaging, true interest story theme, something to serialize, make readers want to keep coming back for
more. There are plenty of heroic people who have resisted
and keep on resisting and blowing whistles. If not for those
guys at the *Washington Post* who dug up people willing to
put their lives on the line to tell the truth, Nixon would have
kept on deceiving us." She stopped and pointed to her list of
categories. "I want to showcase women's rights, civil rights,
the poor who have no rights and then, of course, gay rights. I
could ease into this last one."

Leaning back on the couch, her aunt tilted her head side-to-
side, and then looked at her watch. "It sounds like a promising
idea, but a big one for sure. Don't you think your uncle might
want to hear it first, I mean, before Ernie?" She stood up and
smoothed over her dress.

Jeannie stood too. "Yeah, maybe, but Ernie's my direct
boss though."

Before leading the way to the kitchen, her aunt gave her

a sideways glance and shook her head. Jeannie didn't know what to make of the look and didn't want to feel any doubt about her plan. Her aunt picked up her pocketbook and headed for the door.

She thanked her for the food, for listening and then gave her a big hug.

"One last thing, sweetheart, please don't dredge up your family's past. In our case, ignorance has served us well. In the meantime, I'll put in a good word with the chief."

. . .

JEANNIE DIDN'T TAKE HER aunt's advice to talk with her uncle first but met with Ernie a few weeks later. Before pitching her idea, Jeannie wanted to make sure he'd have only minimal questions or concerns, so had prepared a thorough plan of who she would contact, when, how, the themes, all of it. He seemed impressed, nodding here and there, as he read her proposal. A few days later, he summoned her to his office, told her the chief was on board, and gave her the green light.

It took two months of running around the city interviewing advocates, activists, professors of history and social science, giving her more than enough copy to fill up her bi-weekly column, titled "Getting So Much Resistance" after a lyric from a Buffalo Springfield song she and her SDS comrades had sung over and over. She completed three two-part articles with first person accounts. The first focused on reproductive rights, and the Supreme Court's recent Roe vs. Wade decision. She managed to get interviews at the New York chapter of the National Organization of Women with a few fiery leaders who then referred her to the small staff of women from the Boston Women's Health Collective. The Boston group gave her an autographed copy of their published manual called

*Our Bodies, Ourselves.* It was the best road trip she'd ever been on, the women she met were so inspiring that she actually considered leaving the paper and joining up with them. The next two-part piece spotlighted the grassroots activists who were organizing in Harlem, Hunts Point and Bushwick for better jobs, wages and health care. This path took her to some of the city's grittiest neighborhoods, where too many times she wanted to abandon the project, frightened by the hungry and suspicious eyes that watched her from alleys and doorways. But witnessing the devotion and tireless efforts of those committed organizers gave her the inspiration to persist. She owed it to them to write an honest account and let the public know that there were many residents who still cared about their communities.

While Ernie and her uncle had been encouraging of her series idea, she worried it wouldn't be the success she envisioned. But, after several letters to the editor praising her work came across their desks, they each took her aside and congratulated her. As a boost to the staff, letters to the editor from readers about stories they liked were posted on the bulletin board in the break room. Howie and some of the guys in her pod actually patted her on the back when a few had her name on it. Now it was finally time for the story she had wanted to write from the beginning.

It wasn't as hard as she thought, though none of the men would give her their real names. Each one told her about growing up in confusion that turned to despair. Their bodies not responding to the girls and women around them and struggling every day to fit in. They shared anecdotes about the tough guys who could sniff out their tendencies and then prey on their fears. Two of the guys she interviewed had been engaged to high school girlfriends; one went through with it and separated from his wife a year later, while the other left his hometown before the wedding and hasn't been back since. They confessed that at great risk, they'd look for others like them in dark bars and seedy hangouts. One man spoke about being in the thick of Stonewall and how it emboldened him to come out and work for change. It took three weeks to gather the stories and write them up in a thoughtful and cohesive piece. A day before her scheduled deadline, she went back and cut out 350 words, leaving her space to add her own story. She started it at work and then finished up on the portable typewriter that fit perfectly on the oak desk Aunt Cindy had bought for her as a housewarming gift.

She woke up early, showered quickly and got to work at 7:45 a.m. Uncle Jack's door was open and as she rounded the corner to his office, she heard him on the phone. Resisting the temptation to eavesdrop, she went back to her desk and stuffed her purse into the side file drawer. The newsroom was a mess after a week of chasing headlines about Nixon's resignation, Gerald Ford's swearing in and then, of course, the pardon. They all knew it was coming. She'd been in her own world, distancing herself from the work chatter and competitiveness for months, until she was finally given her due as an almost equal. She knew that being a woman would keep her on the second rung of the ladder, but maybe those women in Boston would do something about that someday.

She returned to her uncle's office and waited until she heard him place the receiver back in the cradle. It was nearly eight and he wouldn't have another quiet moment before her deadline.

"Good morning, Chief." She peeked into his door frame.

"Hey, you're here a little early. C'mon in. What's up?" He picked up his Yankee mug and took a sip out of it.

"I have the final column ready, and I wanted you to read it

before I gave it to Ernie." She put the pages on his desk blotter.

"Right this minute?"

"Could you? It's important."

He put on his bifocals, picked up his pen and leaned over her work.

As always, he started to make edits. Then he must have gotten to her new addition, because he dropped his pen and stared at her.

"What are you doing?"

"I'm finishing up the piece." She kept her head high.

"This isn't going in."

"But it doesn't use any names, it's a story I found in my travels. It's the right ending. No one is going to get it except you, Aunt Cindy and me. But the men I talked to, and everyone like them, will understand. It's going to raise awareness about the outrageous penal codes in places like Georgia, and maybe, prevent anyone else from losing hope."

He scribbled some more, then looked into her eyes. "It's a more controversial piece, you'll get questions, including from your mother and grandmother."

She didn't back down. "I'll answer them, don't worry, I've kept the secret, haven't I?"

"I'll run it by Ernie. But don't be upset if he goes with some stronger editing."

She got up and walked to the door. "Oh, I won't. I'll just find another paper to get it published in if I have to."

• • •

***The NY Globe Series: Getting So Much Resistance***
By Jeannie Glazer
*(continued from page 1)*
**Nobody's Right if Everybody's Wrong: Untold Stories**

MY LAST STORY WAS shared by an older, southern man who decades before, had stopped at his local watering hole for a nightcap. Seated at the bar was an out-of-towner who wandered in after hours of highway driving. The regular sat down on the adjacent stool and slowly, with each round, engaged the stranger in honest talk, encouraging an easy flow between them. The regular took a risk with deeper glances into the stranger's eyes, deciphering a coded language. He'd seen it before. By the last round, the regular leaned in so close that the intimate moment between them was unmistakable. Closing time, they walked out together. The stranger had too many drinks and when he nearly tripped over his own feet, the regular took hold of his arm, leading him to his car at the far end of the lot. The stranger fumbled at the door, the regular gently took the keys from his hand, then guided him to the surrounding brush, where together they let their bodies take over. Bright beams of light blinded them from a car with a red blinking top, the regular escaped through the woods. The stranger, paralyzed with fear, was arrested for sodomy, a law punishable by up to 10 years in prison in the South. Circling the confined cell in helpless torment, the stranger searched for options, and found only one. He pulled off his belt, hooked it to the window bars and adjusted it around his neck. He'd left a mother, father, brother, wife, and two children to a fate none of them deserved.

These stories of pain and suffering are intended to plunge deep into our awareness, creating a ripple effect that can free our hearts and minds to act with more compassion and understanding. It has taken and will continue to take all of our courageous voices, though, speaking out and marching side-by-side to break through barriers and demand justice. I believe it's in *us*. Do you?

. . .

AFTER HER UNCLE'S RELUCTANT approval and Ernie's sign-off, the article was slated for the Sunday edition. On that weekend morning, Jeannie woke up to sunlight seeping through the blinds. She put on a kettle of water and shuffled to her front door. The bulky paper was held together by two large rubber bands. Placing it on the coffee table, she made a cup of tea and returned to the couch. Her piece was bumped up to the lower left column of the *City Highlights* first page. She sat down and read it slowly, taking in her bold words, and thrilled Ernie didn't change a word in the last paragraph. It was too early for the family calls, even Grammy would wait another hour before her ritual acknowledgement of anything she wrote. Jeannie wondered if she'd be as gushing for her gay rights theme as she had been for the others. Then her mother, naturally, would also phone in her praise, and maybe Marty would get on the extension. Jeffrey and Roz would likely check in later in the day. She had wanted to tell them all the truth, that it was *her* family who lost a son, brother, husband and father decades ago in a dingy jail cell. But neither a blue moon nor hell freezing over would ever change her uncle's mind about that copy going into his paper; and if she had taken the article anywhere else in the city, a risky bluff, he'd never forgive her. It wasn't just to protect Grammy, she knew that, and so did Cindy. It was also senseless to tell her mother; as the years passed, she'd become even more incapable of handling emotionally difficult things. It was time though to tell Jeffrey, him and only him. Now that the piece was out, she had no more reason to delay. Unlike her uncle, Jeannie believed her brother had the right to know.

She stood, stretched out her arms and went to the window.

Pulling up the blind cord, she gazed down at the angular view of her street. She watched a few people strolling along, coffee cups in hand. A young couple sat on a bench outside a popular breakfast spot sharing the contents of a white paper bag. Shoulders touching, Jeannie could see animated smiles as the sunlight passed over their faces. She lingered for a minute or so and then, as she'd done every morning for the past three months, went to her bedroom and lifted the receiver to her ear. Every time before, she'd hang up before dialing the last number. But not today. After five rings, it was his voice that answered.

"Hey Phil, it's Jeannie."

# ACKNOWLEDGEMENTS

THIS NOVEL COULD NOT have arrived at its final destination without a train full of dedicated supporters. My love and gratitude to Renee Roberts, her eyes and ears from cover to cover were invaluable. From insightful advice to that uncanny gift at finding typos of all shapes and sizes hidden in plain sight, your encouragement was a godsend.

To Joy Gould Boyum for truthful reviews that sent me down dark tunnels, but always with the assurance that my hard work would pay off one day.

To author and professional editor Nina Schuyler for her expertise in helping me develop stronger plot links while staying close to my characters.

To Book Passage, the best independent bookstore west of the Mississippi, and author, Leslie Keenan for her motivating workshops and valuable writing groups. Huge gratitude to daughter Emily Rath, who provided loving guidance through all the years of sweat and toil. To Mary Marshall for her unwavering praise over the decades of plot twists and angst all the way to her invaluable (x-ray vision) line-by-line editing, Gil Murray for his 11th hour line edits and insightful feedback, and to my wonderful posse of dedicated readers: Caroline Gould, Amy Gould, Helen Henry, Richelle Delevan, Jessica Warren, Laurie Kappe, Donna Savona, Kirti Withrow, Deirdre Kidder, Marjorie Castillo-Glantz, Merry Cohen, Jeff Karlin, Susan Deluca, Al DellaPenna, Sandy Wald, Rick Roberts and Paula Farmer—thank you so much for your time, focus and encouragement.

To Jennifer Tejada for inspiring women everywhere to embrace their power. To die-hard friends Carol Leifer, Carolee Goodgold, Linda Rait, Amy Sussman, Ron Sepielli and Ken

Marshall. To Pamela Livingston for providing referrals to Nina Schuyler and Jim Shubin, but most of all, to Jaqueline Gilman, whose artistry, patience and sharp eye led me through the windy curves of independent publishing. You're the best.

This book is dedicated to my mother, Caroline Gould, who gets the extra acknowledgement award for being an amazing role model, for never letting me quit, giving me honest feedback, cheering my highs, lifting me from lows, and her support in all ways. I love you with all my heart.

Lastly to my three netherworld muses, Helen Adams, my grandmother extraordinaire, Jack Biello, who taught me that fighting injustice is the path to freedom, and my spirited friend, Lauren Catuzzi Grandcolas, whose tragic death on Flight 93 inspired me to write this book.

## ABOUT THE AUTHOR

WRITING HAS BEEN BOTH a career and personal passion for Cathy Rath. She completed her education at UC Santa Barbara and San Francisco State University where she is a professor. Her research in health and social justice was published by the American Public Health Association. As a director of a county-wide violence prevention project, Cathy's achievements were published by the National Resource Center on Domestic Violence, which contributed to her receiving the Marin County Millennium Leadership Award on behalf of women and girls. She is also a writing coach who guides debut writers in completing their books. *Ripple Effect* is her first novel. Ms. Rath resides in the San Francisco Bay Area.